THEODORA'S DIARY

Also by Penny Culliford

Theodora's Wedding

THEODORA'S DIARY

Faith, hope and chocolate

PENNY CULLIFORD

GRAND RAPIDS, MICHIGAN 49530 USA

This novel is a work of fiction.
The names, characters and incidents portrayed in it
are the work of the author's imagination.
Any resemblance to actual persons,
living or dead, events or localities,
is entirely coincidental.

ZONDERVAN™

Theodora's Diary
Copyright © 2001 Penny Culliford

First published in Great Britain in 2001 by HarperCollins*Publishers*

This edition published in 2004 by Zondervan.

Scripture quotations are taken from the *Holy Bible, New International Version*®, NIV®. Copyright © 1973, 1978, 1984 by International Bible Society.

Penny Culliford asserts the moral right to be identified as the author of this work

A catalogue record for this book is available from the British Library

ISBN 0 00 711001 4

Printed in the United States of America

04 05 06 07 08 09 10 /❖ DC/ 10 09 08 07 06 05 04 03

This book is dedicated to
Terry Simpson

1942–1999

He laughed at my jokes.

Contents

June

Monday 29 June

Chickenpox! How can a grown woman, who spends her whole life avoiding children, have contracted chickenpox? It must have been one of that hideous brood of Hubbles. They always look as if they're harbouring some disease or other. Anyway, the doctor says it will mean at least four weeks off work, two of them in isolation, so it does have its benefits.

Tuesday 30 June

This chickenpox is a blessing in disguise. I am determined to use the time to grow spiritually by reading all the latest Christian books, listening to proper Christian music (not just Cliff Richard) and by keeping a journal. It will be a record of events at St Norbert's and will document my journey through the year. I know it's a bit unusual to start a diary at the end of June, but I've never been one to pander to convention. I'll try it for a couple of weeks – I don't think I've ever stuck to anything for longer than that. Then I can look back at how I've rocketed spiritually upwards in this time of enforced solitude.

St Norbert's is a funny sort of church. Perched on top of the hill, squinting down at the village like a benign, geriatric vulture, its solid grey bulk veers more towards cuddly than sinister. It's not quite Norman (more Nigel, really), not quite Victorian, and definitely not quite modern. I've been going there for as long as I can remember. I sometimes think it's easier than finding anything else to do on a Sunday morning. Practically everyone else I know goes there too. I suppose our outlook is basically evangelical, as long as it doesn't involve actually talking to anyone. Our major concessions to the twenty-first century are the overhead projector and the tea urn.

St Norbert's itself would probably be all right, but for the fact that it seems to attract the strangest people – an assorted assemblage of 70 or so, as diverse in age and temperament as it is possible to get. Kevin, who hardly ever sets foot in the place, says that it's no stranger than any other collection of deranged cranks, psychopaths and simpletons. That's rich, coming from a man who thinks nothing of spending the entire weekend at a draughty football ground watching 22 grown men kick a ball up and down a field. Sometimes I wonder why I go out with him. I think he must be spiritually degenerate!

Ariadne persuaded me to keep this diary. She said it would stop me sitting here feeling sorry for myself and worrying about things like why there's only one Monopolies Commission, how the person who wrote the first dictionary knew how to spell the words, and who owns the copyright to the copyright symbol. 'That, and scratching your spots, then phoning up to whinge at me,' she said.

Honestly – sisters! Does she think I'm completely neurotic? No, this journal is going to be a record of dynamic living and a fascinating insight into the mind of a modern Christian woman. I would list as my major influences the Acts of the Apostles, the diaries of Samuel Pepys and Adrian Plass's *Sacred Diary*, probably in reverse order.

July

Wednesday 1 July

Kevin was rather short with me last night, when I rang him in the middle of the televised match to ask him to call into the Christian bookshop for some spiritually uplifting material for me. I must still have been in bed when he called round this morning, because I found a package on the doormat with a scribbled note:

> Theo,
>
> Sorry I didn't have time to call into the bookshop. Hope these will do.
>
> Love Kev.

Inside the package were a *1982–1983 Goal of the Month* video and a book entitled *Astro-Turf – A Guide to Players and their Star Signs*. The latter lists the zodiac signs of all the premier league footballers. I really think he is spiritually degenerate. Still, his heart's in the right place.

Friday 3 July

I read two famous and very elderly books today – *The Screwtape Letters* and *The Cross and the Switchblade*. Some would describe them as classics, but I think it just goes to show that it's been a very long time since I last bought a Christian book.

Out of desperation, I also listened to a cassette I found right at the back of a drawer. I must have bought it at the Greenbelt Festival over 10 years ago, when I first met Kevin. It was by a Christian heavy-metal band called The Ungrateful Lepers. Kevin and I had gone to hear them in a damp field after a veggie burger and two cans of Albatross cider. It was during the song 'Send Down the Plague' that we had our first kiss. Now I remember why I haven't played it for 10 years.

My spots itch. Mustn't scratch.

Saturday 4 July

Kevin came to visit today. It was all rather unsatisfactory, as he was petrified of catching chickenpox and wasn't in full command of his faculties because he's still coping with his grief over his team's relegation at the end of last season. He insisted that I should prop open the letterbox and sit on the opposite side of the hall before he would talk to me.

'How are you feeling?' he bellowed across my flat from a distance of about 30 feet.

'Terrible!' I yelled back.

'Me too!' he screamed.

'Why? You haven't caught it, have you?' I shouted.

'No, haven't you heard the news? We're selling the goalkeeper . . . and he was our best scoring player!'

Sunday 5 July

I couldn't go to church today, but someone dropped a copy of St Norbert's newsletter, *The Church Organ*, through my door. My eye was drawn to one of the notices:

> *The first notice is an apology relating to an item which appeared in last week's newsletter. The item announced simply as 'Reverend Graves – slides in hall' was in fact referring to the vicar's photographic slides. The PCC apologizes sincerely to those disappointed members of the congregation who turned up hoping to see the shoe-less vicar run very fast and slither from one end of the hall to the other.*

Monday 6 July

Well, that's it. I've read every Christian book and nearly every other book I own – except, of course, *The Complete Works of Shakespeare*, which everyone has on their bookshelf but no one has ever read. Ariadne suggested I tried reading the Bible for once. I think she was being facetious. I've watched Kevin's football video forwards and backwards (backwards was vastly more entertaining) and am currently reading a women's magazine from 1972 that I found in the airing cupboard. Aesthetically challenged as I am, I find it hard to believe that people *ever* really made crocheted toilet-roll covers 'in co-ordinated shades of lilac, tangerine and lime'.

A 'get well soon' card arrived through the letterbox at lunchtime. It was from Jeremiah Wedgwood, whose purpose in life seems to be boring or frightening sick people better. It read:

To comfort you in your time of infirmity and affliction.

How nice, I thought, until I read the Bible verse he'd included:

My body is clothed with worms and scabs, my skin is broken and festering.   *(Job 7:5)*

Please God, don't let him visit me.

Things are getting so bad, I may have to resort to watching one of those daytime DIY shows which tell you how to 'update' a perfectly acceptable wardrobe using zebra-striped paint effects with a 'fashionably kitsch' neon pink silk lining.

Tuesday 7 July

Much to my disappointment, there were no daytime DIY shows on. My wardrobe remains untransformed. Instead, I watched with horrified fascination the American interview show where people with deep-seated emotional and relationship problems come to a television studio to hurl abuse (and occasionally chairs) at each other in front of millions of viewers.

I wonder why they do it?

After several hours of 'entertainment', including repeats of American detective shows from the 1970s and cookery programmes for incompetent or unwilling chefs, I have come to the conclusion that daytime television is a government conspiracy to deter malingerers. If you can endure daytime television, you must be *really* ill.

Wednesday 8 July

Every inch of my skin itches, I look like the one who got turned down for a part in *101 Dalmatians* for being too spotty, I want to strangle Cliff Richard, and if I spend another day alone I shall start talking to the fridge.

Thursday 9 July

Just as I was asking the fridge what it thought I should have for lunch, the buzzer on my entry phone sounded.

'What do you consider to be the purpose of life?' enquired an earnest-sounding voice. I pressed the entry button and soon two smartly dressed young men carrying briefcases and magazines appeared at the door of my flat. They eyed my spots apprehensively.

Three hours later, after giving them the benefit of my opinion on the purpose of life, heaven and who would get there, blood transfusions and the meaning of the Book of Revelation, the two young Jehovah's Witnesses finally persuaded me to let them leave.

Friday 10 July

I got a phone call this morning from Charity Hubble, the chintz-upholstered curate's wife. I was so desperate to communicate with another member of the human race that even Charity seemed bearable. She reminds me of a well-manured cottage garden – covered in flowers and extremely fertile.

'Hello, Theodora. How are you feeling?'

Even though I couldn't see her, I just knew she was smiling in that seraphic, 'I'm just brimming over with joy' way I find so utterly nauseating.

'Oh, I'm just fine thank you, Charity,' I lied.

'How are the spots?' she enquired.

'A bit itchy, but they're getting better,' I fibbed.

'Look, Theodora, I hope you don't mind, but I wonder if we could come and visit you. I've had chickenpox already, but none of the children have. If we came round today and they caught it from you, they would all get it over and done with in the school holidays.'

My stomach lurched. All eight Hubble children in my flat! Like a priest in a department store who has accidentally wandered into the ladies' lingerie department, I frantically searched for a way out. I found none.

'Yes, that would be fine,' I said through gritted teeth. 'About four o'clock?'

The visit of the Hubble tribe, though lasting less than an hour, was simply too hideous to record. Suffice it to say that I lost my temper with six-year-old Bathsheba, who spent half an hour following me around with a felt-tip pen in her hand, eyeing me in anticipation. I tried to dodge into the bedroom, but she followed me in there. I nipped smartly into the bathroom and whipped the door shut, but when I turned round, there she was, standing by the washbasin. I started to wonder if she was some sort of apparition.

'Why are you following me?'

Two blue eyes stared out from a puffy gerbil face. She said nothing, but studied my face and bare legs. The felt-tip pen in her hand twitched slightly. I unlocked the door and flung it open.

'Go away,' I snapped. 'Leave me alone.'

'But I only wanted to play join-the-dots!' she wailed, and ran to find her mother.

Saturday 11 July

The visitor I was looking forward to about as much as a turkey looks forward to Christmas arrived this afternoon. Jeremiah Wedgwood strode into my flat wearing an expression which made me think of a vulture watching a creature about to take its last breath. 'Greetings in the name of the Lord! When I noticed you hadn't been to church, I feared you had backslidden. Then, to my great relief and joy, I heard you were ill. How is your poor, tortured body today?' he enquired in a voice that sounded like a very bad impersonation of a Conservative politician.

'Oh, er . . . not too bad, thank you, Jeremiah. Still a bit . . . spotty.'

'Visiting the sick is my "ministry", you know.'

I nodded vigorously, trying to humour him.

'Bringing succour to the afflicted and relief to those in tribulation! You look very pale. Are you sure it's only chickenpox?' He peered at me with watery, blue eyes.

'Yes, yes, that's what the doctor said.' My mouth started to feel dry.

'Doctor? You've had the doctor in?' He shook his head and tutted. 'You want to be careful of doctors, you know. It was a doctor who told my Uncle Sid it was only chickenpox. She prescribed him calamine lotion, but—' and he glanced behind him, lowering his voice to a chilling whisper, '—dead within a week'.

'Really!' I ran a finger around the inside of my collar, which had suddenly become two sizes too small.

'Yes, he was on his way to the chemist to collect his prescription when he got run over by a bus.'

I could feel the perspiration beginning to break out on

my forehead. How long was I going to be able to endure
Jeremiah's 'ministry'?

'I don't feel too good. Perhaps I'd better not keep you.'
I tried to sound as if I was suffering bravely, which of course
I was.

'Nonsense, I've got all afternoon. I always allocate the
whole of Wednesday and Saturday afternoons for my ministry of visitation.' Jeremiah's immediate departure was
clearly not going to be that easy to secure. 'Anyway,' he
continued, 'I haven't given you your present yet.'

'Present! Oh, that's extremely kind of you. You really
shouldn't have bothered.'

He rummaged around in his holdall and, to my astonishment, pulled out a five-pound bag of King Edward potatoes. My mind searched frantically for a suitable response.

'M-m-most people would have brought grapes,' I stammered eventually.

'No, no, no. Potatoes are *much* better for you. Vitamin
C and loads of roughage. You look as if you need more
roughage. How are your—'

I leapt in before he could quiz me on the workings of my
digestive system and thanked him profusely for his generous gift. It was clear by now that he was here for the
duration and little short of an atomic bomb would deflect
him from his intention to 'minister' to me. Desperately, I
tried to engage him in conversation. If I kept him talking,
he couldn't lay hands on me.

'So how did you come to this ministry, Jeremiah?'

That was the wrong question. Apart from intestines, his
ministry was his favourite subject. His already watery eyes
welled up, threatening to burst their banks.

I made mental arrangements for my funeral.

I was sure I wasn't going to make it through this visit

alive. Even if I survived the boredom, I feared I might drown in his tears.

'Oh yes! I've been doing it ever since I had The Dream.'

I didn't ask.

'You'd be amazed how many people can barely stagger from their bed of pain when I arrive, but by the time I leave, they're changed and restored. I've witnessed people who start off looking pale and drawn, becoming flushed with health and positively leaping across the room to see me out by the end of my visit, sometimes after only three or four hours. It's little short of miraculous, truly it is. It's so precious to be able to bless people in this way.'

He withdrew a handkerchief from his pocket and mopped at the deluge.

'D'you know, there was one poor soul I used to visit – a Mr Barrymore, who drove a really splendid little red sports car. He lived right at the top of the steep hill in the village. Anyway, he became unwell and I used to walk up that hill to visit him every Wednesday. I would pray for him, then we would talk about his garden and his car. He really loved that car. He used to polish it every day until it shone, even when he got really poorly and couldn't drive it any more. One day something truly wondrous happened. God worked mightily in that situation. It was nothing short of a miracle.'

I was stunned. Maybe I had misjudged him. 'You mean he was healed and got better?'

'No! He died and left *me* the car. Lovely condition, beautiful bodywork. As I said, a miracle!'

I felt a sensation of overwhelming weariness. I would have to grasp the nettle and ask him to leave. 'I'm suddenly feeling rather tired. I think you'd better go so I can get some rest.'

'But I haven't prayed for you yet!'

That was the final straw. He *had* to go. Pray for me, like
he did for Mr Barrymore? No thank you! When most people ask God to undertake in a difficult situation, they don't
mean it literally.

'By the way, that's a lovely china figurine you've got on
your table,' Jeremiah said. 'I've always wanted one of those.
Do you have any plans for it when . . . well, you know . . .
Have you made a will?'

I couldn't believe my ears. He was supposed to be making me feel better. Instead he was practically measuring me
for my coffin!

'I'm perfectly all right,' I hissed through clenched teeth.
'It's only chickenpox, you know.'

'Are you absolutely sure about that? It could be some
deeply concealed, unconfessed sin – greed, perhaps, some
demonic attack upon your psyche, some heinous iniquity
festering away in your subconscious, manifesting itself in
physical affliction.'

'No it isn't! It's chickenpox!' I snapped.

'You look a little tense. It could be a stress-related anxiety disorder.'

I had a desperate urge to say, 'Look, you will be suffering from a boot-related backside disorder if you don't leave
pronto. I'm supposed to be ill. You come in here with your
potatoes, scare me half to death with stories about dead
uncles, try to worm your way into my will, then accuse me
of being demon-possessed and mentally unstable!'

Instead, I summoned the dregs of my energy, hoisted
myself to my feet and opened the door. 'Please, Jeremiah,
you really can go now. I'm suddenly feeling much better.'

To my utter amazement, Jeremiah seemed delighted to
be evicted. His moist eyes shone and he rubbed his hands

together with glee. He was beaming, as I stood pleadingly by the open door.

'You see,' he chuckled with delight, 'a miraculous recovery! Works every time. What a gift!'

Sunday 12 July

Kevin popped round to bellow at me again through the letterbox and drop in some supplies. One of the items he deposited through the letterbox was the latest copy of *The Church Organ*. I've always been sure that church magazines only exist to stop people nodding off during the boring bits of the service, and it looks as if that's right. Among the notices about the Ladies' Guild and the Sunday School outing was a note in very small print, right at the bottom of the last page. It read:

> *If you are reading this, the sermon must be really dull.*

Monday 13 July

I have the feeling that my period of solitary confinement is nearly at an end. Today I sat and thought about all the things I could have done, even *should* have done while I had the time and still didn't do. I thought of the painting-by-numbers set, still in its box under my bed. I thought of the copy of Stephen Hawking's *A Brief History of Time* that Ariadne made me borrow. I haven't even opened it. I guess now I'll never understand how to synthesize the theory of general relativity with quantum physics. Oh well!

There have been benefits. My time hasn't been entirely wasted. I now have beautifully manicured hands and nails, my eyebrows no longer look like Eric Cantona's, and I have a bikini line smooth enough to skate on.

Tuesday 14 July

Hooray! I saw the doctor this morning, and I'm no longer contagious. Theodora Llewellyn is now able to receive visitors.

2 p.m.
No visitors yet.

8 p.m.
Still no visitors. Where are they all?

11 p.m.
Fed up. Spent all day hoping someone would visit me after what seems like years in solitary confinement.
    No one.
    Not one single person.
    Not even Kevin.
    Nobody loves me.
    I'm going to bed.

Wednesday 15 July

It occurred to me this morning that perhaps I should phone people to tell them I can now have visitors. That might do the trick.

11 a.m.
Kevin popped in on his way back from a plumbing job near-by. He was positively bubbling over with excitement. I thought it was the joy of being allowed near me again, but then he let slip that the reason for his effervescence was that his new football season ticket had arrived in this morning's post. Who said romance is dead?

Friday 17 July

I fell asleep on the sofa after lunch. It's the sort of thing you're allowed to get away with when you're convalescing. I was in the middle of a very pleasant dream involving Mel Gibson and an enormous bar of chocolate, when the entry buzzer sounded.

'Theodora, are you there, dear?' called a quavering but genteel voice. If a slightly damaged Royal Doulton tea set could speak, it would sound like Miss Chamberlain. I reluctantly dismissed Mel Gibson and pressed the button to admit the elderly lady. I opened the door of my flat and galloped halfway down the stairs to take Miss Chamberlain's arm and assist her up the last flight. Slightly breathless, she carefully manoeuvred herself into an armchair.

'I hope you don't mind me visiting,' she said, 'but I thought you must be feeling a bit fed up, so I brought you this'. She pulled a huge bar of chocolate out of her string bag. I hugged her.

'I know grapes are healthier,' she said, her eyes sparkling with mischief, 'but chocolate is much more fun'.

As far as I know, Miss Chamberlain doesn't have a first name – she has always been called 'Miss'. A retired school-teacher, she has been a Christian for so long and her faith is so seamless that you genuinely can't see where Jesus ends and Miss Chamberlain begins. If I was asked how long I spent praying or reading the Bible, I would probably multiply the real amount by four or five so that I wouldn't appear spiritually degenerate. I suspect Miss Chamberlain would divide hers by four or five to avoid making me feel inadequate.

When we had eaten our fill of the chocolate, had a good chat and I had helped her back down the stairs, I sat on my sofa and looked round my flat. Everything appeared a little brighter, a touch less jaded. Apart from Mel Gibson (of course), I can't think of anyone in the world I would have preferred to visit me this afternoon.

Monday 20 July

I was lying on the sofa under a blanket, finishing off the chocolate and giving daytime television a second chance, when the phone rang. It was my sister, Ariadne.

'Get off the sofa, switch off that television, stop stuffing your face and do something useful, you lazy slug!'

I jumped up, electrocuted by guilt. How did she know?

'You were, weren't you?' she laughed. 'You're so predictable, Theodora.'

'No, no ... actually, I was...'

'I can also tell when you're lying.'

Even when we were children, Ariadne had the knack of being able to catch me out whenever I was doing something iniquitous. She was my unofficial conscience and took great delight in recounting my misdemeanours to Mum or Dad. As we grew older, she no longer told on me, but prefaced her remarks with, 'Do you really think that's a good idea?' or, 'You could do it that way, but...' which in some ways was far worse. It was like living with Jiminy Cricket.

'I've been reading,' I said piously. That, at least, was true. *The Adventures of Noddy* is an excellent book – if you're six.

'Why don't you do something useful for a change? Something for somebody else.'

'What exactly do you have in mind?' I asked, my suspicions aroused.

'Well, a guy from my church, Steve, has just gone out to Nepal with a missionary organization and various people have been writing to him – you know, to help him keep in touch with what's going on in England. As you have so much time on your hands at the moment, I thought you could send him a letter.'

'But I don't know anything about him,' I protested. 'I can't just write to him out of the blue!'

'I don't expect you to write anything profound, just chitchat, really. He's a doctor, about 30-ish, likes football. You could even send him extracts from that diary of yours.'

I felt quite sure that Steve, whoever he was, would not wish to learn the gruesome details of Jeremiah Wedgwood's visit. Whatever else I might write about, the diary would stay private.

'Well, OK,' I sighed. 'Let me have the address.'

Football! I've spent the last 10 years trying to avoid knowing anything about football. Perhaps I should get Kevin to write. They'd have plenty in common.

Tuesday 21 July

Ariadne came round with Steve's address and a photo. Steve, it turns out, is totally drop-dead gorgeous – tall and dark, with a smile that would melt concrete. Surely missionaries aren't allowed to be gorgeous? They're supposed to be earnest, balding, middle-aged men in khaki shorts and pith helmets, not Mel Gibson's better-looking brother. I've decided I *will* write to Steve (nothing to do with the photo, of course).

5 p.m.

I hate writing letters. After 13 attempts to write something vaguely interesting, which doesn't make me seem like an eight-year-old writing about the Pony Club, I've decided this isn't a good idea. Trying to appear light-hearted and chatty makes me sound like a character from *Little House on the Prairie*, and if I try a more formal approach I sound as if I'm writing to my bank manager.

11 p.m.
It's not my writing style that's the problem – it's my personality. I'm just not *interesting* enough. Who wants a letter from a convalescent office worker from a boring little village near Sidcup?

I know. I'll invent a person to write to Steve. It's not as if I'm ever likely to meet the guy. Ariadne said herself, the content of the letter isn't important. I could say anything I want, be anyone I like.

11.45 p.m.
Inventing a personality is harder than I thought. I can't pretend to be a doctor: Steve would see straight through that one and, even if he didn't, he might want to discuss the gory details of his latest operation. Yuck! I can't even pretend to be amazingly spiritual: he'd see through that even more quickly. Of course, I could say I'm a teacher – that sounds a suitably worthy profession – and pretend that I'm thinking of becoming a missionary too. That will instantly give us something in common. I'll be single and totally unattached. I live only for the children – no, the *socially deprived* children – I teach. I shall be tall, blonde, attractive – in the spiritual sense, of course, a sort of cross between Pamela Anderson and Mother Teresa.

Midnight.
Letter finished. That was fun! The new, improved Theodora Llewellyn lives. Now comes the difficult part: getting the

letter past Ariadne. Even if God forgives the subterfuge, Ariadne certainly won't.

Wednesday 22 July

Success! She doesn't suspect anything. She didn't even look at the letter. She just asked if I got Kevin to write anything about football. Kevin? Who's Kevin?

Thursday 23 July

I tried to cook a romantic meal for Kevin to celebrate my not-being-contagious. Unfortunately, as I hadn't been shopping, I had very limited ingredients with which to create my culinary masterpiece. He nibbled politely at the food, forcing himself to swallow by sheer willpower. Maybe, with hindsight, 'Kippers with Garlic Mayonnaise' was a mistake.

'You don't *have* to eat it, you know,' I said eventually.

'It's very nice; it's just that I'm a bit full up tonight.'

'It is not nice, it's disgusting!' I put my cutlery down with a clatter, pushed my plate away and sat with folded arms.

'Theo, it's just . . . different . . . unusual . . . distinct . . . unconventional . . .'

I stopped Kevin trying to think of any more adjectives to describe the meal and sent him out to hire a video. He came back with *Fever Pitch*, the story of an obsessive football fan and his relationship with his long-suffering girlfriend. It was better than I expected – funny and romantic, not too much football. We even had a cuddle at the end.

'Theo,' Kevin whispered, 'promise me, if I ever start getting like that bloke in the video, you'll take me out and shoot me'.

I hadn't the heart to tell him.

Friday 24 July

I needed to go to the chemist's to buy a very large spot-concealer stick to hide the remaining scabs and chickenpox scars, in preparation for my return to work. My neighbour Doris Johnson very kindly offered to give me a lift there in her gigantic old Volvo. The car has huge rust holes in the wings, but I accepted her offer gratefully.

'Righto! I'll go and get Matrimony out of the garage and get her ticking over.'

'Matrimony?' I asked. 'Why on earth do you call your car Matrimony?'

Doris giggled. It was a giggle which seemed to start at her feet and work its way up through her body, making the whole of her little, round frame shake with mirth. 'Because it's a holy estate, of course!'

I should never have asked.

Saturday 25 July

I went out with Mum this afternoon to book our annual holiday. Kevin can't get time off this summer and Dad won't travel abroad, so it's just the two of us.

After much wrangling – she wanted Athens, I wanted Tenerife – we agreed on Kos. Mum's into Greek culture and architecture and I'm a complete beach bum, so obviously some compromise was necessary.

I've just tried on all last year's holiday clothes. Am now deeply depressed. I squeezed into my linen shorts and caught a glimpse of my backside in the bedroom mirror. It looked like a sack full of footballs. Had to have a bar of chocolate to cheer myself up.

Sunday 26 July

Back to church today. My return after several weeks of absence wasn't greeted, as I'd hoped, with hugs, kisses and tears. Most people didn't even seem to notice I'd been missing. In fact, the only person who offered to hug me was slimy, oily Roger Lamarck. I declined. I know where he likes to put his hands.

After the service, I wrestled with the lock on my driver's door in the car park for a good five minutes before I admitted defeat. I was just climbing in through the passenger side when a sudden, violent impact from behind catapulted me across the front seats. I extracted my head from the driver's door side pocket, clambered out backwards, tugged down my skirt and turned, red faced and fuming, to face a seraphically smiling Charity Hubble. One of her progeny had swung open the door of their prehistoric, text-covered minibus and nearly sent me into orbit.

'So sorry!' she beamed. 'Nebuchadnezzar, say "sorry" to Theodora.'

'Sorry I hit you up the bum with the door,' replied the chastised but unrepentant Nebuchadnezzar.

'Now, now, that isn't a nice thing to say, is it?' chided his mother.

'No,' concurred the grinning brat. 'It was a good shot, though.'

Seven other toothy faces grinned and grimaced at me through the sticker-covered bus windows like a pack of deranged hamsters. All the children appeared identical, varying only in size and degree of tooth protrusion. They looked like the result of a genetić experiment to cross a cabbage-patch doll with a gerbil. Nigel Hubble glided up, still in his curate's robes, and put his arm around his rose-and-wisteria-clad spouse as she smiled up into his eyes.

The bus and its inhabitants jolted and bumped out of the car park. As I rubbed my sore head and bruised backside, I caught a glimpse of the door with which Nebuchadnezzar had clouted me. It bore the text of Psalm 141:5, 'Let a righteous man strike me – it is a kindness.' Talk about rubbing salt into the wound.

Monday 27 July

Must be ready to go back to work. Had an overwhelming urge to organize my underwear into alphabetical order.

Tuesday 28 July

I had a discussion with Kevin about football hooliganism. Of course, Kevin denies even knowing anyone who has ever even been associated in any remote way whatsoever with violence on the terraces. I reminded him of the time he was sitting at the back of the stands with his half-witted mates and accidentally dropped a bag of mint imperials just before the national anthem. The acoustics of the stadium amplified the sound of the rock-hard sweets as they bounced down the concrete steps. Both teams thought they were under machine-gun fire and flung themselves face first onto the pitch. They were still visibly shaking during the first half. I made him write to the Football Association to apologize.

'But me, Paul, Jez and Kev 2 – we're model supporters!' His voice squeaked in incredulity.

Model supporters? Smaller, non-working versions of the real thing.

Wednesday 29 July

It's nearly August and I have no signs of great spiritual growth to report yet. It's a bit embarrassing, really. This diary is supposed to be a record of my pilgrimage through life, but I don't feel as if I've even got as far as the front door. I'm consoling myself by thinking this must be a waiting period, a time of preparation. I feel God must have some work of great importance for me to do, a project, a mission – a ministry, even. Everyone else seems to have one. Charity has her committees and good works, Miss Chamberlain has her lovely way of bringing happiness to people, Doris Johnson runs the playgroup and Sunday School, Jeremiah Wedgwood has his 'ministry of visitation'. Even Kevin seems to find the time to do odd jobs for some of the elderly people in the village. Oh well, I'm sure God has something up His sleeve. Does God have sleeves? Does He have arms? Why am I even asking that?

Friday 31 July

Rang work today to tell them I'd be back on Monday.

'Good, we've saved it all up for you,' said Declan. 'Bring a stepladder. It's scraping against the ceiling.'

I think I'm about to have a relapse. A return to an office where whoopee cushions, foaming sugar and soap which turns your face green pass as normality is enough to set back anyone's recovery.

God must have arms. The Bible says, 'The eternal God is your refuge, and underneath are the everlasting arms' (Deuteronomy 33:27). Can't find anything about sleeves, though. Logically, if God has arms, He must have sleeves. But does He wear clothes?

I'm rambling. The chickenpox must have affected my thought processes.

August

Sunday 2 August

Went to church. Reverend Graves (a most unfortunate name, I've always thought, especially as he's originally from Australia and has the nickname 'Digger') gave a very uplifting sermon from 1 Corinthians 12 about knowing your gifts. I had a slight guilt pang about giving Kevin's Mum the bottle of cheap perfume Auntie Gwen gave me for Christmas as a birthday present, until I realized he was talking about *spiritual* gifts, so that was all right.

He spoke about the different kinds of jobs the Holy Spirit gave to people in the early Church: apostles, prophets, teachers, workers of miracles, healers, helpers, administrators, and the gift of speaking in different kinds of languages. He said that people in the modern Church could also have these gifts. I spent the rest of the sermon and final hymn trying to decide what my gift was.

I was still pondering the subject over coffee in the hall afterwards, when Nigel Hubble came in carrying a tray loaded with polystyrene cups of coffee and tripped over Mrs McCarthy's zimmer frame. It was like a slow-motion film. He stumbled, regained his balance, then trod on one of his children, who started yelling indignantly. He eventually lost his grip on the tray, which toppled onto Mr Wilberforce's dog.

In the ensuing mêlée of damp cloths, apologies, muttered curses and agonized yelping, it became very clear
which members of the congregation possessed what gift.
The 'apostles' in the room were sent for more coffee;
the 'helpers' pulled the dazed Nigel to his feet, picked up
the cups and mopped the carpet; the 'teachers' showed him
the correct way to carry a tray of coffee; the 'miracle-
workers' managed to persuade Mr Wilberforce that Nigel
was really very fond of Rex and the scalding was merely an
unfortunate accident; the 'healers' rubbed Germolene into
Rex's scalded fur; the 'administrators' calculated the cost of
hiring a carpet-shampooing machine; the 'prophets' said, 'I
knew that would happen!'; and many of the words uttered,
mainly by Mr Wilberforce, were in a totally indecipherable
language.

Monday 3 August

Back to work today. The security guard peered closely at
me over his glasses as I waved my pass and went into the
building.

''S funny, you don't look any different,' he said. He
sounded disappointed.

I've had chickenpox, for goodness' sake, I thought, *not
grown an extra head*. When I reached my office, Declan had
mysteriously disappeared. All through the morning, every
time I looked up from my pile of papers, I found groups of
people peering at me from behind files or round filing cab-
inets, whispering. I spent the rest of the day wondering why
everybody was looking at me so strangely, until I tortured
a filing clerk into divulging that Declan had told all my colleagues that I'd been off work having plastic surgery to
make me look like a supermodel.

This is Declan's idea of a joke. That man puts clingfilm across toilet bowls and superglue on door handles for 'a bit of a laugh'. Some days it's like working with Jeremy Beadle.

He's going to need more than plastic surgery to remove the filing cabinet from where I'm going to put it when I find him.

Tuesday 4 August

All that chocolate and daytime television while I was off sick has taken its toll on my figure. Only three weeks until I go on holiday, and some serious measures are called for. I went out at lunchtime and bought a large tub of cottage cheese. I really hate cottage cheese. In fact, no one actually likes cottage cheese. It's one of those things that's so disgusting it must be doing you good.

Wednesday 5 August

Joined the gym at the local sports centre today. I was pleasantly surprised to find that it wasn't completely bursting at the seams with lycra-clad supermodels with leotards that look in danger of vertically bisecting their bodies and more silicon than IBM. Instead there were a couple of pleasant-looking young mums, a very large Italian lady and three elderly men.

A girl who looked about 12 years old showed me how to use the equipment. There were cycling machines, rowing machines, stepping machines, machines to make your arms bigger, machines to make your backside smaller, and even a machine to develop your 'pecs'. I didn't like to admit that I hadn't a clue where my 'pecs' were, or even if I had any to develop. I decided to use the machine anyway: at the end of the session, by a process of elimination, I'd know that the bits which felt developed must be pecs.

After an hour of pulling, stretching, lifting, cycling and walking, I felt sweaty and slightly wobbly. There was no sign of anything developing. The three old men, who looked in far better physical shape than I did, nodded to me as I left. I climbed gratefully into my car and drove the 200 yards from the leisure centre to my home – I didn't want to overdo it on my first day.

Cottage cheese lasagne for supper tonight – I can hardly wait.

Thursday 6 August

Woke up unable to move. The gym is entirely out of the question today. Can't work out where my pecs are, because everything hurts. I can't have pecs all over, surely?

Friday 7 August

Stiff muscles even worse today. At work it took me 10 minutes to ease off my jacket and hang it on the back of the chair. I barely had the strength to pick up a coffee cup. No sympathy from my colleagues.

At lunchtime, Declan asked me to take some letters down to the postbox. In agony, I struggled to put on my jacket – only to find that I couldn't get my hands down the sleeves. Declan had stapled up the ends of my sleeves while I was in the loo. I needed two people to help ease my arms and shoulders out again. I could hear Declan howling with laughter from the other end of the office.

Kevin was rather more sympathetic and enthusiastically offered to massage my sore pecs for me. I know where they are now, and there's no way he's getting his hands on them this side of an engagement ring!

Sunday 9 August

I'm still concerned about what God has up His sleeve for me to do. I bet Declan wouldn't dare staple up God's sleeves. I prayed that God would send a thunderbolt to strike down Declan right in the middle of one of his pranks. That would be revenge indeed – the best practical joke ever.

Monday 10 August

Felt guilty and repented of wishing Declan struck by lightning. He might be a pain in the neck, but I'm sure God loves him.

At lunchtime, as a reward for a week of cottage cheese, I met Ariadne for coffee at a little Italian café halfway between her office and mine. While we waited for what seemed like three days for the waiter to bring our order, I asked her what kind of thing she thought God had in mind for me.

'If God has some important work for me to do, I should be getting on with it, not just sitting here wondering what it is,' I complained. Our cappuccinos arrived, but the chocolate powder had yet to put in an appearance. I drummed my fingers on the table. 'I'm just wasting my life. All this unfulfilled potential.'

'Well,' she said, sipping her coffee and leaning thoughtfully back in her chair, 'perhaps God's teaching you about patience, endurance and forbearance, learning to live tolerantly with others and forgive their faults.'

'OK, fair enough, but if God's teaching me these things, I just wish He'd hurry up about it.'

Ariadne started to cough and splutter into her cappuccino. Honestly – sisters!

Tuesday 11 August

Forgot to ask Ariadne about God's sleeves. I woke up three or four times last night wondering what God wears. My mind flitted back to a school trip to the National Gallery. There were plenty of pictures of God there. He was usually sitting in clouds casting thunderbolts at cowering mortals beneath. But what was He *wearing*? I searched through my sluggish brain, trying to remember what this terrifying, vengeful deity wore. As far as I could remember, it looked like some sort of tablecloth. The more I thought about it as the night wore on, the less the image of God in the paintings seemed to fit my experience. Where had I gone wrong?

Had the Church of England misled me when I dared to believe that God might actually love me and accept me, warts (actually, I don't have any warts) and all? Doubts, fears and the looming gargoyles of my insecurity roamed my mind. I cowered like the mortals in the paintings, uncertain whether my duvet would afford adequate protection against a celestial blast. I became more and more convinced that what God had up His sleeve for me was a thunderbolt.

Wednesday 12 August

After another night of torment, I rang Ariadne first thing this morning in a state of feverish agitation to talk through my questions.

'Ariadne, does God have sleeves?' I blurted out. 'On His arms, I mean, like a sort of jacket . . . to keep things up, you

know, things for us . . . thunderbolts . . . or something. . .'
Realizing I was talking gibberish, I ground to a halt.

'Have you been drinking, Theo?' she enquired, in the
sort of voice people use when talking to men wearing
trousers held up with string who wave empty whisky bottles on station platforms late at night.

'Of course I haven't been drinking! It's only 7.15,' I
replied huffily.

I was rather put out by the suggestion and carefully
explained my theological predicament. She laughed and
said, 'You do find the strangest things to worry about. Try
Psalm 104.'

I grabbed my Bible and flicked through it frantically.

> . . . clothed with splendour and majesty.
> He wraps himself in light as with a garment . . .

It isn't a tablecloth, then. But it still doesn't help much.

Thursday 13 August

Dad phoned me at some unearthly hour this morning. 'I'm
sorry to spoil your day,' he said, 'but I've got a bit of bad
news, see. Auntie Ivy's just died.'

'Who's Auntie Ivy?' I murmured, pulling the duvet back
over my head.

'You know, Auntie Ivy, one of your Grandpa's sisters.'

Grandpa Llewellyn was one of 17 children, all girls
except for him. They all lived into extreme old age and the
surviving old ladies were sprinkled liberally around remote
parts of South Wales. Although Grandpa died when I was
very young, I remember him as a very quiet, tormented-
looking man. Not surprising, really.

'Oh. Have I met her?'

'Course you have – blue hair, kept racing pigeons, had a thing about greaseproof paper.'

'I don't remember her.'

'You'd know her if you saw her.'

'Well, I'm hardly likely to see her now, am I? She's dead.'

'True, true. Anyway, just thought I'd tell you. Funeral's on Monday 24th down home. Ariadne's got to work, and goodness knows where your brother is. See if you can make it. Mam and I are driving down Sunday. We'll stay overnight at Auntie Madge's.'

Saturday 15 August

I've been busy at work recently, so the diary has been put on the backburner rather. Likewise the diet. Cottage cheese was invented by sadists. It isn't a food, it's a form of punishment.

Sunday 16 August

Today's sermon was based on the sufferings of Job. Job 10:10 caught my eye: 'Did you not pour me out like milk and curdle me like cheese...' Obviously a sign to persevere with the diet!

Monday 17 August

Have lost only three pounds after all that effort. I asked Kevin what he thought about my diet. He said, 'I think you look fine the way you are. Nice and cuddly. I like curvy women.'

That does it. The diet hots up. 'Cuddly,' indeed!

Tuesday 18 August

Only a week to go to my holiday, and I still look like the Michelin man's overweight sister. No more food until I can get back into my bikini. Not even cottage cheese.

Thursday 20 August

I fainted at work today and Declan had to call Ariadne to come and take me home early. Ariadne tutted and shook her head as we sat together on the station platform, me with my head between my knees – which undignified position, she insisted, would prevent me passing out again.

'You can never do things sensibly, can you? You always have to take everything too far.' She unwrapped a chicken roll she had bought from the buffet and broke bits off to feed me.

'I'm sorry, I just felt fat and unattractive.' I sat up and accepted another bite before returning to my extremely unattractive pose. I felt like a gigantic sparrow fledgling with an inferiority complex.

'Who are you trying to attract? You've got a boyfriend who likes you the way you are. No one else is remotely interested in whether your waist is 26 or 24 inches. You're just making yourself unhappy and ill with this diet. Eat a bit less chocolate and walk a bit more. Give your poor old car a rest. And for goodness' sake, smile! That's what makes you attractive.'

I smiled and gave her a hug. I just wish she wasn't always right.

Friday 21 August

I decided to resolve the issue of what God has up his sleeve for me once and for all today.

Digger Graves was mowing his lawn when I called at the vicarage. 'G'day!' he called, waving cheerily. He pulled out two folding chairs and we sat on the newly mown grass. The smell of roses filled the still evening air and with only the sound of distant birdsong to accompany my discourse, he sat and listened patiently, nodding occasionally as I poured out my worries and fears. About God, His plans for me and what now seemed my ludicrous dilemma about His sleeves. Digger is the only person who doesn't laugh at my fears or dismiss them as a symptom of too many Enid Blyton books as a child.

'Well, Theo love, I can't be sure about the Heavenly Father's clobber, and He hasn't told me what He's got up his sleeve for you, but I can tell you exactly what He has in His hand.' He picked up his Bible and began to read to me from Psalm 73. 'This is what the psalmist says about God: "Yet I am always with you; you hold me by my right hand. You guide me with your counsel, and afterwards you will take me into glory. Whom have I in heaven but you? And earth has nothing I desire besides you." I can't think it's much different for us Christians now. If God's holding your hand, I don't think you need worry about anything else.'

Saturday 22 August

Told Kevin about my impending trip to Wales and tried to persuade him to come with me for the weekend. 'It's part of my heritage, you know. "Land of My Fathers" and all that.'

'As far as I'm concerned,' Kevin said, 'any nation that spends its winters running up and down a field with a ball shaped like an Easter egg and goalposts you can go over as well as under, where handballs and flying tackles are not only legal but part of the game, where you pass the ball backwards to move forwards and the whole team has the same surname, will just have to do without me.'

Sunday 23 August

Got to Auntie Madge's just in time to go with her to the evening service at chapel. Afterwards, while she was chatting to some of her friends, I slipped away and had a quiet wander around the graveyard. I love reading the names on old headstones and trying to imagine what life was like for these people who lived in another age, so distant, so separate. Glorious Welsh names caught my eye:

Griffith Ap David Ap Meredith Ap Jones
God took his soul,
Now God rest his bones.
Laid to rest in the year of our Lord 1875

So did the inscription on a monument to a former minister of the chapel who had met a tragic end:

Reverend Ifor Cowryd Thomas
Departed this life 12th day of March 1910
Struck by lightning whilst walking to chapel
for the morning service
This memorial was erected by his grateful
parishioners

Monday 24 August

6 a.m.

I've just spent the night sleeping on what felt like a sack stuffed with marbles in Auntie Madge's spare room. With an overnight temperature of 15°C outside, the stone cottage managed to maintain an indoor temperature of just above freezing. Even with an extra blanket, two jumpers and my socks, I still shivered.

5 p.m.

Just got back from the funeral. It was what people call 'a lovely send-off'.

'Such a pity, she was so young,' lamented Auntie Madge. Young? She was 92!

Still, the funeral served to dispel one myth. Not all Welshmen can sing. I know this for a fact. I had one sitting behind me, belting out the hymns in a monotone all the way through the service. I mentioned this to Dad on the way back.

'I know him,' Dad said. 'That's Owen Thomas, that is. Used to have a beautiful singing voice. He worked down the pits, singing hymns as he toiled at the coalface. Then one day he got crushed in a rock fall, mid-descant, and now he sings in the key of A flat miner.'

What a sad story! Dad, for some reason, seemed to find it funny.

Tuesday 25 August

Packing! Such a nightmare. Better make a list.

Something for the beach. Bikini or swimsuit? Both.

Towel (the ones in the hotel are usually about the size of a postage stamp).

Something for the evening, and a jumper in case it gets cold (make that three).

Shorts and top for sightseeing.

Shoehorn to squeeze bottom into shorts. (Only joking.)

Something to wear on the journey (both directions).

Something in case it rains. Yes, it does rain in Kos in August. Not often, but better be prepared.

Shoes, sandals, flip-flops, wellies (no, forget the wellies).

Sunhat (makes me look like Daisy the Blackpool Donkey, but it's the only one I've got).

Mosquito repellent, suncream, sunburn cream, hot-water bottle.

Something to read on the beach. Something a bit more respectable to read on the beach, in case I meet any other Christians.

Greek phrasebook (it's arrogant to expect the rest of Europe to speak English just because we're too lazy to make the effort).

Travel games.

Iron.

Washing powder.

Washing line and pegs.

Toiletries and make-up.

Emergency back-up mascara brush.

Actually, forget the travel games. My Travel Scrabble only has 17 letters. I think the rest got lost the last time Ag played 'rude words Scrabble' with Auntie Rosie after too much sherry trifle one Christmas. If you could buy a two-piece jig-saw, my brother would be sure to lose one of the pieces.

2 a.m.

Eventually laid out my entire wardrobe and nearly all my portable possessions on the bed. Too tired to sort it out tonight. I'll slide into bed under all the clutter.

Wednesday 26 August

Slept really badly. It felt as if a large, hairy yak was lying on top of the duvet. Every time I turned over, things rolled off and crashed to the floor. Woke up sweating with a mouth full of jumper. Leapt out of bed, trod on the travel iron and stubbed my toe on the parasol. Said some words that were not in the Greek phrasebook.

Mum rang at 7.30 just to check that I was up and dressed. I lied and said I was. Then I looked despairingly at my two small suitcases and put half the stuff back in the wardrobe.

Ended up with my ski boots, a Laura Ashley ballgown and two pairs of tights left on the bed. Sat down and read an article in a Christian women's magazine entitled 'Packing the Evangelical Way – a short guide to a spirit-filled suit-case'. I was rather disappointed that it contained no references at all to the duty-free allowance. The article ended rather puzzlingly with Luke 9:3, 'Take nothing for the journey – no staff, no bag, no bread, no money, no extra tunic.'

Best leave the barley sugars behind, then.

9.30 a.m.

Starting to panic. Need to leave by 10.30 and still not packed. Mum rang again to check I'd packed travel sickness tablets. Feel more in need of Valium. Confessed my packing problem.

'Don't worry. If you forget anything you can always buy a replacement. They do have shops in Kos, you know,' was her less than helpful reply.

10.30 a.m.
Kevin came round to give us a lift to the airport in his van.
I'd intended to drive, but Mum is a very nervous passenger
and, quite frankly, I couldn't face driving round the M25
with Mum in the passenger seat, her eyes tightly closed and
feet braced against the floor, screaming, 'We're going to
die! We're going to die!'
     It doesn't make for a relaxing start to the holiday.
     Kevin had promised to remove the immersion heater and
old toilet from the back of his van. I didn't quite expect him
to leave them in the communal front garden. 'They won't
be in anyone's way,' he protested.
     Suitcases still not packed. Kevin gallantly offered to help,
but I had to send him off to buy a newspaper, as he seemed
to be rather too enthusiastically inspecting my piles of clean
underwear.

11 a.m.
Mum rang again to find out where we were.

11.20 a.m.
Packed. We're off!

11.30 a.m.
We're back again! Realized I'd forgotten to cancel the milk,
switch off the gas and water the plants. Also, I'd forgotten to
pack toothbrush, underwear, tickets, money and passport.
     I gave Kevin a big kiss when we said goodbye. He looked
a bit pathetic. 'You haven't got room to pack me in your
suitcase, have you?' he asked.
     Wish he was coming.

September

Wednesday 9 September

Back again after a wonderful, relaxing holiday. Mum was right, you could buy most things in Kos. The only thing I'd forgotten that I couldn't replace was my diary. The apparent inconvenience didn't cause me too much irritation, however, as the entries would have been extremely monotonous:

> Got up.
> Went to beach.
> Went to bar.
> Went to bed.

That was the composition of at least 12 of the 14 days of my holiday. The other two varied only in that 'went to bar' happened a good deal earlier and 'went to bed' didn't appear on the itinerary at all. Not that I drank a great deal, not alcohol, anyway. Most of the time was spent eating, reading or chatting to the other holidaymakers. I now have a figure that would send a sperm whale rushing to Weight Watchers and the pattern of the sun-lounger seat permanently imprinted on my backside.

Thursday 10 September

Mum called round with some of my clothes which had been packed accidentally in her suitcase. The packing routine was no smoother on the return leg of our journey than it had been on the outward leg.

Mum had a wistful look in her eyes. Although she was physically in England, her soul had stayed among the purple bougainvillea that sprawled over the ancient walls of Kos Town.

Although born in Sidcup, my mother has a deep, intense affinity with Greece. We have a family joke that if you cut her, she would bleed ouzo. The affiliation started when she went on a Mediterranean cruise in 1960 when she was 15 years old, courtesy of a maiden aunt who still believed that 'gels should be "finished"'. Mum, in spite of originating from one of London's less culturally distinguished suburbs and being far removed from the finishing-school type, had the foresight to seize the opportunity to travel and broaden her mind. In short, she became hooked. Homer, Alexander the Great, Hippocrates, all came to life for my mother along with the myths and stories of that country. Chaperoned by the maiden aunt, she drank retsina in Athens, danced to the bouzouki in Rethymnon and bathed in the Aegean at midnight.

Ever since, she has been obsessed with the nation, the people, the history, the language and the food. We were the only kids in the street who regularly ate moussaka and meze instead of sausages and chips. That was over 20 years ago, and people's taste in food was not as cosmopolitan as it is now. Having schoolfriends to supper was a complete nightmare. Sitting round the dining room table, they would look from their plates to our faces and back again with a mixture of pity and disgust. One child even ventured to ask, 'Do you *eat* this?'

'No!' I shouted back, red-faced with anger and embarrassment. 'You rub it on your verruca. What do you think you do with it?'

So great was Mum's love of anything Greek, she decided to make a return trip when she was 20 to find a Greek man to marry, preferably a rich one. Much against my Granddad's wishes, she saved her money, quit her job and caught a train to Dover. It was when she was buying a ticket for the ferry to Calais on the first leg of her journey that she met my Dad. He was tall, blond and called Dai Llewellyn. His family was from Newport and the only thing remotely Greek about him was that he had once owned a Nana Mouskouri record. Much to Granddad's relief, she fell in love with him and, instead of a Greek shipping magnate for a son-in-law, he ended up with a Welsh ticket office clerk.

My father, lanky and yellow haired, with a temperament as fiery and Mediterranean as damp asbestos, humours my mother by allowing her annually to indulge her passion for Greece, courtesy of Thomas Cook. His only other concession to her love of all things Greek was to allow her free reign in naming their three unfortunate offspring. That's how Ariadne, Agamemnon and myself came to have pretentious Greek forenames while being saddled with the surname Llewellyn.

Friday 11 September

The parish has arranged for some refurbishment work to be carried out on the rather dilapidated vicarage over the next few weeks. I volunteered Kevin for the plumbing work, but they had already appointed a 'Christian' plumber who calls his business Living Waters Plumbing Services. Apparently he's one of Nigel Hubble's distant relatives and lives somewhere in Dorset. I asked Jeremiah, who had arranged for the work to be carried out, why the plumber was travelling so far when we have a perfectly competent plumber on our doorstep, so to speak. He replied that Nigel's cousin (or whatever he was) was a Christian and Kevin was, in his opinion, 'of uncertain religious persuasion'.

I leapt to Kevin's defence. 'Kevin is just as religiously persuaded as most people at St Norbert's!' I protested.

'Exactly,' retorted Jeremiah.

I decided to try a different tack. 'So what difference does it make, anyway? The water would still come through the pipes, the toilet would still flush, the central heating would still heat up if the work was carried out by a Christian, a Muslim, or someone who thought we were all controlled by little green men from Mars. Kevin's just as reliable and I'm sure his price is just as reasonable.'

Jeremiah shook his head sympathetically and pulled his handkerchief out of his pocket to mop his watery eyes. He was obviously having to deal with leakage problems of his own. 'How could I possibly trust the Reverend's private plumbing to the hands of one of the unchurched?' he said earnestly.

I managed, by sheer willpower, not to laugh.

Just.

Saturday 12 September

11 a.m.
Still feeling relaxed and at peace after my holiday. Nothing in the world can make me stressed or anxious. I'm just floating along on a cloud of tranquillity, spreading my inner calm to everyone I encounter.

2 p.m.

That blasted woman! If anyone was designed to test me to breaking point, it has to be Charity 'Stepford Wife' Hubble. I bumped into her outside the greengrocer's this afternoon and forced myself to resist the urge to comment on the new car sticker she had on display in the window of her beaten-up minibus: 'Anglicans do it on their knees.' I'm sure there's something not quite wholesome about this, but Charity is blissfully innocent about any form of innuendo. In spite of the proliferation of children, she can be alarmingly naïve sometimes.

'Charity,' I enquired, 'why have you got so many stickers and texts all over your van? Don't you think it's a little over the top?'

'Well,' she smiled beatifically, 'two reasons, really. One is to show I love the Lord, and the second is that it's a way of telling non-Christians about Jesus. I drive around all the time, taking the children to school, travelling to Mothers' Meetings, going to my arc-welding classes. How many people see my old bus in a day? Must be hundreds. So few people bother to read the Bible these days, that Nigel and I decided [she couldn't make a decision without consulting the omniscient Nigel] to bring the Bible to the unsaved.'

I had to admit, grudgingly, that she had a point. Lots of people at church have little shiny fish, *ichthus*, stuck on their cars. These fish are supposed to tell people that the people in the car are Christians, but I'm sure it's only other Christians who know what they mean.

I mentally flicked though images of cars belonging to other people I knew. Mary Walpole has a sticker saying in tiny letters:

If you can't read this, contact an optician.

Underneath is her optometrist practice phone number in very large print.

The Boswells, next door, have a sticker proclaiming their support of the 'Keep Sidcup Nuclear Free' campaign. I didn't even know Sidcup was under nuclear threat.

Even Kevin has a little wobbling football kit in his team's colours in the back of his van.

You can tell a lot about someone's personality by looking at his or her car.

I stood in the street and surveyed my own rusting automobile. What did it say about me? It was bare of decoration, except for a sticker proclaiming where I'd bought it:

MULDER & RUST

Quality Used Cars,
Emergency Vehicle Repairs and Recovery Service

'We'll drive you to a breakdown'

It seemed characterless and impersonal. I don't have any shiny fish or texts stuck to my windscreen, no indication that I belong to any clubs, groups or societies, no record of my holidays. It doesn't bear any evidence that I support a charity or good cause. There's nothing to tell any of the hundreds of people who see *my* car every day anything about its occupant.

I don't even have furry dice.

A horrible thought struck me. Maybe there's nothing to tell. Perhaps my life really is so empty and void that there's nothing to write on a car sticker. Maybe I'm a non-person. How depressing! I'm glad there isn't a Bible passage proclaiming, 'By their cars shall they be judged.'

I could buy a sticky fish to show other Christians that I'm one too. Then we could smile and nod in a 'we're in the club' sort of way when we drive past each other, but that would mean forfeiting the pleasure of shouting and making gestures at people who cut me up at the traffic lights. Blow that! It's my only vice. I'd rather remain anonymous.

5 a.m.
Can't sleep. I've been haunted by dreams about car stickers. At one point I dreamed that Nigel and Charity had nailed a giant crucifix to the roof of my car and were decorating it with fairy lights. Now I'm worried that I'm not using opportunities to tell people about Jesus, like Charity. I can't even get away from her in my sleep. A fortnight's worth of relaxation wrecked in one afternoon.

Sunday 13 September

HARVEST FESTIVAL
A cynic would call it an opportunity to empty your kitchen cupboards of all the tins of marshmallow-and-aniseed-flavour rice pudding, anchovies and pasta wheelbarrows and inflict them on the less fortunate. Not that I'm a cynic, of course. I'd never dream of fobbing off the contents of my cupboards on distressed pensioners in the parish. I went to Tesco specially and spent a not inconsiderable sum, which humility forbids me to record, but it was more than you normally win over the counter on a scratch lottery ticket.

Not that I do the lottery, of course.

Anyway, I thought that just because people are elderly or poor, it doesn't mean they shouldn't be able to enjoy life's little luxuries occasionally. It will make a change from all those Rich Tea biscuits.

Kevin came round with a few tins and some tap washers which he insisted the poor and deprived in the village should have in their store cupboards just in case. Tried to talk him into coming to the service.

'Don't you think this "patty dee foy grass" will be too rich, and the caviar might stick to their false teeth?' enquired Kevin, peering into my shoebox.

'Plebeian,' I sneered.

'Thank you very much,' said Kevin.

The church looked beautiful. Jeremiah Wedgwood had donated a giant marrow and people had brought flowers and produce from their gardens to decorate the building. Charity had made a cornucopia-shaped loaf of bread, complete with pomegranates, dates and figs and decorated with woven grapevines. She said she felt it was important to be faithful to the historical and geographical context of the Bible and portray only authentic Middle Eastern fruit. It was a shame someone had propped their tin of curry-flavoured beans with pork sausages against it. I found a single vacant seat next to Miss Chamberlain.

Kevin had ignored the invitation to come with me and had stayed back at my flat to realign my ball cock and grind my cistern valves. Apparently it's an essential plumbing job which shouldn't be delayed. Sometimes I think he's just finding excuses for not coming to church. I told him he would be condemned to hellfire for all eternity, but he started up his blowtorch and pretended not to hear.

We sang 'We plough the fields and scatter' and took our little boxes to the front. I helped Miss Chamberlain carry hers, filled with Rich Tea biscuits and packets of tea. Surely she should be receiving Harvest gifts, not giving them. 'Just a little something for the old folks,' she sparkled.

At the end of the service they asked for volunteers to take the boxes around to the old, sick and needy in the parish tomorrow afternoon. I looked across at Charity, beaming over her basket of home-made delicacies, and felt a pang of envy. I could do that, I decided. I'm due a day off. My hand shot up.

I'm going to visit those in need with provisions and a word of comfort. This could be the ministry I've been searching for.

Monday 14 September

2 p.m.
Collected my four boxes and loaded them into my car ready to deliver to the names on Nigel Hubble's list of needy people. Made sure one of the boxes was the one that I'd donated. I must admit, I really want to see the look of surprise and gratitude on the face of the person when I hand it over. I won't tell them it's from me, of course.

Just time for a quick cup of tea before I start my 'ministry of deliveration'.

5 p.m.
I am never ever doing that again!

The first house I visited had a brand-new Mercedes parked in the drive. An elderly lady with a complexion like a sun-dried tomato and wearing a cashmere sweater opened the door.

'This is from St Norbert's as a gift to the poor and needy in the parish,' I explained.

'Oh, how kind! That will come in very handy. We've just got back from a month in the Algarve and I haven't a thing in the house.' She took the box and shut the door before I could draw breath.

The second address appeared to be inhabited by four or five savage Alsatians, which slavered and snapped behind the six-foot-high security gate. I threw the box over the gate like a champion shot-putter. There was a whimper as the box landed and I swear I could hear the sound of teeth piercing tin as I drove away.

The third address was on a small council estate where the inhabitants had purchased most of the houses and decorated them in a variety of styles ranging from neo-classical and Georgian to stone-cladding. The address for the package was a dingy, unmodified, mid-terrace house. I rang the doorbell and waited. I could hear feet shuffling up the hall.

'Wha'd'ya want?' came a husky voice from the other side of the door.

'I'm from the church. I've brought you a Harvest gift.'

'Push off. I don't want yer blinkin' charity.'

'It's, um, just a few things—' I peered into the box, '—fruit, and that.'

'Fruit gives me the trots.'

'All right, I'll take it away and give it to someone else. Sorry to have bothered you.'

'Wait a minnit.' The door opened a crack. 'Got 'ny booze in there?'

'No,' I snapped. 'You'll have to brew it yourself from the fruit.' I prised the box through the crack in the door and left.

I had trouble finding the fourth address, so I stopped to ask a couple of workmen who were sitting on the back of a delivery lorry enjoying the autumn sunshine.

'Do you know where number 42 is?' I asked. 'I've got this box to deliver.'

'Yeah, it's just round the back, love. Do you want me to take it round for you? It looks a bit heavy.'

'No thanks. I can manage.'

One of the men hopped down from the tailboard and opened the gate for me. He peered into the box. 'What's all that food for, then?'

'It's from the church. For the old people.'

'What, do they get to choose what they want and you deliver it, then?'

'No, it's Harvest. People in the church give food, then we put it in boxes and take it round to old people in the village.' He shrugged and shook his head. He didn't look very old. I tried to explain. 'Don't you remember doing it at school? Harvest Festival ... "We plough the fields and scatter..."'

He looked blankly at his mate, who also shrugged and looked blank. 'Sorry, love. We're from Croydon.'

I rang the doorbell and an old lady with a large hearing aid opened the front door. 'Oh, is that for me?' she exclaimed, clapping her hands together in delight. She peered into the box. 'What's this? Pâté, caviar ... oh dear, I can't eat that, I'm afraid. I was hoping for a nice packet of Rich Tea. What a shame. Never mind, I really am most grateful. I can give the pâté and stuff to the cat – I'm sure she'll enjoy it, and it saves me buying cat food. Thank you so much.'

Any hopes that I'd found my ministry gurgled noisily down the drain.

Tuesday 15 September

Came home to find Dad sitting on the front doorstep with his knees tucked up and his hands clasping his shins like a lanky garden gnome. Felt an instant sense of foreboding. There could only be two reasons for Dad to turn up unannounced – bad news, or his need to borrow some kind of obscure plumbing device from Kevin's toolbox. I prayed it was the latter.

'Dad, what a surprise! Is anything the matter, or do you urgently need a pipe-bender?'

'Does anything have to be the matter? Can't a man just visit his daughter sometimes?' He pulled his long face into a kind of grimace, which I guessed was supposed to be an ingratiating smile.

'Come on, I don't normally come home to find you sitting there on the doorstep. What's wrong?'

'I don't suppose I could stay for supper?'

'Won't Mum have cooked you something?'

He let out a shuddering sigh. 'That's just it. I couldn't stand it. I just couldn't take any more.' His voice trembled with emotion.

I felt my eyes widen. 'Whatever have you done?'

I glanced at his hands for traces of soil, in case he had done away with Mum and buried her under the patio.

'It's not what *I've* done, it's what *she's* doing that's driving me crackers.'

'What is she doing?' I had visions of him enlightening me about my mother having a sordid affair with the milkman, or running up thousands in gambling debts, or even running off to join the Salvation Army.

'Moussaka. Blinking moussaka. I'm sick of the sight of it!'

'But Mum's always cooked moussaka at least once a week.'

'Once a week would be bliss! Heaven! I'm getting it twice a day at the moment.'

'How come?'

'It all started when the two of you went away on holiday. Your mother left me a freezer full of her home-cooked Greek delicacies, enough for the whole fortnight. One evening when I got back from work, I really fancied fish and chips. I knew I shouldn't. I knew I'd get into trouble if I didn't eat the supper she'd made for me, see, and I didn't want to waste it, so the next day I took it to work with me and gave it to Georgie – his Mam's Greek. Well, the next night I just thought, "I could murder a curry." So I did the same again. The next night was Chinese and the night after that, pizza. So Georgie and his family was getting all your Mam's suppers. Lapping them up, they were. Turns out Georgie's brother Nicky runs a restaurant and catering business. Reckons your Mam's moussaka's the best he's tasted outside of Athens. When she got back I made the mistake of telling her. That's where the trouble started.'

'You mean, she was angry with you for not eating them?'

'No, she was delighted. Got the idea into her head of making this stuff and selling it to Nicky as a takeaway. Only trouble, see, is that she's got to get the recipe absolutely perfect – bit more spice, bit less aubergine, make the béchamel a bit thicker. And guess who has to eat the flaming stuff all the time. I'd call myself a guinea pig, but at least a guinea pig gets to eat dandelions once in a while.' He hung his head. 'I'd do anything for a spot of steak and kidney pie or a couple of sausages.'

'Is she serious?'

His look said everything.

'But that's great!'

'Not if you're me it isn't. She's contacted the bank, put her name down for one of these food hygiene courses, even designed the packaging.'

'Hang on. "Doreen Llewellyn, Authentic Greek Cuisine" – doesn't sound quite right.'

'Calling herself Aphrodite.' His face suddenly broke into a grin and he let out a little snorting laugh. 'That'll be the day.'

'Come on, I'll see what I can find in the fridge,' I smiled. I took his arm, unlocked the door and went up to search for something without olive oil, aubergines or tomatoes in my fridge.

Wednesday 16 September

Declan is off for a couple of weeks' leave from today. He has told everyone else he's off surfing in Cornwall, but confided to me that Katherine has insisted that he goes round and decorates her flat. I'm to be promoted temporarily to Trainee Assistant Deputy Manager. It means that I get an extra £3.84 per week and am permitted to use the executive coat rack.

Thursday 17 September

A memo arrived on my desk this morning. In my capacity as temporary Trainee Assistant Deputy Manager, I'm required to take over Declan's post as secretary to the divisional committee at their AGM. My duties will comprise agreeing and compiling the agenda, taking the minutes and later distributing copies to those who were present at the meeting. Shouldn't be too difficult – I just need to sharpen my pencil, brush up on my shorthand and practise crossing my legs in a ladylike manner. I'm quite looking forward to being an integral part of the cutting-edge, decision-making process, a vital cog in the managerial machinery. In fact, I think I'll go and compile that agenda right now.

10.30 p.m.
Actually, I'm quite worried about this meeting. What if I can't keep up with the cut-and-thrust dialogue? What if I'm way out of my depth in the higher echelons of management? I'm to meet the Area Manager. He's only just below

the Regional Administrator, who ranks slightly below the Divisional Director, who reports directly to the Managing Director. I can't do it! I am too lowly.

Too late to phone Declan now.

Friday 18 September

2.30 a.m.
Phoned Declan, whose voice, through the yawns, sounded comforting and reassuring.

'Sorry, did I wake you?' I said.

'Well, no. Whatever makes you think I'd be sleeping at this time of the morning?'

I explained my dilemma.

'Don't worry about it, Theo, it's all bluff. You'll be fine. Just dress smart and pretend you know what you're doing. If you believe yourself, so will they. Then all you have to do at the meeting is write down what they say, work out what they mean, and Seamus is your uncle!'

'But what if I get it wrong?'

'You'll find that most of them are so well lubricated from the pre-meeting booze-up that you could write anything you like. They'll never remember what they said. What do you think you're there for, but to write down what they *would* have said had they been sober enough to think straight? Just one little tip, though. Don't you be going sinking any of the brown stuff before the meeting.'

'You know I hardly ever drink.'

'Aye, you're a good girl. Best of luck! Good night.'

Sunday 20 September

There was a notice in *The Church Organ* today which caught my eye:

Vicarage Refurbishment

Due to the refurbishment of the vicarage kitchen,
it has been suggested by the PCC that
parishioners might like to have the vicar for
Sunday dinner. He has offered to bring his
own jar of mint sauce.

I think, on the whole, I prefer chicken.

Monday 21 September

AGM at our City office today. I wore a black suit with a white shirt, black shoes with heels that were high but not too high, and carried a briefcase. The briefcase was empty apart from my sandwiches, because I couldn't think of anything useful to put in it (I'm one of the few people who still doesn't own a mobile phone). I toyed with the idea of removing the lenses from an old pair of sunglasses so that I could perch them on the end of my nose and peer over them to give myself an air of efficient authority, but decided against it.

The meeting started at 2 o'clock and Declan was right: the Area Manager, two of the Regional Managers and their assistants had obviously spent a rather well-lubricated lunchbreak at the local wine bar. Consequently, their behaviour was rather peculiar. One of the assistants kept falling asleep and had to be nudged awake by his boss. A Regional Manager took frequent and embarrassingly long trips to the Ladies, while the rest of the committee made small talk and tapped their pencils on the conference table. She once disappeared for the best part of half an hour. The other Managers, now completely fed up, decided not to wait for her to return before resuming the meeting. When she eventually returned, she remained three agenda items behind the rest of the committee for the remainder of the meeting. She didn't seem to notice.

The Area Manager was obviously also suffering from the lunchtime hospitality. A man not known for his diplomacy and economy of speech at the best of times, he floundered around with the most extravagant and bizarre metaphors. I just did as Declan had told me, wrote down what they all said and then tried to turn it into what they meant to say. For instance, when the Area Manager said that the proposal for the new office site had 'gone down like a damp squid', I assumed he actually meant a 'damp squib' – ineffectual firework rather than soggy marine creature. When he said we would run up and down the flagpole saluting the idea of more flexible working hours, I translated it as running the idea of more flexible working hours up the flagpole to see who salutes it. (Actually that didn't really make sense either.) Finally, when he said that all the employees who belonged to the union were a bunch of idle troublemakers and slackers and that all the union representatives should have their philanthropic, socialist principles shoved up their backsides, lit, and then be launched off extremely tall buildings like rockets, I toned it down considerably and just reported that they would be instantly dismissed without recompense.

I felt quite pleased with myself at the end of the meeting, as the Area Manager shook my hand warmly. I gained even more Brownie points when I offered to order him a cab to his hotel, although I declined the invitation to join him.

Wednesday 23 September

I decided to tackle the problem of Kevin's spiritual degeneracy head on, to ask him why, despite my persistent efforts, he still refuses to come to church with me. Since I've been going out with him, he's gone from being a 'Christmas/ Easter/weddings/baptisms' attendee to a 'wouldn't set foot inside that place if rabid dogs were chasing me up the high street' person. Surely not even Kevin could be beyond redemption? So, no beating about the bush, I resolved to come straight out with it and ask him why he refuses to go.

'Kevin,' I wheedled, 'there's a family service at church this week.'

'Yeah ... and...?' he replied sulkily.

'Well, I just wondered if you'd like to come with me.' I said this in my best baby-bunnies-and-kittens voice.

'No thank you,' he answered curtly.

'Well, you should. It'd do you good, pagan!' I snapped.

'I just don't want to.'

'But why?'

'You know I hate family services.'

'But why?' I persisted.

'Do you want to know the truth? Do you really want to know why I hate family services so much? Would you like to know why I'd rather walk naked up Oxford Street, or have my legs waxed, or go to a Barry Manilow concert, than go to one of your family services? Would you?'

I nodded dubiously.

'Well, I'll tell you. I don't have a problem with the God bit. The Creator who made me, loves me and sent his son to die for me. Yeah, that seems reasonable enough. If it's true, and I think it probably is, I'm happy to hand over my life to him. He'd probably make a better job of it than me. Reading the Bible and talking to God – I can buy that.'

It sounded good so far. I was beginning to hear choirs of heavenly angels singing the *Ave Maria* and was mentally deciding what I would wear on the occasion when Kevin finally stood up in the pulpit and humbly told how he had been led to Christ.

My reverie was cut short as he continued speaking.

'But what I just can't take, the part that gets right up my hooter, is the thought of spending over an hour sitting on a hard bench in a freezing cold building with people I wouldn't normally be seen dead with in a plague pit, and *singing*. Theo, you know me. I've got a voice like a walrus with laryngitis. I don't even sing at a match. And doing a Placido Domingo in church, where people can actually *hear* you . . . I'm sorry, that takes the biscuit, that really does.'

I sat open-mouthed. Singing. He didn't like singing. Was that all?

'Do you know the most embarrassing kind of song?' he continued unabated. 'The "Children's Action Choruses". The ones where you have to wave your arms about, being a chimpanzee or a Dutch girl, and looking a complete moron in front of the greengrocer, the doctor and the bloke who cleans your windows. And do you know the worst thing about it? They sneak these blooming choruses into the family services, when us ordinary blokes have been bullied *by their girlfriends* into setting foot inside the church. But these choruses aren't just for the kids to sing. Oh no. They expect all the grown-ups to join in with the catchy tunes, confusing actions and oh-so-jolly words. It's all right for you Christians; you must be immune to it. After years of exposure to "Children's Action Choruses" you must get used to looking like a bunch of complete idiots. The other day, I even caught the postman humming "I want to be God's pancake, stodgy, round and flat" *out in the street*! Forgive me, but that can't be normal.'

Well, singing children's choruses! Was that it? That's the reason he refuses to become part of the St Norbert's flock? I must admit, I often find those choruses the best part of the service. 'Drown Those Sinners' and 'I'm as Happy as a Puffer Train Bound for Glory Halt' – I love them all. 'His Love is Bigger than the Widest Elephant' was always a particular favourite, until I got a bit carried away with the actions and gave poor Mr Wilberforce a black eye.

I tried to look thoughtful, as if I were weighing his comments. I knew arguing with him would be useless, and quoting scriptures (if I could think of any) would be futile. I had to try a new tactic.

'OK,' I conceded. 'You've got a valid point. I can see exactly what you mean and I respect your opinion. If you really hate it that much, I won't pressure you to come any more.'

'What?' He looked stunned. 'You won't try to blackmail me into going to church with you ever again?'

'Of course not.' I tried to look hurt.

'Really?'

'Really.'

'Promise?'

'Cross my heart.'

'You'll never make me sing those songs?'

'Never. If you don't want to come, it's completely your decision. I respect that. I know that you're a resolute and determined man who knows his mind. If you don't want to come, I wouldn't dream of trying to influence that decision. Conversely, if you do decide to come to church, I know full well that it's a decision arrived at by an independent-minded man who couldn't possibly be swayed by the opinions of any other person.'

Evidence of a deep mental wrestling match appeared on Kevin's face. He was weighing up the arguments. I'd just told him I didn't care if he came or not. I'd just said I respected his opinions and he was free to make his own decision. That was obviously a new one to him. He had to think independently. He'd never done that before. He always found out what I thought and did the opposite. I was refusing to state my opinion for him to contradict. Was it possible that I actually *didn't* want him there? If not, why not? What was I hiding? His brows knitted together in a deep frown of suspicion. He looked up to the ceiling, then down to his feet. Finally he sighed deeply.

'OK then, I'll come.'

'If you like.' I shrugged with a feigned indifference.

'But I'm not singing.'

'Fine. Whatever you say.'

He stood up, covered in confusion. 'Save me a seat on Sunday.' He picked up his coat, planted a kiss on my forehead and started off home, still looking puzzled.

Massage his ego, confuse him by refusing to give an opinion, then make him think it was his idea in the first place. The perfect strategy!

I hadn't thought about it before, but, when you consider it, it *is* an extremely strange thing to expect people to do. In fact, the whole procedure of a church service is quite bizarre. A group of people from different backgrounds and of different ages, with very little in common, gathers once or twice a week in a draughty stone building. They talk, not to each other, but to someone who died 2,000 years ago. They sing about gathering at the river, putting on armour, washing in the fountain and the blood of the lamb. They sit and listen while a man in a long dress tells them how to behave. They read from a book no bigger than a James Clavell novel, the same book people have been using for hundreds and hundreds of years, sometimes in an obsolete version of English. Occasionally they queue up to sip a tiny drop of wine and eat a crumb of bread, given to them by the man in a dress. The only part that really seems to make sense is the coffee at the end. Thinking about it like that, it's a wonder that Christianity as a whole and the Church of England in particular have survived as long as they have.

I suppose it shows it must be true.

Either that, or all Christians are two quiches short of a bring-and-share.

Thursday 24 September

I'm in deep trouble. I may have to leave the country under a false name, change my appearance and take on a new identity, or at least get another job. I'll probably never work in an office ever again. My name will be blacklisted.

I got a phone call from one of the Regional Managers who had been at the committee meeting. He'd just received the minutes.

'What's wrong with them?' I enquired rather shirtily.

'What's wrong with them? You've just said, in black and white, that the Area Manager stated that all trade union officials would be instantly dismissed!'

'So? That's what he said, wasn't it? In fact, I even toned it down. Considerably.'

'Did you ever consider the possibility that he didn't actually *mean* it and that he was just sounding off? That he didn't actually want that part written down and circulated?

Don't you think that, if the union officials themselves ever get hold of it, they might just be the tiniest bit upset? Didn't you contemplate for one moment that, if this ever gets out, there'll be a strike? Industrial relations would completely break down. It would be curtains for the Area Manager. And as for you. . .' He paused to draw in a hissing breath between his clenched teeth. 'As for you, it would make the Spanish Inquisition look like the Teddy Bears' Picnic, Miss Llewellyn.'

Aaagghh!

Friday 25 September

Finally calmed down enough to pluck up the courage to ring Declan at a quarter to one this morning. 'You seem to be making a habit of these nocturnal phone calls,' he said. 'I'd better not let on to Katherine that you're phoning me at all hours. She's a suspicious woman, that one.'

'Yes, sorry. It's just that it's really important, Declan,' I sniffed. 'I've well and truly blown it.'

I explained what had happened and for a while Declan was very quiet. He didn't try to tease me or make a joke of it.

'I see your problem.'

'What can I do?'

'Have you thought about the Foreign Legion?'

I thought it was too good to be true. I was sunk, and Declan was indeed laughing at me.

'Wait a minute!' he exclaimed suddenly. 'Theo, did you send all the minutes out?'

'Yes. I sent them to the Regional Managers a couple of days ago, but I only sent the Area Manager's copy yesterday.'

'Great. We're saved! Leave it to me, Theo. Go and get some sleep and I'll ring you this evening.'

7.30 p.m.

Declan is the most wonderful person in the whole world. He should be knighted. No, sainted!

After years of being secretary to the committee, Declan has enough sleaze on every single Regional Manager to ensure that they will instantly and unquestioningly do whatever he asks. He spent the morning phoning each Regional Manager, reminding them of their little foibles and peccadilloes, and suggesting that they might like to 'lose' their copy of the minutes in the vicinity of the shredder and await an amended copy.

He spent the afternoon charming the Area Manager's secretary into handing back his copy of the minutes unopened and unread.

'Thank you so much, Declan, you've saved my life. How can I repay you?'

'I'll think of a way.'

A thought struck me. 'Hang on, though. The Regional Managers all know what the Area Manager said, even if they no longer have the paper copy, including the ones who didn't attend the meeting. It went out to the entire team.'

'Theo, you just don't understand the workings of a great bureaucracy at all, do you? You see, it doesn't matter what the Area Manager said. It doesn't matter that the Regional Managers know what the Area Manager said. What matters is that the Area Manager doesn't know that the Regional Managers know what he said. He doesn't know that they know, and they don't know that he doesn't know whether they know or not. You see, as long as nobody knows exactly what anyone else knows, no one is going to give the game away and you're in the clear. Simple as that!'

I'll take his word for it.

Saturday 26 September

Mum phoned me this evening. She was checking up on Dad, as his frequent disappearances, which mysteriously coincide with their suppertime, have aroused her suspicions. Firstly, I was able to reassure her that he had been to see me and he definitely wasn't seeing another woman – yet. Secondly, I was hoping to squeeze in a tactful suggestion that she started varying the menu a little, before Dad left home completely and ran off with the woman from the fish-and-chip shop.

Just as I was about to make this suggestion, however, Mum launched into a description of a business meeting where she'd met Georgie and his brother Nicky, and of how she was about to go into partnership with the brothers and their mother and father. There was just one problem. The parents spoke little English, so for the venture to succeed, she would really need to learn to speak Greek. She seemed so excited and I really didn't want to throw cold retsina on the idea, but I have serious doubts about Mum's capacity to converse in eloquent business Greek.

Despite her long association with the country, one area in which Mum has failed to make progress is the language. During our recent trip to Kos, Mum marched confidently down the town's main street, phrasebook in hand, wishing everyone we saw 'good morning'.

Or so she thought.

Part of the problem is that Mum's Greek accent is actually very good and she exudes self-assurance, which unfortunately makes things worse. Her downfall is her vocabulary. She muddles words. Instead of saying '*kalimera*', which is 'good morning' in Greek, she greeted everyone we met with '*kalimari*', which means 'squid'. An easy mistake to make – the words sound very similar. But that goes no distance at all to make up for the perplexed expressions on the faces of the local populace that morning, as my mother waved at them and greeted them all with a cheerful cry of 'Squid!'

Sunday 27 September

Kevin came to church. He sat through the entire service and even opened his eyes and unclenched his fists for part of it. Unfortunately he refused, even metaphorically, to 'raise his hand for the altar call', in spite of a rip-roaring sermon from Digger. Still, as someone said, 'A journey of a thousand miles begins with a single step.' I think it was Elvis Presley. Or that astronaut.

Monday 28 September

The suntan from my holiday started peeling alarmingly today. I noticed it after my shower. It looks as though I've got all-over body dandruff.

Tuesday 29 September

MICHAELMAS
That's a funny idea. Fancy naming a diary date after a type of daisy.

October

Thursday 1 October

Could hardly get my front door open for all the junk mail that had arrived while I was at work. I'm one of the few people who don't mind receiving bills. After all, if I've used it, I expect to pay for it. What I object to are the glossy brochures suggesting I need double glazing, my drive paved, hideous leisure suits or a new three-piece suite.

I also received a newsletter from a neighbouring church that was almost as entertaining as *The Church Organ*. Its headline read, 'NEW BELL TOWER HELD UP BY RED TAPE'. Sounds rather precarious! Still, it got me thinking about fundraising. St Norbert's doesn't seem to do it, but just about every other church and organization does. We haven't got a huge hardboard thermometer outside our church. Why not? There must be something we need. I want to belong to a proper church with a proper fundraising campaign like everyone else. Perhaps I'll start one at St Norbert's.

Hang on, this could be my ministry. I can see it now: I could be the campaign co-ordinator and have my picture in the local paper presenting the cheque. In a humble, modest, self-effacing way, of course.

Sunday 4 October

Rev. Graves's sermon today was about members of the church supporting each other and learning to be tolerant of each other's faults. Felt rather peeved. People who tell me to be more tolerant get right up my nose.

'Be completely humble and gentle; be patient, bearing with one another in love,' intoned Jeremiah Wedgwood from the lectern, reading from Ephesians 4:2. 'And would somebody please keep that baby quiet!'

At the end of the service the vicar announced that, in order to put the principles of the sermon into practice, the church was setting up a system of 'Prayer Partners'. Two people would be randomly chosen (to avoid the problems of either cliques or personal antipathy) and would meet once a week to share problems and joys and to pray for each other. There was a general murmur of approval from the congregation. Greasy Roger Lamarck caught my eye and wiggled his eyebrows at me suggestively. We'll each find out on Tuesday who our randomly selected partner is to be.

I made a list of people I *don't* want to be partnered with. Unfortunately, it accounted for most of the congregation.

Tuesday 6 October

The church secretary rang today to tell me who my Prayer Partner is. I thanked her politely, put down the receiver . . . and screamed. Then picked up the receiver again and rang Ariadne. When I explained the principle of the idea, she thought it was an excellent notion.

'But how am I going to get out of it?' I pleaded. 'They've partnered me with Charity Hubble! I'd rather die.'

'Stop being so melodramatic, Theo. Who is she, anyway?'

I tried to explain the phenomenon that is Charity Hubble.

'Oh, I remember, Kew Gardens on legs. I must admit, she makes Pollyanna seem clinically depressed.'

'I could leave the country, convert to Islam or develop a tropical disease. Anything has to be better than spending an hour with her. Help me, Ariadne!'

'I think it would be good for you. After all, isn't the point of the exercise to practise patience and forbearance? The best thing would be to try it, see how it goes.'

Why is it that those closest to you make you suffer the most?

Wednesday 7 October

Spent most of last night wrestling with the idea of Charity being my Prayer Partner. Came to the conclusion that, deep down, I don't mind praying for her. I just can't stand the thought of her praying for me. The idea of having to expose my hopes, doubts, fears and insecurities to her makes me want to lock myself in the cupboard with the dusters.

I've known Charity since we were at school. One day, when we were about 14, the teacher, Miss Tyson, asked our class to write down what we would like to achieve in life. The class frantically scribbled their hopes and dreams onto pieces of paper. I scribbled a bit, crossed it out, chewed my pencil, scribbled a bit more, stared out of the window, then spilled my ambitions onto the paper. Miss Tyson asked us to stand up, one by one, and read them out to the rest of the class. Some wanted to be politicians, actresses, doctors, lawyers, professional boxers (it was a very progressive girls' school). My ambitions, I remember, included being a successful businesswoman, owning a large house and a beautiful car, being a patron of the arts and supporter of humanitarian causes, and being universally respected and accepted. Charity wrote that she wanted to get married and have lots of children.

Everyone laughed at her.

The thought has struck me that I'm still light years away from achieving my ambitions, whereas Charity has realized hers. And she's happy. That's why she irritates me so much.

Thursday 8 October

Charity is coming round for our first Prayer Partner meeting tonight. Must think of something she can pray for – can't bear the idea of telling her my real worries.

6 p.m.
Done it! Have composed a list of things to ask Charity to pray about:

1 Button has fallen off my best coat.
2 Auntie Maggie's cat has a bald patch.
3 Declan has lost the key to the ladies' toilet at work. (Genuine need for prayer there!)
4 I was tempted to eat three doughnuts at lunchtime.
5 Actually ate two. Prayer for forgiveness for sin of gluttony.

10 p.m.
List not required. Charity brought her own list, which, from what I can remember, included:

1 Forgiveness for forgetting to iron Nigel's shirt.
2 Thanks that Nebuchadnezzar's missing biro has been found safely.
3 Prayer for success in Bathsheba's spelling test.
4 Release from bad habits (which sounded interesting, until it turned out to be thumb-sucking) for three-year-old Ahimelech.
5 That a Christian home might be found for Solomon, their budgie, when they go on holiday soon.

Apparently Charity is deeply concerned that the budgie, which can say 'Praise the Lord' and recite parts of the Nicene Creed, might learn bad language while they're away, if left with 'unsound elements'.

I offered to look after the budgie for her. Can't wait to increase its vocabulary!

When we'd got about halfway through the list the phone rang, as arranged, and I answered it.

'I'm not doing this again next week, you know,' said Ariadne's irritated voice.

'Ah, Mrs Barrie!' I said in a jolly tone. 'How nice to hear from you.'

'Next time, you're on your own. I mean it!' came my sister's voice.

'What's that? You've lost your cat?' I sounded concerned.

'You know how I hate covering up for you,' she hissed through her teeth.

'And you'd like me to help you look for it?'

'Right, that's it! I'm going now. You can find someone else to do your dirty work for you,' grumbled Ariadne, and hung up.

'Of course I can come now, Mrs Barrie. See you in a minute.'

I put the phone down and turned to Charity. 'That was Mrs Barrie, the old lady from downstairs,' I lied. 'She's very attached to her little cat and it appears to have gone missing. I hope you don't mind ending our prayer time early so I can go and help her find it.'

'Not at all. I'll help you search for it.'

'Er . . . no, that's perfectly all right, thanks.'

'But it will be quicker with both of us looking, and it's a foul night for a poor little creature to be out.'

I looked out of the window at the grey sky. A fine, tenacious drizzle hung in the air along with the autumn smell of bonfires. 'Really, I'd hate you to get soaked. Didn't you need to get back to iron some shirts, or something?'

'I insist. Nigel's shirts are of secondary importance to helping alleviate a poor old lady's distress at the misplacement of her beloved pet. I'm sure he'll forgive me for deserting my wifely duties this once.'

Charity and I put our coats on, I found two torches, and we went out into the cold wet night to begin our totally pointless search. We peered under cars, called 'Puss, Puss!' into gardens and swept our torches like searchlights into trees. I didn't even know if Mrs Barrie owned a cat.

'What does this cat look like?' asked Charity.

'Er . . . it's black, I think. With white bits.'

'What's its name? I feel silly just calling it "Puss".'

My brain worked frantically. I glanced around and my eyes alighted on Mr Barrie's old car. 'Allegro,' I blurted.

'That's a funny name for a cat,' remarked Charity.

After about half an hour we called off the search. 'Oh well, I'm sure Allegro will turn up. We'd better go in,' I said wearily.

'I suppose you're right,' said Charity, 'but I think I'll just see how Mrs Barrie is.'

'No!' I exclaimed. 'I really don't think we should disturb her.'

'Nonsense. She'll be worried.'

It was too late. Charity had marched up to the old lady's door and pressed the buzzer. After a few seconds the door opened and there, framed in a rectangle of light, stood the short, stout figure of Mrs Barrie, cradling a small, black and white cat.

'Oh, you found him. How super! I am pleased,' said Charity.

Mrs Barrie stood there looking puzzled.

'Goodnight then, God bless.'

Damp, cold and feeling sour, I trudged back up the stairs to my flat. Charity had remained good-humoured throughout the totally futile cat hunt and had positively glowed at seeing the old lady reunited with her very-much-in-residence feline.

Why do I do it, God? Why do I have to make life so complicated?

Saturday 10 October

I received a photocopied sheet among my junk mail (just how do these people get my address?) proclaiming that Professor Ignatius Hardy-Larkin of the Worldwide Evangelism in the Community Fellowship Training Institute was offering a training course every Tuesday in the Scout hut, starting next month. *Eight Easy Exercises in Enthusiastic Evangelistic Endeavours*, it was called.

Evangelism – could this be my ministry? Decided instantly to go along. It sounds right up my street. Must phone

Ariadne for moral support. After all, they might turn out to be some kind of cult and try to brainwash me. No one would dare try to brainwash Ariadne.

Sunday 11 October

Visited Ariadne and Tom's church today. Even *they* are involved in fundraising. They have an appeal fund for a new organ. Apparently a colony of a very rare species of bat has been found nesting in the pipes of the old one and wildlife conservationists are reluctant to have them disturbed from their slumber by the Evensong hymns. Instead, the church is fundraising for a new, digital, state-of-the-art electronic organ, which is the size of a small suitcase. They will, of course, keep the old one for show.

Feel even more jealous now. We don't need a new organ. There are no rare bats in our organ loft, although someone once suggested to the vicar that he might have some in his belfry. I don't think so. The bells would have frightened them off. There must be *something* we need to fundraise for. Overseas mission? New hymn books?

Monday 12 October

Kevin refused to come round this evening. He said I've been snappy recently, always barking up the wrong tree and then biting his head off. Makes me sound like a cross between a Chihuahua and a Rottweiler.

'You're like a bivouac and a marquee, Theo.'

'What are you jabbering about in that half-witted way?' I drummed my fingers on the tabletop.

'You're just two tents.'

Tuesday 13 October

I'm refusing to talk to Kevin until he explains yesterday's comment. He doesn't seem to understand that those things get me really wound up.

Wednesday 14 October

Informed Kevin on the phone that I was very sorry, but, un-Christian as it was, I was going to have to kill him unless he told me what on earth he was talking about. He laughed so hard I thought he was going to choke. I eventually hung up on him.

Declan asked me today if anything was wrong. When I asked him why, he said that if my shoulders were scrunched up any higher around my ears, I would go deaf. He also threatened to take away all my pens and pencils if I didn't stop tapping them on the desk. He said it was like working with Ringo Starr. I explained my predicament over Kevin's comment.

'Oh Theo,' he laughed, 'he's quite right. You're definitely two tents!'

Thursday 15 October

Gritting my teeth all day. Prayer Partner meeting with Charity again tonight. Ariadne is still not speaking to me after I made her lie for me last week, and Declan fell off his chair laughing when I told him about the cat search.

Hoped I would get run over by a bus on the way home from work tonight, but it didn't happen. Nobody has phoned, urgently requiring my attendance at something. War has not been declared. So, there's no choice. I'll just have to endure it.

I wonder if she'd notice if I wore my Walkman.

11 p.m.
When Charity arrived this evening, her usual, beaming,
'I'm completely at peace and my Christian life is advancing
in leaps and bounds' smile was missing.

'What's up, Charity? Has Naphtali lost his school tie
again? Or have you and Nigel had a tiff about whether to
buy chunky or thin-shredded marmalade?'

'Actually, it's my Granddad,' she said. 'I'm desperately
worried about him. He was rushed to hospital last night. I
just thought I'd call in on my way to see him. I wanted to
ask if you'd mind praying for him.'

'What's the matter with him?'

'They think he's had a stroke. Things don't look too
promising.'

'I'm sorry to hear that. Of course I'll pray for him.'

She forced her lips into an impostor of a smile.

I sat alone and thought of Charity's grandfather. I
remembered when I was a child, seeing him in church. He
seemed prehistoric then. Now he must be well over 90. He
used to sit very upright in his dark suit, blinking slowly as
he listened to the sermon. He had bushy white hair and
long white whiskers. The general appearance was decidedly
feline, like a very old, dignified cat. During silent prayer, I
swear I could hear him purring.

It was difficult to know what to pray. After all, he's an old
man and old men die. I thanked God for his life and then
prayed for Charity. She might make me want to reach for a
bucket every time I speak to her, but I really don't like her
to be unhappy. It makes me feel guilty about detesting her.

Friday 16 October

Two tents – too tense! I've got it!

Now, where's that large, unpleasant cactus? I have an overwhelming desire to use it to inflict something very nasty upon Kevin.

Saturday 17 October

Finally got round to reading last week's copy of *The Church Organ* and was intrigued by an item of village news about the new curtains purchased for the Scout hut as a result of funds raised by the WI, who held a sponsored 'cream-cakeathon'. (See? More fundraising – it gets everywhere.) Rather than allowing the occasion to go unmarked and just putting the curtains up in the windows, inhabitants of the village have been invited to a 'public hanging' at the Scout hall next Friday evening. Apparently refreshments are available (not cream cakes, sadly) and visitors are welcome to take photographs.

Sunday 18 October

Rev. Graves is on holiday for the next two weeks, so we have what are known as 'visiting clergy' to officiate at the services. A succession of visiting clergy certainly makes you appreciate your own vicar. A rather worrying notice in *The Church Organ* read:

> *During Reverend Graves's leave of absence, the visiting clergy will be found pinned to the noticeboard by the front doors.*

It's little wonder that none of them comes back for a second visit.

Monday 19 October

Ariadne accosted me at lunchtime, just as I was about to sneak out to the cake shop.

'I got a letter this morning,' she said curtly, brandishing a blue airmail envelope at me. 'I think you need to do some explaining.'

She seized me by the arm and marched me up the street to Gianni's Italian Café. There she sat me down and slapped the letter on the table in front of me like the bad cop in a police drama.

'Well?' she demanded.

'I don't know what this is all about,' I protested.

'You remember Steve, the missionary?'

'Um, yes...' I replied rather more cautiously.

'I've just received this letter from him. Shall I tell you what he says?'

I had the feeling she was going to tell me anyway, regardless of what I said.

'He wrote to our church to thank everybody who had written and to say how grateful he was for their prayers and support. He also said he was fascinated by one of the letters. One from a young teacher, a young, female teacher who is thinking of becoming a missionary. A young, female teacher who is thinking of becoming a missionary, by the name of Theodora Llewellyn. He's asking for a photo and has enclosed this *personal* letter to the young lady in question. What have you been up to?'

'Well, I might have exaggerated a bit.'

'You didn't exaggerate. You lied. What you wrote was a

blatant pack of falsehoods to make yourself out to be something you're not. How could you?'

My face glowed with shame. I suppose that, technically, I had lied. I had also known full well how upset Ariadne would be if she found out. Put like that, I felt second only to Jack the Ripper in the ranks of all-time low-life scum.

'I didn't mean to hurt anyone. I just wanted to, well, to improve on myself a bit.'

Ariadne sat, arms folded, and snorted in disgust. Honesty has always been of paramount importance to Ariadne.

'Let's face it,' I continued, 'people like us are boring. We're short and dumpy with mousy hair, we're pushing 30, we do boring jobs, drive boring cars, live boring lives. We never write books, compose music, or do anything that doesn't perpetuate our own boring existence. We're from Sidcup, for goodness' sake! Nobody in their right mind is going to be interested in us, particularly a handsome doctor who travels to exotic parts of the world to change things, to make a difference. People like us – people like me – don't make a difference. I wanted to live in that other world, just for a little while, and pretend I was someone else, someone worthwhile.'

'How can you say that? No person is more or less important than another because of what they look like, what they do for a living, or where they were born!'

'It feels that way.'

Ariadne took my hands and held them in hers. 'If that was the case, what future would there have been for a carpenter, "pushing 30", from the backwater town of Nazareth? At least Sidcup's got a McDonald's! I know you're finding it hard to see what God wants you to do at the moment. Just being yourself might be a start.'

She passed me the letter. 'Here, you'd better have this.'

'I'll have to write back and . . . explain, I suppose,' I said reluctantly.

'Look, Steve's a really nice guy. He won't be angry, really.'

'No, he'll probably have a good laugh, though.'

10 p.m.
Read the letter from Steve. It was kinder than I deserved. He gave details of a missionary society and some books to read if I really thought God was calling me to be a missionary. He suggested, however, that if I really looked how I'd described myself in the letter, perhaps I should think about a career in modelling instead. He also asked me to pass on his regards to my brother Ag. Apparently they were in the Scouts together.

Steve?

Steve! All of a sudden I remembered a tall, gangly boy who used to play football with my brother. I once asked him what he thought the offspring of a basketball player and a guppy would look like. He shook his head and looked down at his shoes.

'Look in the mirror, then,' I had taunted.

That was Steve.

Please God, make the world end tonight.

Tuesday 20 October

The world didn't end. No sign of a ministry of any sort and, to cap it all, I've just discovered irrefutable proof that I'm getting old. I watched a gardening programme on television – and enjoyed it.

Wednesday 21 October

Phone call from Charity. Her Granddad died last night. I didn't know what to say. Suddenly all my problems seemed trifling and insignificant.

Her voice was full of tears. 'I just wanted to thank you for praying for us, Theodora,' she said. 'It makes a difference, knowing someone cares.'

'If there's anything I can do to help,' I said sympathetically. It felt good. I was offering a fellow human being my compassion in her time of trouble. This was what Christian living is really about.

'Well, there is just one teensy-weensy little thing. I hate to ask, but...' She paused, and then took a deep breath. 'The funeral will be a week on Friday. I wonder if you could just look after baby Ezekiel for a couple of hours?'

Noooo! Anything but that! Please God. I'm psychologically incompatible with babies, especially hamster-faced Hubble babies.

What could I do? I had offered. I had backed myself into a corner. I was only saying what anyone says in these circumstances. I didn't really *want* to do anything for her; I was just making the right noises. A sigh escaped. There was no getting out of this one. I would have to do it.

'Just for a couple of hours, you say?'

'Oh yes. I'll leave everything you need – his toys, bottles, nappies. You're a gem, Theodora.'

I groaned and sank to my knees. What have I done?

Thursday 22 October

Toyed with the idea of borrowing a book on baby care from the library, then thought better of it. Surely *anyone* can manage a baby for a couple of hours? I remembered the selection of childcare books Mum and Dad had on the bookshelves at home. Most of them seemed to have been written by Dr Spock. How could my parents possibly have entrusted the upbringing of their children to a man with pointy ears?

Friday 23 October

Having decided that visiting is definitely not my gift, the more I think about it, the surer I am that God is grooming me to become an evangelist (perhaps with a bit of fund-raising thrown in for good measure). After all, I enjoy talking to people, I've been a Christian for absolutely ages, so I know what it's like, and I happen to own a very large Bible. I think I'm well qualified. Anyway, after missing the 'public hanging', attending Professor Hardy-Larkin's course will be a good opportunity to admire the new curtains in the Scout hall. Training starts on 3 November.

Saturday 24 October

I can't do it. I can't possibly look after a baby for a whole two hours. By the end of it I'll be clinically insane. Will phone Charity and explain the problem. Perhaps I could tell her I'm suffering from a contagious disease.

Sunday 25 October

Why do there always seem to be more people in the queue for coffee after the service than there were in the service itself? Where do all the extra people come from? Mentioned this to Nigel Hubble.

'I'm not sure,' he said as he scratched his chin. 'Perhaps it's the thirst after righteousness.'

Monday 26 October

Passed Charity on my way to work today. I've never seen anyone looking so crestfallen. Started to tell her that it had all been a mistake and that I couldn't look after Ezekiel after all. Before I could say anything much, however, she told me she had just had to cancel their holiday. Racked with guilt, I told her how much I was looking forward to looking after Ezekiel.

Tuesday 27 October

Work is hectic this week. They've just finished installing a new computer system. It seems to be one of those systems that allow you to do half the work in double the time.

Wednesday 28 October

Declan sent a memo to all staff today. It was entitled 'Working Towards a Paper-free Office' and appealed to staff to use e-mail and electronic data storage systems to reduce paper consumption. He sent the memo, to all 140 staff, on A4 paper.

Thursday 29 October

I must confess, I'm quaking at the mere thought of Ezekiel Hubble. What if I lose him or drop him or do something you're not supposed to do with babies and damage him for the rest of his life? Fingers will point and everyone will accuse me.

'It was her!' they'll say. 'Never let her near your children!'

In the end I phoned Mum, who absolutely refused to come round and help me. 'Just two things you need to know about babies, Theo. Firstly, they bounce. Secondly, they're too young to remember. Just don't forget those two things and you won't go far wrong. That's what got me through bringing up you three.'

That explains everything.

Friday 30 October

8 p.m.
Just getting ready for bed. Absolutely exhausted. Looked after baby Ezekiel for almost two hours today. I need a drink.

Saturday 31 October

Finished wiping the trail of slimy rusk and congealed snot from my walls and furniture this morning. I didn't know it was possible for one small person to produce so much bodily effluent from so many different places.

I started off hoping that yesterday would be a quiet day – a stroll with the pushchair in the park to feed the ducks, a story after lunch and an afternoon nap for both of us. Some chance! I thought babies just sat there and looked cute. Not Ezekiel.

The panic I felt at the thought of being in sole charge of such a frail little object evaporated when I actually saw Ezekiel, who is built like a miniature sumo wrestler. I was convinced that Mum was right and that he definitely would bounce. I'm not sure about his capacity to remember things, though. The look he gave me as Charity heaved him up the stairs seemed to say, 'Watch it. I'll remember you.'

'He's just started crawling,' Charity informed me proudly as she dropped off the department store's worth of paraphernalia a baby seems to need. 'You'll have to keep an eye on him. Oh, and I'd rather you didn't leave those magazines lying around. They wouldn't be good for him.' She nodded towards my pile of *Cosmopolitan*s that had slipped out from under their surreptitious covering of back issues of St Norbert's *The Church Organ*.

Was this child genius able to read as well? Did Charity seriously believe reading the candid yet curiously discerning articles would damage him? I promised that I would move them, gave Charity a 'chin-up, old girl' hug and watched her descend the stairs. When I returned to the living room, I understood immediately what Charity meant. Ezekiel was sitting in the middle of the carpet, devouring the glossy pages of my magazines. I also understood what she meant by the magazines not being good for him, as he proceeded to hawk up large, slimy globules of paper on my living room carpet.

Feeding the ducks was equally stressful and almost as messy. Ezekiel, restrained and thankfully immobilized by a four-point harness like an overweight parachutist in his pushchair, solemnly chewed his way through the stale crusts intended for the ducks. I stopped him, just in time, from eating the plastic bag as well.

Lunch was a holocaust. Apparently, even after the magazines and the ducks' bread, there was still space in his stomach for the home-made braised vegetable mush Charity had supplied. I valiantly dipped, shovelled, scraped and scooped the mush into his mouth. Most of it ended up dribbled down his chin, in his hair or over me.

I cleaned him up as best I could and laid him in his pushchair for an afternoon nap. He went to sleep surprisingly quickly. I gazed at his food-encrusted face, plump fingers and soft, wispy hair – and wondered how Charity managed, day in, day out. After two hours I was a physical and mental wreck. At least I hadn't dropped him.

The buzzer sounded and I helped Charity load her van with Ezekiel's impedimenta.

'How was he?' she enquired.

'Oh, fine. No trouble at all. Good as gold,' I lied.

'How many times did you have to change his nappy? Only he does seem to have rather rapid digestion at the moment.'

Change his nappy? Oh, so that's what the smell was.

November

Sunday 1 November

ALL SAINTS' DAY

Jeremiah Wedgwood stood up after the prayers today to bear witness to the depravity and pagan idolatry that gripped our village. There were shocked gasps as he recounted how, on his way home from his 'ministry of visitation of the sick', he was mistaken for a trick-or-treater. The horrified gasps gave way to stifled sniggers and muffled chortles as he described the episode. Even the normally imperturbable Rev. Graves was biting on his handkerchief and crossing his legs for fear of embarrassing himself.

Jeremiah Wedgwood's long black coat and dark trilby leave very little of the man exposed, except his watery blue eyes. No one could describe Jeremiah as portly. Indeed, cadaverous would be an apt description. On Halloween night, he would look something like a cross between the Phantom of the Opera and Freddie Kruger.

He described how a group of small children – dressed as a ghost, a pirate and a Teletubby – had run up to him in the street, screaming and whooping. They skidded to a halt a few feet in front of him, performed a perfect U-turn and vanished, screaming, into the nearest house. When he knocked on the door in order to reprimand the parents for allowing their children to participate in such a profane ritual, the door was opened a fraction, five pairs of anxious eyes peered through the gap, then a bag of sweets and biscuits were pushed into his hand and the door was slammed in his face. A moment later, the door opened a crack and a man's voice requested, in quavering tones, that Jeremiah kindly give their house a miss next year, as the children were scared rigid.

'How they thought that I would dream of participating in such a heathen activity is just beyond reason!' he exclaimed, his hands trembling and his eyes streaming with outrage.

Poor Jeremiah. I have the feeling that he had unintentionally succeeded in his aim of ridding the streets of ghouls, spectres and local children.

Monday 2 November

Practised walking around with my Bible tucked under my arm and an air of calm assurance, trying to look like an evangelist. Think I ended up looking more like an unsuccessful but deeply religious double-glazing salesman.

Tuesday 3 November

Ariadne and I walked into the Scout hut and nearly walked straight out again. It was full of earnest-looking people all smiling too much. Some of the women were wearing long skirts and had lurid headscarves tied under their chins. Some of the men wore baggy grey cardigans with leather elbow patches and zip-up fronts. They all seemed extremely tense and grinned inanely whenever they weren't actually speaking. Ariadne muttered something about suddenly having an overwhelming urge to powder her nose, and disappeared.

Before I could turn and run, a woman with a grin like the Cheshire cat at Billingsgate Fish Market came and introduced herself as Peggy, pumping my hand enthusiastically and almost crushing my fingers. This, she explained, was Professor Hardy-Larkin's first rule of evangelism: 'A bright, cheerful smile and a firm, confident handshake gives an impression of overflowing joy and assurance.'

Professor Hardy-Larkin, it transpired, existed only on video. Presumably he was too busy out evangelizing to come to the Scout hut in person. I glanced around desperately for the still-absent Ariadne.

Peggy then introduced me to her boyfriend, Paul, who repeated the bone-crushing assault on my right hand. He spoke in a strangled 'John Major' sort of voice. 'Greetings, sister.'

I leaned forward and removed his large, bottle-bottom spectacles. 'Paul Browning?' I said, and looked him up and down. Paul had once been the hunkiest youth leader St Norbert's had ever seen. Everybody had a crush on him, even Ariadne. I used to stay behind after Youth Group to help him collect up the ping-pong balls and scrub the cigarette burns off the church hall lino. We lost touch when he went to university.

'Paul, is that you? What the blazes happened to you . . . er . . . I mean, how the blazes are you?' I stuttered in disbelief. He looked like the one who got turned away from the sci-fi convention for looking too nerdy.

'Come, Sister Theodora,' he intoned. 'Come drink of the joy and become as we are.'

Peggy, sensing that her boyfriend was in the proximity of a woman who didn't look as if she had just stepped off the set of *Little House on the Prairie*, homed in and took hold of Paul's arm. 'We're brimming over with the joy of the Lord, aren't we, Brother Paul?' she said through gritted teeth.

'Yea verily, Sister Peggy.'

I suppressed an overwhelming urge to laugh. 'I don't doubt that for one minute.' I searched frantically for something sensible to say. 'You're looking. . .' I fumbled for the appropriate word, '. . .well.'

'Thank you. And how is your eternal soul, Sister?'

The question took me aback. Just how do you answer that one? 'Just fine, last time I looked. Thank you for asking.'

'Alleluia, Brother. Praises be!' said Peggy rousingly. They leered joyfully at each other. My curiosity got the better of me.

'Look, I'm sorry to ask, but why are you being like this?'

'Like what, Sister?' Paul looked puzzled.

'Well . . . strange. You came to St Norbert's for years, you did a brilliant job with the Youth Group, then you disappeared off to university and we never heard from you again. Now, when I finally do see you, you've become – there's no other word for it – strange.'

Peggy clung to him even more tightly, like a jealous boa constrictor. 'The Professor and his teachings have transformed our lives. We have gone from being indistinguishable from "the world" to being those who really stand out as different, a light, a beacon to a dark world. The Bible tells us to be "an holy nation, a peculiar people".'

'Surely that's peculiar as in "special or separate", not peculiar as in "nutty as a fruitcake".'

'Unlike you, Professor Hardy-Larkin doesn't believe in twisting Scripture to suit his own purposes,' Peggy offered icily.

Paul tried to patch up the situation. 'It is biblical, Theodora. The Professor knows his theology. He stressed that we were not to be of this world. We should stand apart. Easy Exercise Number Seven.'

'Did he specify which world you *were* to be part of? Planet Plonker, by any chance?' I probed.

Paul fiddled nervously with his cross.

'And this "standing apart" – is that working?'

'Well,' replied Paul thoughtfully, 'it seems to be. Whenever we go out on street corners to proclaim the message, I haven't noticed many people standing very close to us.'

'What a surprise. And the eminent Professor Hardy-Larkin, what else did he have to say about evangelism? Do tell me. I'm dying to know.'

They grinned inanely. At last they had found someone to talk at. 'He said we should bear the outward manifestation of the joy within at all times. That's the second of the Eight Easy Exercises in Enthusiastic Evangelistic Endeavours.' Their grins distorted into grotesque grimaces. I recoiled involuntarily and my chair slid backwards on the polished floor.

'I'm fascinated. Do continue,' I said from my new position, six feet away from them.

'We are called always to be ready to give account of ourselves, explain why we are as we are,' chipped in Peggy.

My initial incredulity was giving way to a sort of perverse enjoyment. 'Sound advice. Go on then,' I said.

Peggy looked perplexed. 'What?'

'Give account of yourselves.'

'I don't understand,' said Paul.

I spoke very slowly and distinctly, like someone talking to a child. 'Tell me what you're doing. How do you evangelize? Tell me what you actually say. How do you convert people? Isn't it a bit difficult if, every time you approach anyone, they run in the opposite direction because they think you've escaped from somewhere?'

'Are you mocking us?' asked Peggy suspiciously.

'No, really I'm not. I just want to know how you manage it.'

Her face brightened. 'Ah, Professor Hardy-Larkin's fifth Easy Exercise. "Make the most of every opportunity. Proclaim the word at all times and in all places to all peoples." You're here with us. We can evangelize *you*!'

They nodded at each other and grinned like gargoyles.

'But you can't evangelize me. I'm already a Christian!'

'It is not for us to question, just to proclaim the word,' quoted Peggy.

'Another of the "Eight Enormous Endeavours", I suppose,' I sighed. I could see this was leading nowhere. Evangelism, at least Professor Hardy-Larkin's brand of evangelism, was clearly not going to be my cup of Darjeeling.

I was about to say goodbye and make my departure when another of the Professor's proselytes introduced herself as Gloria and seized me by the upper arms. I sensed she was intending to shake my hand, so I quickly plunged both hands into my pockets to avoid further injury. For a moment I thought she was going to hug me instead, and braced myself. She didn't. Instead, she propelled me through a door in one corner of the Scout hut, into the vestibule near the toilets, and sat me down in a grey plastic chair. The rest of the hall, she explained, had a long-standing booking with the WI. It all got rather crowded, but the jam came in handy.

From my position at the end of the third row, I could see Ariadne, pinned between two grinning acolytes in the back row. They had obviously ambushed her on her way back from the toilets. The look she gave me was set on 'shoot to kill'. Gloria rose to her feet and took the platform. The talk, entitled 'Evangelism – Grab 'em and Hold on Tight', began.

Apparently, Professor Hardy-Larkin was full of helpful hints for attracting crowds and keeping their attention while you proclaim the gospel. As Gloria explained, 'Three Techniques for Trendy Theologians in the use of the Thespian and Theatrical to Teach Truths' showed how the performing arts – mime, music and dance – could be used to get the message across to people.

At last, I thought, someone's beginning to make sense. My hopes were dashed, however, when Peggy stood next to Gloria and demonstrated the techniques as Gloria described them. When Gloria spoke eloquently about the effectiveness of mime, Peggy started a truly appalling parody of 'walking against the wind' and 'person inside a glass box'. It was enough to make Marcel Marceau turn in his grave, if he was dead, which he isn't, but this performance would surely have made him wish he was. As Gloria expounded the virtues of music in evangelism, Peggy produced a battered, tuneless guitar and started strumming and singing 'Jesus Bids us Shine' at breakneck speed. The only redeeming factor in the performance was its merciful brevity. During Gloria's articulate address on the beauty and power of dance as a medium of worship, Peggy performed a kind of *Swan Lake* affair, pirouetting and gyrating, arms flailing like a windmill in a hurricane.

I could suppress the laughter no longer. I stuffed my handkerchief into my mouth and pretended I was choking. As Paul patted me on the back, I heard the scraping of a chair. I knew without looking that it was Ariadne's chair. I knew she wouldn't let it pass. I knew that her honesty and integrity would force her to speak out. She just had to say something to this strange, fanatical, misguided group of people. I prayed for an earthquake. It didn't happen.

'Excuse me,' Ariadne's steady voice rang out. Heads swivelled and 10 pairs of eyes gazed impassively at her.

'Look, don't get me wrong, I think it's fantastic that you want to tell people about Jesus, but I don't think you're likely to have the desired effect. After all, I'm a Christian and you scare me rigid!' She gave a little laugh, trying to sound light-hearted. The eyes continued to gaze. 'I think you're trying too hard to be something you're not. I'm sure God loves and accepts us as we really are, not how *you* think some Professor thinks we ought to be. I've known Paul here for a long time.'

Peggy ran over and clung to Paul as if Ariadne was about to prise him from her grasp. Ariadne stared at her, and continued speaking.

'He used to be really nice, you know – normal. He used to run a Youth Group at my church. He cared for the youngsters and they respected him. If he told them about Jesus, they listened because they knew that what he said came from his heart, not the regurgitated ramblings of some half-baked professor.' There was an audible gasp from the throng. 'You've changed him into a freak. You're all freaks. You're probably all nice, normal people underneath, like Paul was. If you forget Professor Hardy-Larkin and start behaving like human beings, you might find that people will start listening to you rather than running screaming down the street to get away from you.'

Chairs scraped as the Professor's disciples rose, presumably to eject the heretic from their midst. I didn't wait to find out. I mouthed 'Leg it!' to Ariadne and we were out of the foyer and through the hall faster than greyhounds on steroids. The women of the WI looked perplexed as we flew through the middle of their talk on Armenian quilt interpretation. There was no time to admire the curtains.

When we felt sufficiently distant from those strange, zealous, misguided people, we stopped running and leaned on a wall to get our breath back, laughing. Ariadne had lost a shoe and my hair hung in my eyes like an Old English Sheepdog's. An elderly man commented on our breathless state.

'Cor!' he exclaimed. 'You're either trying to get to something very good or away from something very bad!'

He was right, but I'm not quite sure which way round it was.

Thursday 5 November

At Prayer Partners tonight, I'd just made the obligatory cup of tea and handed Charity the Bourbons when she asked me to sit down.

'I have a burden for you, Theodora.'

For a moment I thought she wanted me to help her carry something heavy and was about to offer Kevin's services. 'What kind of burden?'

'A spiritual burden.'

In my experience, telling someone you have a spiritual burden for them is usually a roundabout way of criticizing them and blaming God for it.

'It's Kevin,' Charity went on. 'I'm worried about him.'

'So am I,' I blurted.

'I mean, we rarely see him in church and as far as I know, he's never even attended an Alpha course. Last week he admitted that he'd never even *heard* of Graham Kendrick. Have you ever asked yourself if he's really the right man for you?'

'Frequently.'

She shuffled her chair closer. 'Have you ever thought you might be . . . unequally yoked?'

I couldn't hold my tongue this time. 'I have no intention of being "yoked" with Kevin or anyone else, unequally or otherwise. I know he's got his faults, but prying isn't one of them.'

Charity retreated to the sofa with a wounded look and we continued to pray for her children and their many petty adversities.

I'll have to think of a way of wriggling out of these meetings.

Friday 6 November

Still unnerved about events at the Scout hut on Tuesday. I called round to consult Digger Graves. He pushed a can of lager towards me and took a sip from his own can. I've yet to see him wear a hat with corks suspended from it, but I'm sure he has one stowed away somewhere in the vicarage.

'What I really want to know is, who's right?' I said. 'Those strange people who seem so keen to tell people about Jesus but go about it in such a peculiar way? Or someone like me who never seems to know the right thing to say and seems to miss more opportunities to talk to people than a workaholic misses lunches?'

'Well, Theo love,' he replied, 'what you have to remember is that there's more than one way to skin a cat. Some people ram it down your throat until it gets right up your nose and you just can't stomach it any more. They like to lay it on with a trowel and rub your nose in it. The way I figure it is, if you're straight with people and don't pull any punches, if they want you to lay it on the line they'll ask, and Bob's your uncle.'

I think I know what he means.

I'll have to have a quiet word with him about using clichés. Some of those images are positively bizarre.

Saturday 7 November

Have just sat through the longest firework display in history. Kevin told his mates, Paul, Jez and Kev 2, to bring some fireworks round so we could have a barbecue and let them off in his back garden. There must have been enough rockets, Catherine wheels and Silver Rain Fountains to arm a small European country. Kevin had gathered the children from the neighbourhood and we all stood expectantly in the crisp air as Kevin first described then lit the fireworks one by one. We oohed and aahed as the Traffic Lights fizzled and rockets soared. We ate gritty black sausages and burgers as the Catherine Wheels spun.

After two hours of fizzing and flashing, the children started to drift away home. Kevin continued methodically lighting the blue touch paper and retiring. No one else was permitted to light them. An hour later, Jez was found asleep in front of the television. I tried to liven things up a bit with some sparklers, but by midnight Kevin was alone in the garden, his presence only detectable by a wavering torch followed by a flash and a crackle. At 1.30 I felt I'd done my duty, and left. Kevin's armoury was still stocked, however, and the bombardment continued unabated. Paul and Kev 2 bedded down on Kevin's sofa. The display would have carried on all night, had one of Kevin's neighbours not come round and threatened to insert a rocket into him before lighting it.

Sunday 8 November

Another mysterious notice has appeared in *The Church Organ*. Rev. Graves's attempts at ecumenicalism in the village have involved St Norbert's, the Baptists and the local

Christian Fellowship, which meets in the Scout hut, advertising each other's midweek services.

Healing Service

Please note that the Healing Service that was due to be held on Wednesday at the Scout hut has unfortunately had to be cancelled due to ill health.

A case of 'physician, heal thyself'?

Monday 9 November

Still having problems with the new computer system. Although, as Ariadne explains, a computer is only as clever as the person who programmes it, our computer seems to have done some very strange things with people's pay. We stood in the office comparing pay slips. It had paid the cleaners the accountants' salaries, and vice versa. It had missed the decimal point out of my pay and paid me £126739 for the month and, much to Declan's disgust, had deducted his entire year's tax contribution in one month.

'How can it possibly pay me a minus figure?' he demanded.

'Well, you seem to have so much fun, perhaps they thought is was time *you* paid *them* to work here,' I suggested.

He stalked off to have a little word with the pay department.

Thursday 12 November

Digger Graves rang just as I was about to leave for work this morning. The church secretary is going to Eastbourne for a week and he was wondering if I could come and lend a hand in the office. At last, a ministry I *know* is within my capabilities! The main duties will be answering the phone, booking in weddings, baptisms and funerals, and compiling St Norbert's weekly newsletter, *The Church Organ*. Digger asked if I thought I could cope. I coughed modestly and explained that, with my wide range of administrative experience, a few days in the church office should be a piece of cake.

Maybe I'll have a look round the office tonight after work. It means missing the Prayer Partners meeting, of course. Great, a credible excuse!

I've booked a week's leave and have just rung Charity to cancel Prayer Partners – 'indefinitely'.

Friday 13 November

Good thing I'm not superstitious. Touch wood.

Sunday 15 November

Got chatting to Jeremiah Wedgwood over coffee after church, and he described to me an Advent service he'd been to last year at the cathedral. Digger was unable to attend and had appointed Jeremiah to go on his behalf. Apparently it was packed wall to wall with bishops and clergy. Jeremiah, being a mere layman, had been instructed to sit at the back and felt it had been a complete waste of time. He complained that he couldn't hear the service properly and that people had shown scant respect for the occasion and for the Almighty, whispering and chatting throughout.

'Honestly,' he complained, 'the agnostics in that place were terrible!'

'I think you mean acoustics,' I corrected him with a wry smile.

'I know exactly what I mean,' answered Jeremiah darkly.

Monday 16 November

Like an uncle you only ever see at Christmas, it's hard to believe that St Norbert's has a life other than at Sunday services. When I turned up for work at the church office this morning, however, instead of a tranquil building smiling benignly at hatted and suited worshippers, I found a small business buzzing with life and activity. During the week, sleepy old St Norbert's leads a double life and becomes the centre of village activities.

As Digger turned the foot-long key in the lock and shoulder-barged the heavy oak doors, the smell of lilies and old hymn books skulked out. We walked up the aisle, past the empty pews, to a door next to the vestry marked 'Private'. I hadn't managed to see the office on Thursday evening after all, so didn't know what was waiting for me on the other side of that door. It wasn't promising.

'The old computer's a bit, um, temperamental, I'm afraid.' Digger indicated a machine which looked as if God could have used it to type up the Ten Commandments if he'd been a bit short of stone tablets that day.

'I see. Where's the photocopier and fax machine?'

'Er, here.' He pointed to a hand-operated duplicating machine. My heart sank. The disappointment must have distilled through to my face. 'I'm sorry if it's not what you're used to, Theo love. But we'd be grateful if you'd give it your best shot.' He left on his first parish visit of the morning.

I looked around the office. It was no more than eight feet square, with a large, old-fashioned desk along one wall. Under the desk was a swivel chair which looked well past retirement age. There was a wooden cupboard containing the choir robes and lost property box. Next to it was a bookcase. Other low cupboards stretched the length of the third wall and a large noticeboard hung above them.

I found a pile of articles and scribbled notes on the desk and prodded the computer's 'on' button. As the ancient programme clicked into life like a choir of cockroaches, I felt a presence behind me. I spun in the chair. It was Jeremiah Wedgwood, clutching a watering can.

'Good heavens, you nearly frightened the life out of me!'

'The fear of the wicked, it shall come upon him: but the desire of the righteous shall be granted.'

'Please, just don't creep around.'

'Watering the flowers,' he explained, brandishing the can.

I returned to the keyboard and began to type. The letter R kept sticking, I noticed. Fortunately, the layout for the pages of *The Church Organ* was standard and saved on a floppy disk. Typing it all in would only take me half an hour, I thought.

Fat chance! I hadn't bargained for a keyboard which types the letter it feels like rather than the letter I press, a printer that won't print and an office chair with a broken hydraulic system, which means that every 20 minutes or so you have to stand up, turn the chair over and press the height adjuster with an elbow while standing on the arm of the chair with one foot. If this task isn't carried out on a regular basis, you find that you're typing with your chin resting on the desk.

I finally managed to type in all the news, the births, christenings, marriages and funerals. The village fête was duly advertised and Mr Wilberforce's remedy for relieving hard pad and distemper were committed to print, along with Mrs McCarthy's recipe for egg-free sponge cake. I wonder if anyone's ever told her the war has finished?

I pressed 'Save'. A message flashed up on the screen.

Error. This file cannot be saved.

'No!' I whimpered. This couldn't be happening. A whole morning's work! 'It's not true. This document *must* be able to be saved, you stupid machine!'

I pressed 'Save' again.

Error. Disk full. Close document or replace disk.

'It can't be full!' I searched for a new disk. No new disks in the office. If I closed the document, I would lose all the work. A brainwave! I could save it on the machine's hard disk. I tapped frantically at the keyboard.

Error. File will close. Information may be lost. File cannot be saved.

I stood up and put my hands where the computer's neck would be if it had one. 'I've just about had it with you! You're useless and worthless and I feel nothing but utter loathing and contempt for you! You have one last chance to redeem yourself.' I placed both hands on the screen and screamed at the recalcitrant document. 'YOU *WILL* BE SAVED!'

'Theodora! What on earth are you doing?' I whirled round to see the normally imperturbable Digger Graves standing in the doorway frowning. 'Just remind me never to take you on an evangelical mission.'

I blushed. 'I . . . I'm sorry. I just can't get the computer to save my work and I. . .' My voice trailed off to nothing.

'I don't think shouting at the equipment is the approved method. Look, have you tried. . .' His fingers tweaked at the keys and he opened a file in the computer's memory. The document was miraculously saved.

'How did you do that?'

'Just a knack. You look as if you could do with a coffee. I'll put the kettle on.'

We sat sipping the coffee, and Digger put his feet up on the desk.

Tuesday 17 November

Today's duties included consoling Mrs Epstein whose budgie had just flown away, organizing the next PCC meeting and listening to a blow-by-blow account of Miss Cranmer's gallstone operation. The flow of interruptions meant that two-thirds of the letters I was supposed to be typing were still in a pile when the vicar returned from his morning visits.

'I'm sorry, I didn't manage to get as much done as I'd hoped.'

'Never mind, Theo love, the paperwork will still be there tomorrow.' He looked exhausted.

'Busy morning?'

'Been to see a young couple at the far end of the village. Just lost their three-year-old kiddie to cancer. Words of comfort! What can you say? Old people are one thing, but kids. . .' He released a hissing sigh. 'Gets me every time.'

I couldn't do his job.

Wednesday 18 November

More chair wrestling, organizing the organist and ensuring that church hall bookings for the Brownies and Guides don't clash with the Medieval Re-enactment Society. Doris Johnson, who runs the playgroup, found that their toy Noah's Ark had been run over by a tricycle and had lost its bow doors. I offered to take it home and ask Kevin if I can borrow his glue-gun to mend it over the weekend.

Ariadne phoned me. She and Tom are having a video and pizza evening on Saturday. Could I bring my favourite video? I've decided it has to be the classic with the gorgeous Hugh Grant, even though we've seen it hundreds of times. Hopefully it will cheer Ariadne up a bit. She also asked me to bring a couple of bottles of sparkling mineral water to pour into her punchbowl with the wine to make Ariadne's Special Spritzer. I left myself a note on the jotter on the desk and went out to lunch.

When I returned, I found Digger looking flustered.

'Theo, I'm not Superman, you know!' He thrust a note into my hands. It read:

Saturday

Four weddings and a Funeral.

Water into wine.

Rebuild Noah's Ark.

'Streuth! You wouldn't like me to feed the five thousand and part the Red Sea while I'm at it?'

Thursday 19 November

I was just about to print out the copy of *The Church Organ* when Gregory Pasternak, the organist, rushed in with an urgent lost property notice. I half expected him to shout, 'Hold the front page!' He didn't, though.

How he managed to lose his shirt (his *shirt*!) in the organ loft, I didn't quite like to ask. Still, I suppose it's better than leaving your pants in the vestry.

Friday 20 November

Or your vest in the pantry.

Had a few problems with the duplicator when it came
to printing off the copies of the newsletter. After copying
one side, I couldn't work out which way round to put the
original to copy the back. Ran off over 50 copies before I
realized that half the newsletter was printed upside down.
Still, I'm sure the congregation won't notice.

Saturday 21 November

Great evening with Ariadne and Tom. I'd forgotten how
many times Hugh Grant says a rude word in the film,
though. Had to keep coughing in the appropriate places.
Ariadne is rather sensitive about that sort of thing. Tom's
now convinced I'm a consumptive. Ariadne seemed rather
quiet. I wonder if I should have timed my coughing better?

Sunday 22 November

I wouldn't describe today's sermon, given in slow motion
by Jeremiah Wedgwood, as boring, exactly. Suffice it to say
that it was fortunate that *The Church Organ* was issued
today. The sound of people falling off pews has been known
to wake the verger. About halfway through the sermon,
there was a rustling noise like a hurricane in a paper bag
factory. It was the sound of 70 people turning over their
newsletters and trying to read the end of Mr Wilberforce's
distemper cure. The congregation twisted and turned their
Church Organs, leaning their heads first to one side, then
the other. It looked as if 70 people were trying, simultaneously, to navigate their way round Spaghetti Junction.

Digger came to see me afterwards. 'Well done this week, Theo, never an easy job.'

'Oh, it was no problem.' I blushed modestly.

'Just one thing. I know that old keyboard can be a bit temperamental. That's why it's a good idea to proofread what it chucks out. Look at the article under "Lost Popety".'

I scanned the item. It explained how Gegoy Pastenak, the chuch oganist, would be extemely gateful fo the etun of an aticle of clothing which he had unfotunately mislaid in the ogan loft last Thusday. My blush deepened. Why couldn't he have lost his jacket?

Monday 23 November

Back to work for a rest! Even Declan's practical jokes seem bearable compared with lost cage birds (now safely back) and gallstones (still thankfully out). At least my office computer doesn't suffer from a lack of R's.

Wednesday 25 November

Charity phoned me yesterday to say that she didn't feel she could carry on being my Prayer Partner. She said something about us being 'spiritually incompatible'. I tried to sound suitably downcast but resigned. I sighed deeply and said that I thought it best in the circumstances, as I was unsure how much time I could commit and it wouldn't be fair to her. Inwardly I was punching the air in celebration.

What does she mean, 'spiritually incompatible'?

Thursday 26 November

Alarm didn't go off this morning. Had to run to the station. Arrived panting and sweaty, to find Ariadne tapping her foot and looking at her watch.

'Sorry I'm late,' I puffed.

'Don't talk to *me* about being late,' she huffed. Funny, it looked as though she'd been standing there for ages.

Friday 27 November

A brainwave! I know the thing the church needs more than anything else, more than a new bell tower, or a new organ, or a new roof, or even a new congregation. It needs a new computer! In fact, all the office equipment needs replacing. I'm sure that communications would be vastly improved, though *The Church Organ* may prove less entertaining. It would benefit everyone. And if we connected to the Internet, people could e-mail their prayer requests. Hall bookings would no longer rely on the diary, so the tea dances would never clash with the model railway exhibitions. The accounts could be computerized, too. It would be fantastic! St Norbert's would be catapulted into the twenty-first century.

And I would be the instigator. They might even want to name the computer after me – a kind of memorial, only I wouldn't be dead. The Theodora Emily Amaryllis (Mum also liked flowers) Llewellyn Electronic Administration Foundation. TEALEAF for short. Of course, I would humbly decline the offer of having it named after me. Nice of them to suggest it, though.

All I need to think of now is a method of fundraising.

Saturday 28 November

Digger was in favour of the idea when I suggested it to him. ''Bout time we got rid of that awkward, cantankerous old thing,' he said.

I don't think he was referring to the church secretary.

The church secretary herself couldn't see anything wrong with the old equipment, which she said had served her faithfully for the last 18 years. That rather proved the point.

I phoned around some friends and family to try to glean some fundraising ideas. Ariadne was still in a funny mood and wasn't very helpful at all. The only thing she could suggest was a 'Beautiful Baby' competition. Seeing as Nigel and Charity are the only couple in the church with small children, it would hardly be a fair contest. Mum suggested a 'Greek Night' with traditional Greek dancing, plate smashing and Greek delicacies. In view of the potential wear and tear on the carpets, I decided against that. Kevin suggested producing and selling a calendar with pictures of some of the Mothers' Union in 'artistic' poses. I suggested that if he wanted to walk down the high street and remain in one piece, he would keep that idea to himself. Finally, Digger suggested a Christmas Fair.

'There isn't much time to get organized, but if you're up for it, I'm right behind you. We could hold it in the hall and people could come and buy last-minute presents. I'll be Father Christmas, if you like, for the kiddies. The choir could sing carols and we could cook some snags on the barbie outside. . .'

His eyes misted over. *Barbie*? I guess the kind of Christmas he's used to is very different from the ones in England.

Now for the first important step for any new idea in the Church of England: we must form a committee.

Sunday 29 November

ADVENT SUNDAY
There's always an air of anticipation on Advent Sunday.
Makes you realize that Christmas is just around the corner
and it's time to start booking next year's summer holiday.

Monday 30 November

ST ANDREW'S DAY
Declan decided to celebrate St Andrew's Day by treating
the whole building to nonstop bagpipe music, courtesy
of a looped tape and a cassette player he'd managed to conceal somewhere in the office ventilation system. He had
to reveal its whereabouts after lunch, when two of the
accounts team tied him up with parcel tape and threatened
to dangle him by his ankles from the fourth-floor window.

December

Tuesday 1 December

Must start my Christmas shopping early this year. Last year I left it until Christmas Eve and wore myself out buying unsuitable presents at exorbitant cost.

Wednesday 2 December

Made a list of presents. I shall start my shopping at lunchtime today.

Kevin	? (Socks)
Mum	Anything Greek
Dad	Socks
Ariadne	Mobile phone case
Tom	Socks
Ag	Socks
Miss C	Lavender bags
Declan	Whoopee cushion (and socks)

Hmm. Perhaps I'd better ring and ask what they actually want before I embark on a shopping trip.

Thursday 3 December

First committee meeting about the Christmas Fair. The date has been fixed for Saturday 12 December, less than two weeks away. I was starting to panic, but Digger tried to reassure me. 'St Norbert's has a fantastic bunch of people. I know that if we all pull together we can pull it off.'

During the meeting, everyone was amazingly helpful. Charity has offered some home-made gifts and food. The choir will dress up and sing carols, holding lanterns. The village school has offered to lend a Santa's Grotto, complete with Father Christmas outfit. Even Jeremiah has offered to help run a stall, provided that there's no gambling or maypole dancing (!). I believe I may finally have found my ministry.

Friday 4 December

Phoned round to ask everyone what he or she wanted for Christmas. Fat lot of help that was! Kevin reeled off a list of obscure plumbing tools that I attempted to write down as he rattled through them. The final list looked like a combination of an inventory from a medieval torture chamber and an order from a Chinese takeaway. I'll probably buy him another football video.

Mum's ideas ranged from the wildly extravagant (a yacht) to the totally mundane and cheap (a tube of hand cream). If she carries on like this, she'll get the leftover raffle prizes from the Christmas Fair. Dad helpfully suggested 'anything except socks'.

'I'd love a pair or two of socks,' said Tom. Bless him. Ariadne had gone to the chemist, so I couldn't ask her.

I'm not sure where Ag is this week, so can't phone him yet either. Last I heard, he was just about to embark on a

fact-finding trip to Uzbekistan. Bet it won't involve
Christmas shopping. He always has some excuse for not
buying presents.

Didn't bother asking Declan or Miss Chamberlain. I buy
them the same things every year and they always seem suitably grateful.

I need to find a shop which sells lavender bags, socks and
whoopee cushions. Hmm.

Saturday 5 December

Kevin was at football this afternoon, so I went to the local
shopping centre. I embarked upon my own fact-finding
mission to establish the range of gifts available and get an
idea of the prices. Didn't actually buy anything apart from
some raffle tickets for the tombola at the Christmas Fair.
Plenty of time, though.

Sunday 6 December

A notice advertising the Christmas Fair appeared in *The
Church Organ* and served to confirm that we are indeed
doing the right thing in buying a new computer. As well as
mentioning the 'tombalo, mice pies and coral singing', it
announced that there would be 'a personal appearance by
Satan and his Reindeer'.

I do hope it was a typing error.

Monday 7 December

Have been reading a really good set of Bible notes and medi-
tations for Advent. Decided to pass on the benefit of my
increased wisdom and deepened spiritual insight to Kevin.

'If there's anything you'd like to know, just ask,' I said.
'About what?'
'About Advent, the Christmas story, anything like that.'
'I've got one question, about the conception and birth.'
'Fire away,' I urged, Bible study notes and notebook in hand. Finally, Kevin was taking a serious interest in spiritual matters, and I felt secretly proud to be there like a sort of sacred tourist information officer, pointing him in the right direction.

'Is it true,' he said, 'that the "Virgin Birth" is Richard Branson's company's attempt to take over the country's maternity services?'

I'm convinced he is spiritually degenerate.

Tuesday 8 December

Must get the Christmas shopping done this weekend. The temperature has been 20°C all week. It doesn't feel very festive yet. Never mind, it's the office Christmas party tomorrow. Nothing like a bit of drunken carousing to get one in the mood. (The rest of the office, that is, will be carousing drunkenly, not me!) We're apparently going to a karaoke night at a new bar in the West End called Floppy's. It's especially for computer operators, so Declan insisted.

Wednesday 9 December

Midnight.
Why am I writing this, no less coherently than normal, after a night at a party? Well, a few days ago, Declan suggested that one person should be randomly chosen to drive everyone home from the party, so that we wouldn't have the bother of finding cabs or catching trains. Everyone agreed

this was an excellent suggestion. We put our names in a hat and my name was picked out as the driver. As I hardly ever drink anyway, I agreed and took my car to work. It cost me half a week's wages to park, but everyone chipped in and at 6.30 we walked arm in arm, tinsel in our hair, feeling very festive, down the street to Floppy's.

Most of the people in Floppy's didn't look much like computer operators, and a lot of them seemed to be wearing leather clothes with holes and studs in very strange places. I thought that karaoke had gone out with red braces and ponytails, but it still seemed remarkably popular here, with strange combinations of men and women and men and men serenading and crooning to songs ranging from 'We'll Meet Again' to 'Relax' and 'The Macarena'.

As the evening wore on and my colleagues became merrier and merrier, I realized that it's virtually impossible to appreciate karaoke fully, either as a participant or an observer, when you're stone-cold sober. After Declan had performed a worryingly accurate impression of Jimmy Summerville singing 'Don't Leave Me This Way', and two women from accounts had sung 'I Will Survive' with such venom that every man in the room felt he should apologize personally for having been born male, it was my turn. The next song was to be a Madonna number. I calculated that, even if I wasn't drunk enough to think I sounded like Madonna, perhaps *they* were drunk enough to think I did.

I was waiting for them to choose 'Like a Virgin' or 'Papa Don't Preach' – something I could interpret as attacking my religious beliefs so I could get out of singing by flouncing off in a huff of righteous indignation. Instead, they chose the lovely 'The Power of Goodbye'. Even I had to admit I didn't do too badly, and revelled in the applause and cheers.

I only discovered the reason for the enthusiastic acclamation when I returned to my seat.

'Theo, you were great, you really grabbed their attention!' Declan's face glowed.

'Yes, I did do rather well. I think they liked my voice.'

'Either that,' Declan whispered, 'or the fact that you have the back of your skirt tucked into your knickers.'

The evening wore on. My colleagues got more and more drunk and I got more and more tired. Just before 11, I pointed out that we all had work in the morning and wasn't it time we thought about leaving. This comment was greeted with raspberries and jeers. They wanted to stay until the bar closed at 2 a.m. and ordered another round of drinks. When Declan let slip that everyone had written *my* name on the pieces of paper in the hat, I left under cover of being terribly affronted, and drove home alone.

Thursday 10 December

I was the first to arrive in the office this morning, so I sat and wrapped up some lucky dip prizes for the Fair. Some of the accounts department turned up and sat in their office very quietly with the door closed. Declan eventually appeared at about 11, wearing sunglasses and looking distinctly green in the face. He wasn't wearing one of his usual immaculate pinstripe suits, but a lumberjack shirt and corduroy jeans which seemed to be three sizes too big. He said he'd inexplicably been taken ill on the way home, gone back to a friend's house and had to borrow the friend's clothes, as his own were at the laundry.

'Oh,' I said, staring at him. 'I thought you might have missed the last train or forgotten where you lived or something, and had to sleep in the park. Perhaps your suit got all crumpled and covered with pigeon droppings and you had to buy some clothes from a charity shop?'

The leaves in his hair and the Oxfam carrier bags were a bit of a giveaway.

'What's it worth to keep Katherine in the dark?' I added.

He winced at the thought. His girlfriend was notorious for keeping him firmly in his place.

I was really enjoying the opportunity for revenge. Part of me thought I should exercise Christian compassion on this suffering human being, but then I remembered the many tricks he had played on me and decided the punishment was just and deserved. I bought the largest, greasiest, fried onion and bacon sandwich imaginable from the canteen and sat at Declan's desk to discuss some files with him.

'Oh Theo, have a heart,' he groaned, gesturing limply at the sandwich, which had started to drip brown sauce onto his desk.

'What? What have I done?' I asked innocently through a mouthful of bacon and onions, as the grease dribbled down my chin. 'Do you want a bite?' I waved the sandwich at him.

He didn't reply as he lurched out of the office and down the corridor.

Friday 11 December

When Kevin returned from work, I announced that in the light of Wednesday's singing success, I thought my ministry might be of a musical nature. He looked at me as if I had grown an extra head.

'Well, there's no way I'm hanging around to be David Beckham to your Posh Spice!' he snorted.

Chance would be a fine thing.

Saturday 12 December

When I arrived at St Norbert's at 8.30 this morning to unlock the hall, I was surprised to find an old gentleman wearing an overcoat and a tweed cap and holding a shopping bag waiting outside.

'Can I help you?' I enquired.

'I 'eard there was some kind of sale on today.'

'That's right, a Christmas Fair. But it doesn't start until 2 o'clock. You're rather early.'

'Oh, that's all right,' he said, glancing at his watch. 'I'll wait.'

Inside, I started setting up trestle tables and putting up bunting. Before long, other St Norbert's regulars started to arrive and soon the hall was filled with stalls. Doris Johnson had agreed to run the second-hand toy stall, Mrs Epstein to oversee the white elephant stall, while Charity brought home-baked cakes and puddings to sell. Nigel Hubble led in the choir, who looked as if they had escaped from a Dickens novel, and Jeremiah stood at the door ready to take the admission fee and hand out leaflets with the cheery seasonal message 'REPENT OR PERISH'.

One of the last stalls to arrive was the Santa's Grotto from the village school. Unfortunately, it was so large that we could only manoeuvre it through the doors with difficulty, and part of the sign and a couple of elves snapped off. When we had finally erected it, Mr Wilberforce pointed out that it no longer said 'Santa's Grotto', but 'Santa's Grot'. Nigel was in favour of keeping it like that, as he felt it rather neatly summed up the usual quality of gifts his children brought home. Digger was relieved to see that the costume consisted of a red suit and long white beard, not horns and a tail. He hurried off to change so that he could participate in his favourite activity – meeting people, especially children, from the village.

At 2 p.m. the doors opened, and it seemed that the whole world flooded in. Out of a village of approximately 3,500 inhabitants, no more than a handful seemed to have stayed at home. I saw the elderly man I'd spoken to outside in the morning. He'd obviously been waiting all that time. Apart from him, however, I barely spoke to anyone all afternoon. I hardly had the chance to draw breath for over two hours. Then, at 4.30, as suddenly as it had started, the tide of people dried up. There was hardly anything left. We cleared up the rubbish and debris and put away the tables. Then we sat down, had a cup of tea and counted the money. Digger removed his red costume and beard.

'Ladies and gentlemen, I am pleased to announce that this afternoon's effort has raised the grand total of...' He performed a little fanfare. My heart beat faster. What if we'd made a loss? '...*one thousand seven hundred and fifty-two pounds, thirty-seven pence!*' There were cheers, applause and cries of 'Praise the Lord!'

Sunday 13 December

Carol service tonight. Kevin couldn't come. Had an emergency plumbing job, he said. The hot tap in the Gents at the Red Lion wouldn't work. I said I couldn't see how that was an emergency, but he mumbled something about 'Health and Safety regulations' and left.

The children looked very sweet performing the nativity tableau. I think the director got a bit ambitious this year, though. I could have told them that using a real donkey would be a mistake. They'll never get rid of the stain. Mrs

Walpole in an old grey blanket may not look as authentic, but at least she's continent.

Tuesday 15 December

Mum rang tonight in the middle of an exciting bit of *EastEnders*. I stood in the hallway trying to watch the TV and talk to her at the same time. I found that if I stretched the cord as far as it would reach and closed one eye, I could peer through the crack in the lounge door.

'What are you doing for Christmas this year?' she asked.

'Dunno, when is it?' I asked absently, while in the lounge someone from the pub looked menacingly at somebody else – I couldn't quite make out who.

'It's on 25 December, same as usual,' came her puzzled reply.

Thursday 17 December

Intended to go Christmas shopping after work today, but a sudden filing rush meant that I had to work late instead. Would have been finished earlier but for Declan, who sent me down to the supplies section. He'd been installing a new printer on my desk and there wasn't enough space.

'Can you go down and ask them for a long stand?' he said.

'Sure, how long should it be?'

'Oh, as long as possible.'

After I'd been standing in supplies for the best part of half an hour, with people appearing, grinning at me and disappearing again, I ventured to ask, 'I came down here for a long stand. That was ages ago. Can I have it now, please? I can't wait all day.'

'Yes, of course,' replied the spotty-faced young store-man, and he disappeared to the sound of muffled guffaws.

It was another 10 minutes before I realized that I'd been had. I went back to the office to tell Declan how much I'd enjoyed my 'long stand' in the supplies section – and to beat him to death with the nearest blunt object.

'Ah Theo,' he chortled, 'did no one ever tell you that patience is a virtue?'

Friday 18 December

We're spending Christmas Eve with Kevin's Mum and hav-ing lunch on Christmas Day with my family. Now that Mum's in the catering business, I hope it means a change from turkey moussaka.

Mum phoned to try to talk to me sensibly about Christmas. Dad has put his foot down firmly about Mum's idea of inviting Georgie's family round to use the occasion as a trial run for her new range of seasonal dishes, including the perennial turkey moussaka, but with extras such as Greek-style Brussels sprouts (cooked in olive oil with toma-toes and garlic) and followed by something she's calling 'Christmas Pudding Baklava'. The battle continues. I can hardly wait for Christmas Day.

Saturday 19 December

Kevin at football. The shops will be very busy this after-noon, so I'll take a day off next week to get it all done. Spent the rest of the day putting up Christmas decorations in the flat. Mum and Dad gave me a box of their old deco-rations when I moved in. The box contained things that Ariadne, Ag and I had made years ago at school. There were three Wise Men made out of papier-mâché and washing-up liquid bottles (Ag), a candle covered in glitter and made from the inside of an old toilet roll (Ariadne), and a nativity scene made from modelling clay with purple sheep (me).

I sat down and looked at the twinkling fairy lights on the balding imitation pine. The slightly torn decorations sagged from my ceiling and the whole room had a faded, tawdry feel, like an elderly lady wearing the 'best dress' she bought 40 years ago for an evening out.

Why isn't Christmas the same as it was when we were children?

Sunday 20 December

Apparently, Jeremiah Wedgwood gave a very powerful sermon today about how the commercialism of the modern Christmas had robbed the sacred celebration of its true meaning. I missed it, unfortunately. Kevin and I had gone shopping.

Monday 21 December

Got a Christmas card from Ag. He's in Singapore. He said he may have a surprise for us, and did we all own hats. Very mysterious.

Wednesday 23 December

Finished buying the last few presents today. Well, it's a day earlier than last year. I was battling my way up the high street when I decided to drop into the Christian bookshop for some last-minute ideas. Apparently, these days it's not good enough just to have a Bible. There on the shelves were Bibles for Babies, Toddlers' Bibles, Teen Bibles, Women's Bibles and Grandparents' Bibles. It was then that I found the ideal present for Kevin – the Bible for Blokes. It included sections on woodworking and fishing, and had a 'Who's Who of Tyrannical Old Testament Warlords'. Disappointingly, it said nothing at all about football. Nevertheless, I bought it and continued my onslaught on the shopping centre. I was dismayed to find that a number of the shops had already taken down their Christmas decorations and had started their January sales! Couldn't they have waited just a few more days?

Thursday 24 December

Kevin picked me up from work in the van and took me to his Mum's house for supper. It was a lovely spread – not the slightest hint of anything Greek. Maybe a 25-pound turkey was a bit extravagant for three, however.

'Oh, never mind,' she beamed, 'there's a couple of old people in the street who'll be on their own tomorrow. I'll invite them in to help me finish it off.'

After supper I took Kevin's Mum to the midnight Communion service at St Norbert's. As we sat and listened to the familiar words and carols, I noticed a butterfly darting and skimming around the building. It must have been among the foliage brought in to decorate the church, and the warmth from the heaters and the candles must have woken it prematurely. It was like a special Christmas present, an unexpected glimpse of summer in the heart of winter.

Friday 25 December

CHRISTMAS DAY
Went to church *before* opening my presents – a sure sign that I'm growing up and maturing spiritually.

St Norbert's was unusually packed, even for Christmas Day. I scanned the faces and felt a surge of what I can only describe as 'goodwill' towards the people gathered in this building: St Norbert's regulars and their friends and families, folks from the village. I considered it a privilege to call them my friends. I felt like hugging everyone. I nearly hugged Jeremiah Wedgwood, but remembered just in time that, considering he disapproves of any form of physical contact, it would not have been the kindest of gestures.

'Good morning, Jeremiah, merry Christmas,' I said, and shook his hand. 'Lots of people here today.'

'Aahh,' he sighed, his watery eyes filling like cisterns. 'Every year, more and more unbelievers enter God's house on this sacred day, bringing their pagan attitudes and humanist philosophies. Christmas to them is just one long orgy...' Bubbles of spittle started to appear at the corners of his mouth. 'An orgy of gluttony, alcohol abuse, licentious behaviour and debauchery!'

I've obviously been going to the wrong parties.

'But,' I ventured, 'isn't it good that they come to church, even if it *is* only on Christmas Day? It must mean something.'

'Yes, but what? What does it mean?' said Jeremiah mysteriously, tapping the side of his nose.

I continued to push my way up the aisle. Most pews were packed to overflowing. I spotted a vacant seat in the pew behind a huddle of Hubbles.

'Good morning! Merry Christmas!' I chimed. All the Hubble heads swivelled simultaneously, the children's hamster faces staring up at me impassively. 'Did Father Christmas bring you lots of nice presents?' I beamed impishly at seven-year-old twins Priscilla and Aquila.

'Father Christmas is merely a marketing strategy to entice parents to spend more money than they have available and detracts from the true reciprocation between giver and receiver,' chirped Aquila.

'And it maketh parenth tell lieth to their children,' lisped Priscilla. 'I thertainly don't want an old man creeping into my bedroom at night. I don't care how many Barbie dollth and chocolate thnowmen he bringth.'

'We just give a small gift to one other member of the family. Naphtali bought me a beautiful stapler. Then we give an extra donation to charity. To help those less fortunate,' contributed Zilpah.

A stapler for Christmas? Could there be anyone less fortunate? My overflowing bonhomie was starting to evaporate.

'Have you seen any good programmes on television?' I asked, fumbling for a nonconfrontational topic of conversation. 'I always enjoy the one about the boy and the snowman and the Christmas specials.'

'We don't have a televithion. Daddy thayth itth bad enough we have to live in the world without welcoming itth wanton ideologieth into our home through the corrupt broadcatht media.'

I was horrified. No television! How are children supposed to grow up to become well-adjusted adults without a twice-weekly injection of *Blue Peter*?

'Oh, I suppose you sit around the piano and sing carols for entertainment.' I congratulated myself on remembering that Zilpah had just passed her Grade 5 piano exam. Here I felt on safe ground.

'Most popular carols are spiritually unsound and incongruous with the accepted account of the nativity to be found in the Gospels,' announced Zilpah darkly. 'Like there weren't three Kings from Orient. They were Magi and we don't know how many of them there were. The Bible just mentions three gifts. . .'

My mind battled with the thought of trying to sing 'We three or possibly two or possibly more than three Magi of Orient are. . .' It didn't work, somehow.

'. . .and Jesus almost certainly wasn't born in the bleak midwinter. Even if it was winter, it's unlikely that in Bethlehem snow would have fallen, snow on snow. . .'

'. . .and a thtable doesn't get mentioned at all, jutht a manger, let alone a lowly cattle thed. . .'

'. . .the holly and the ivy were pagan symbols, and an attempt to justify their inclusion in the festivities by comparing them to the sufferings of our Lord is just. . .'

'. . .and as for three ships coming sailing in. . .'

Fortunately, at this point the organist struck the first chord of 'O Come All Ye Faithful' (apparently not on the unsound carol blacklist) and the congregation shuffled to their feet and belted out the ancient invitation to worship.

Saturday 26 December

BOXING DAY

For the first time in history I have been given a present which is actually functional and fun. My family clubbed together and bought me a computer! It's fantastic! It's got everything – spreadsheets, databases, CD-ROM with multimedia capability, word processor, modem for Internet connection so I can use e-mail – everything. I'm so pleased with it, I feel like a kid with a new toy. The word processor package has just

billions **OF** *different* **fonts**.

It has a spoll chicker too, but I haven't quite got the hang of that yet. It will revolutionize communications in this household. It's the start of my journey into the 'techno-world'. Twenty-first century, here I am! Er ... any idea how to deleteeeeeeeeeee?

It has games, too – which, of course, are childish and a complete waste of time. It also has a diary package, hence the current writings. After using the unruly machine at work, and the piece of antiquity at the church office, this is a marvellous opportunity to become familiar with the workings of state-of-the-art technology.

It's about the only thing I'm likely to get familiar with around here. Kevin's gone to 'the most important match of the season' today. It's funny: they all seem to be 'the most important match of the season'. I wonder if I should put the champagne on ice or look up the number for the Samaritans?

6 p.m.
Kevin came round. Nil–nil, so neither the champagne nor the Samaritans required. He got fed up with me playing Solitaire on the computer, muttered something about being a 'computer widower', and went again. Ha! Now he knows how *I* feel all the way through the football season. Just one more game, then I'll go and do something useful.

9 p.m.
Just one more game.

11 p.m.
Solitaire nearly worked out that time. I was so close, just six cards left.

2 a.m.
Just one more game.

Sunday 27 December

Went to the evening service. It's hard to believe that only two days ago we were all standing here celebrating the Saviour's birth. The carols already seem faded and trite. Everybody seems a little flat after two days of Christmas indulgence, like a bottle of lemonade when the screw cap hasn't been properly tightened.

Digger looked dog tired. I suppose the time of year everyone else regards as a period of holiday and recreation is the time clergymen work the hardest.

Monday 28 December

We definitely overdid the Christmas crackers this year. I bought a box, Ariadne bought a box, Tom won a box in a raffle at work, Ag sent a box from China (apparently he's now working in Beijing), and Mum had already bought two boxes just in case we ran out. Dad insists we use them up. He doesn't want them hanging around cluttering up the house, he says. It's the first time I've ever pulled a cracker and worn a paper crown while eating my boiled egg at breakfast.

Thursday 29 December

Kevin has insisted that I give the Solitaire a rest. He says I'm becoming obsessed and that it isn't normal to be shut in your bedroom playing computer games for 16 hours a day. He's a fine one to talk about obsession. As for normality, just try asking any 12-year-old boy what's normal.

The computer has a dictation facility, so you can speak into a microphone and it types the words for you. You have to train it to understand your voice, but I speak clearly enough for anyone to understand, so here goes. . .

Begin dictation
9 new computer has paid the recent survey into the microphone at the rights to wear its full-year. You have to eat rabbits to understand of or if the guys speak clearly enough what the new one to understand that Higgins.
End dictation

Oh dear! Perhaps I do need to teach it to recognize my voice.

Wednesday 30 December

Dragged away from Solitaire by the phone. Digger and Jeremiah are going to look at computers in the sales and would like me to go with them. The church secretary is away in Eastbourne and, reading between the lines, I gather this would be a good time to replace the office equipment. I wonder if she'll notice.

6.30 p.m.

Constructive afternoon searching computer shops, in spite of Jeremiah muttering about 'dark forces at work' and looking intently at the backs of all the computers. I whispered that perhaps Jeremiah was looking for the number 666. Digger told me not to be unkind.

Thursday 31 December

. I went to the New Year's Eve party in the church hall. Kevin had already arranged to go out with his friends and he looked so pathetic when I tried using emotional blackmail to get him to come with me that I let him go. Everyone brought food and drink. Mum contributed the excess stock from her 'Greek Christmas specialities' range, which was enough to feed the five thousand without a miracle. We laughed, sang, hugged and exchanged the Peace as the clock struck midnight. Most of St Norbert's congregation were there, except Jeremiah Wedgwood, who felt it would be wrong to attend an 'indulgence of fleshly appetites' and intended to mark the night as a vigil of self-denial. I know Digger did his best to persuade him to come, but Jeremiah stood firm.

I can imagine poor Jeremiah standing just outside the gates of heaven, making sure that no one enjoyed themselves too much.

January

Friday 1 January

I have made three New Year's resolutions. The first is to try to keep this diary up to date (and keep the Solitaire within sensible limits). In over six months, I have yet to see the spiritual heights ascended. I am, however, trying to view this as a positive learning experience. Ariadne spent most of last year telling me to stop trying so hard to be someone else and let God use the person I am. I still seem to be trying too hard, getting it wrong and ending up in a worse position than when I started.

I shall have to try harder not to try so hard.

After the Christmas excesses, everything has gone pear-shaped (literally) diet-wise, so it's back to a sensible, healthy eating plan. My second resolution involves cottage cheese and a generous helping of willpower.

My third resolution is to try to be more tolerant towards Kevin. He can't help being spiritually degenerate. I'm sure his time of redemption is at hand. The other day I caught him reading his Bible for Blokes when he thought no one was looking. I also aim to be more magnanimous towards his interest in football. It's his only vice, bless him, and when you spend your day unblocking drains, you need some form of escapism.

That reminds me: he's late. He said he'd be here at seven, and it's gone quarter past.

Saturday 2 January

Kev was at the match this afternoon, so I took the opportunity to go into town and return all those unwanted Christmas presents to Marks & Spencer, like you do. It was interesting to see how many things I managed to exchange which hadn't even been bought there.

I reckon Christmas presents fall into two categories: gifts you buy for people but would really like yourself, and gifts which have the sole function of relieving the obligation to buy *something*. The socket set Dad bought me last year definitely falls into category one. He only buys me things like that so he can borrow them back when he needs to. Three months later, he'll ring up and say, 'I've been trying to undo the nut on my rocker-box pinion-cover and realized I need a 10-millimetre ring spanner. You don't have one spare, do you?'

I'll say, 'Do you know, I think I've got just the thing.'

Never mind, I gave it back to him for his birthday.

The second category includes those presents from aunties – scented coat hangers or notelets for a female and beer-flavoured bubble bath or initialled hankies for a man – which look as if they've come from a WI tombola. Nobody wants them. Nobody uses them. They just get put back into the WI tombola, to be bought and given as presents again the following year. I swear I once received a present that had the raffle ticket still taped to it.

Still, it's good for the environment, endless recycling.

Sunday 3 January

Digger announced today that the service in two weeks' time is to be a joint service for all the churches in the district. It will be held in the United Reformed Church hall a few miles away and will involve representatives from the Christian Fellowship, the Baptists, the Methodists, the local Roman Catholic church and, of course, St Norbert's. Afterwards there will be a buffet lunch and he's suggested that St Norbert's congregation should be in charge of the catering.

Charity's hand immediately shot up. 'I would be only too happy to bake a batch or two of spinach, lentil and pine nut quiche.'

'Ripper!' responded Digger, beaming profusely. 'I'm sure we can rely on the ladies and gentlemen of the parish to come up trumps.'

Jeremiah cornered me over coffee in the church hall. 'Of course I will not be attending that travesty of a service and I intend to persuade other right-minded people to do the same. I trust I have your support in this, Miss Llewellyn?'

'I'm not sure you do, Jeremiah,' I said. 'After all, I think that unity among the Christian churches is a very good thing. Showing that we can put our denominational differences aside and get along is a great witness.'

'But . . . but. . .' he spluttered, 'it would be disastrous. People outside the church will think we all believe in the same thing!'

Monday 4 January

Back to work. I sometimes wonder about Declan's mental state. He thinks Christmas cracker jokes are funny.

'Theodora,' he said, 'what do you get if you cross a chicken with a spider?'

'I don't know, but I've got a feeling you're going to tell me.'

'Eight drumsticks!'

He nearly fell off his chair laughing. Is there any hope?

Tuesday 5 January

So far, so good with the resolutions. I even managed to sound interested when Kevin explained the significance of the player's middle name and its influence on their goal-scoring average. Apparently, players with the middle name of John are 23 per cent more likely to score than those called David or Michael. Amazing!

Wednesday 6 January

Diet going reasonably well too. Have been eating sensibly for five days now and have lost two pounds. I'll have to recommend it to Ariadne; she's starting to look a bit podgy.

(Must remember not to show her today's entry. She'll make me eat it and ruin my diet!)

Thursday 7 January

EPIPHANY

If I was taking gifts to a new baby, even 2,000 years ago, I would have chosen something more practical than gold, air-freshener and embalming fluid.

Friday 8 January

I'm in a state of shock. Can't write any more today.

Saturday 9 January

Ariadne is pregnant! Not just a little bit, but over three months pregnant!

She's been in a funny mood for a while, but yesterday she seemed really upset when I suggested the diet.

'What is the matter with you, Ariadne?' I said. 'You're crabbier than a rattlesnake with PMT.'

'I wish!' She hung her head.

'What?'

'Oh Theo. . .' She took a deep breath, then let it out as a shuddering sigh. 'I'm expecting a baby.'

I searched her eyes to work out whether to congratulate her or commiserate with her.

'I just don't know how it happened.'

She's 32 years old. Did she want me to explain the facts of life? I took a deep breath. 'Well. . .'

'Oh, don't be silly. I know how it happened *physically*. I just don't know how it happened *organizationally*.'

Organizationally? Does she book it in her diary – 'Have sex with Tom' – somewhere between board meetings and appointments at the hairdresser's?

'Theo, I just don't think I'm ready for this. A baby would ruin everything – my career, my freedom, my cream carpets, everything that means so much to me.'

I didn't like to tell her that she didn't seem to have much choice in the matter. She looked close to tears.

'I just don't think I'm a natural mother. I had plans. Oh,

I know I'm being selfish and. . .' A single tear sneaked past the perimeter fence of her composure.

'Things don't always happen as we plan them,' I said, casting about for a helpful idea, 'but it's up to us to make the best of them. You would still be able to work, if you get a nanny or something.' She looked unconvinced. 'Or how about Tom staying home to look after the baby? He's a natural with kids.'

Her lips twisted into a faint smile. 'Yes, he is, isn't he.'

I imagined Tom at the kitchen table, surrounded with nappies and teddies, scooping baby mush into the mouth of a screaming baby while Ariadne sat with her briefcase and laptop, sipping coffee. Tom would love it. Ariadne would love it.

'I think it could work.'

She nodded. 'Maybe.' And for the first time in days, I saw her smile.

Sunday 10 January

Digger Graves arrived at church today with a black eye and a rather sheepish look on his face. After the service he explained that, in the ecumenical spirit he was so keen to foster, he had joined in a 'friendly' football match involving the local ministers and clergy.

'This,' he winced as he tenderly fingered the bruised flesh around his eye, 'was courtesy of the local Baptist minister's elbow. And this,' he rolled up his trouser leg to reveal a graze running the length of his shin, 'was the result of a tackle from the Salvation Army.'

'I thought it was supposed to be a friendly?' I queried.

'Oh, we didn't really mean business. We all shook hands at the end, quite amicable. I'll tell you one thing, though.'

He flinched as he rubbed his back. 'If I ever get set upon in a dark alley, I want that Quaker fellow on *my* side.'

Monday 11 January

A memo arrived on my desk this morning with details of training courses.

'See if there's anything which takes your fancy,' said Declan. 'The company will pay.'

Is he serious? I can never tell.

Tuesday 12 January

Apparently, tensions are starting to mount over the ecumenical service next Sunday. I'm not one to listen to gossip, but I overheard Nigel Hubble, who's on the committee, telling Jeremiah, Rev. Graves and Mr Wilberforce, the PCC treasurer, that it would be a miracle if the service happened at all. To start with, there was a dispute over what to call the service. The Roman Catholics favoured 'Service of Peace and Reconciliation', the Baptists insisted on 'Joint Churches' Celebration', and the local Christian Fellowship said that it would have to be called 'Jesus Together' or they wouldn't join in.

The United Reformed Church, who own the only hall big enough for the service, have invoiced all the other churches for their share of the costs of hiring the hall, its facilities, electricity, heating and rental of the chairs. The invoices were passed around at the start of the committee meeting and apparently the Baptist minister had to be physically restrained from thumping the URC minister and was sent away to sit at the other end of the table.

Nigel felt it didn't bode well. Mr Wilberforce resignedly prepared a cheque for St Norbert's share of the rental.

Jeremiah said, 'I told you so.' Digger suggested we pray like crazy and hope for the best.

I understand that everybody can't be right in this situation, but I *am* worried that everybody can be wrong.

Wednesday 13 January

Charity pounced on me during my evening 'constitutional' around the village, despite the bitter cold. I don't understand how someone that large and that florid could possibly conceal herself. But she did. Meetings with Charity nearly always take me by surprise. For a moment, I thought she was going to 'talk quiche'.

'Ah, Theodora. I'm glad I caught you.'

I sensed I was due either to be criticized or conscripted. 'What can I do for you, Charity?'

'Well, you know I regard involvement in my children's education as one of my most important motherly duties...'

I remembered hearing about the time she was asked to organize a school assembly. She staged a re-enactment of King David's battle against the Amalekites using imitation weapons, papier-mâché severed limbs and several bottles of tomato ketchup. One child fainted, three more had hysterical fits, and the rest of the infant classes were led from the hall in stunned silence. One plucky little chap was apparently heard saying as he left, 'I liked the bit where he chopped his arm off and all the blood came squirting out. It was great – just like a James Bond film!'

'Yes...' I replied cautiously.

'Well, Bathsheba's class are having a "Careers Week" and I thought you'd be just the person to help us out. That is, of course, if you don't mind.' She smiled graciously. Charity obviously recognized in me a certain professionalism, coupled with an innate ability to communicate. 'Most of the other women I know haven't put aside their calling to motherhood in favour of the pursuit of financial gain and worldly status. . .'

'Hang on a minute! I haven't put it aside; I've just postponed it until the right time. And I do a very worthwhile job. Financial gain is not my prime motivation.'

'What is, then?'

'All right, financial gain *is* my prime motivation, but I've got to live. I haven't got a husband to slog his guts out every day to keep me in Fairy Liquid. Everything I have, I've worked for.'

'Precisely,' said Charity.

'In addition to the monetary gain – a substantial proportion of which I donate to charitable organizations – I get satisfaction from doing my job as well as I can and co-operating with my colleagues. Why, in my last yearly review, I got a grade one for "teamwork and dedication". I felt, well . . . valued.'

'My point exactly: worldly status,' said Charity.

'That's without bringing in the intrinsic worth of the job itself. If I didn't input that information or file those records. . .' My mind searched for the logical consequence to my job not being done and I found, to my horror, that it would make very little difference to the great scheme of things if I disappeared in a puff of vapour. 'Well, it just wouldn't be a good thing.'

'Super. I'll tell them you'll do it, then. Thanks, Theodora.' Charity gave a little wave and departed.

Why does arguing with Charity always feel like trying to knit with spaghetti?

Thursday 14 January

Spent the evening flicking through cookery books trying to find a suitable quiche recipe for the ecumenical lunch on Sunday. Just because I'm a key player in the cut-and-thrust world of business and finance, does it mean I can't do a Delia Smith occasionally? If Charity can do it, then so can I. Maybe I should phone Tom for a recipe. On the other hand, things between Tom and Ariadne are a little delicate at the moment. Better not bother them with the trivialities of quiche.

The notion that Christians eat a lot of quiche is a long-established one and, from my experience, seems to have its basis in fact. However, the quiche recipes in my book all look very complex and difficult. (What is 'baking blind'? Would it do if I just close my eyes?) I'll go and buy a quiche on Saturday. I won't tell Charity that it isn't home-made. No one will know the difference. Except that it will be edible if I buy it, whereas if I make it there could be serious doubts.

I wonder if it's possible to buy chocolate quiche?

Friday 15 January

Sat at my desk and studied the list of training course titles from Declan. Apparently he *was* serious – a rare occurrence and an opportunity to be seized with both hands. *Ten Things You Wanted to Know about Assertiveness but Were Too Much of a Wimp to Ask* was tempting. Thought I might like to try *Communicating Utilizing Unequivocal, Condensed and Elementary Techniques Designed to Assist the Average Personage to Impart Information in Lucid Phraseology*. In the end, though, I chose *Counselling in the Workplace*, which was described as a course to help employees understand and

support their colleagues at work. I must admit, as I filled in
the form, that I had one eye on my ministry.

The weather report warned of impending blizzards.
Must check I still have sufficient tread on the soles of my
moon-boots.

Saturday 16 January

Bought one of Mum's feta cheese and aubergine quiches
from the supermarket. She refused to make me one for free.

'I've got a business to run, you know. I can't just go
giving it away free.'

It says on the packet that it tastes just as if you'd made it
at home. I do hope not.

I wonder what kind of quiches other people will bring?
Does the type of quiche reflect the characteristics of the
denomination? For example, would an Anglican quiche be
very traditional, if slightly bland? Is a Baptist quiche particularly wet? A Salvation Army quiche would, of course,
contain no alcohol, whereas a Pentecostal one would be
filled with the Spirit and a Roman Catholic quiche would
surely turn into something else after it had been blessed.

Sunday 17 January

I can remember reading novels where the scene for the
events that were about to unfold was characterized by
the weather. If the heroine fell in love, it was always on a
bright spring morning. A violent disagreement and a fight
where the hero was about to die in tragic circumstances
always unfolded to the accompaniment of a violent thun-
derstorm. This morning I hoped fervently that this only
happened in fiction. The sky was more than grey – it was an

oppressive yellowish-black. The snow didn't come. Instead, there was a vicious, stinging wind, which stole the words from your mouth and slapped your face as it chased through the village. In the wind, shards of sleet threatened to perforate anyone foolish enough to set foot outside their front door.

I called in at St Norbert's to collect the orders of service that the secretary had compiled on her new computer. In the end she was delighted with the system we chose. The orders of service, apart from the catering, were St Norbert's contribution to the event. I toyed with the idea of invoicing the other churches for the ink and paper, but decided against it. Things were bad enough.

There's no doubt that *The Church Organ* has improved considerably since the new computer was installed. It has revealed, however, that many of the mistakes in the publication, previously blamed on the antiquated equipment, are actually attributable to the antiquated secretary. I hoped against hope that no major mistakes had occurred in the order of service. I flicked through and was pleasantly surprised by the content and layout. It was carefully and artistically set out, with appropriate pictures and attractive fonts. I could see no glaring errors. I bundled the sheets into a bag with my quiche and set off, with teeth clenched and eyes half-closed against the stinging sleet, to the United Reformed Church hall.

I arrived to find people bustling around, arranging flowers and setting out chairs. Several people stopped and smiled at me. Most of the St Norbert's regulars were there. Jeremiah, of course, was not among them. A pleasant woman from the Methodist church introduced herself and relieved me of my bundle of service sheets and my quiche. I had removed it from the box, partly because I wasn't sure how 'Aphrodite's Greek Luxuries – Atlas Mountains Quiche Delight' would go down among the assorted churchgoing population of the village. I didn't want to raise concerns about 'food sacrificed to idols'.

I looked around the inside of the building. It was large and old, but warm and comfortable. The wind drove the sleet against the windows and I could hear the roof slates shifting. The ceiling, with its brown watermarks and bulging plaster, was testimony to many leaks and missing slates. Suddenly I didn't begrudge them the money towards the hall's upkeep. It was obviously needed. More people were arriving and I was tempted to go and sit in a St Norbert's huddle at the back with Roger, Doris and Maurice, Miss Cranmer, Mr Wilberforce and the rest. I resisted the temptation and went to sit next to a lady whom I vaguely recognized, as she catches the same train as Ariadne and me in the mornings. It turned out that she attended the Baptist church and we had a very pleasant chat.

The hall filled up and the service finally started with a well-known hymn. There was a warm, friendly atmosphere in spite of the animosity during the preparations. Disputes seemed to have been resolved and differences put aside. The ministers all seemed genuinely amicable and united, each of them taking a different part of the service. We followed the perfectly typed order of service and everything ran smoothly. The Roman Catholic priest led the prayers and a worship group from the Christian Fellowship led the singing. Digger was to read a lesson, and we stood for the Gospel reading, following the words printed in the order of service.

'The lesson is taken from the Gospel according to St Luke, chapter 24, verses 36 to 49. . .' He started to read about the meeting between the risen Jesus and his disciples – and then it happened. Instead of verse 49 saying, '. . .stay in the city until you have been clothed with power from on high,' Digger read in a loud, clear voice exactly what was typed in the order of service: '. . .stay in the city until you have *beer* clothed with power from on high.'

Snorts and giggles broke out all over the hall.

Digger looked embarrassed.

At that moment a slab of bulging plaster gave way and water started gushing through the ceiling as if from a hosepipe, splashing down near to where Digger was standing. Someone rushed to find a bucket. Digger simply picked up the glass of water next to the lectern, emptied it into a flower arrangement and placed the glass on the floor under the leak. The brownish rainwater poured down into the glass, filling it to the brim and forming a foaming head. It looked exactly like a glass of beer.

Digger threw back his head and laughed. 'You see, you sceptics: God always keeps his promises!'

After that, the praise and prayers rose to heaven with a refreshing lightness and joy. All the denominations present in the leaky hall on that Sunday morning, with their different outlooks, their different priorities and agendas, were united by laughter which had been initiated by the ultimate celestial practical joke.

Monday 18 January

Quiche for supper. After the service yesterday, Charity divided up the leftover food among those helping to clear up. I'm sure there was more left over than was brought in the first place. It was just like the feeding of the five thousand.

Charity said, 'Theodora, I saved some nice cottage cheese quiche for you. I noticed you've put on a little weight recently.'

I'm thinking of joining the Baptist church.

Tuesday 19 January

Wore my moon-boots to work today, just in case. Ariadne refused to sit with me on the train.

'I realize, dear sister, that you've been prey to some of the more extreme whims of the fashion industry over the years, but believe me, moon-boots were *never* acceptable office attire and certainly aren't now.'

I think she's jealous. Just wait until she's too big to fit into her Gucci suits.

Wednesday 20 January

I refused to sit next to Ariadne today. She had brought a bag containing marshmallow and pickled onion sandwiches.

'Helps my morning sickness,' she explained.

Thursday 21 January

Still no sign of the blizzards forecast in the weather reports. I think I'll stock up on candles and tins of soup – just in case.

10 p.m.

Had supper with Ariadne and Tom this evening. Or rather, Tom and I had shepherd's pie while Ariadne munched on celery, watercress and chocolate spread. She looked healthy enough on this strange diet, unlike Tom, who had a pale, anxious look.

I leaned over and whispered to Tom, 'She's looking well. How's the morning sickness now?'

'Terrible, Theo,' he shook his head. 'I can't keep a thing down before lunchtime.'

Friday 22 January

Gave my 'Careers Week' talk to Bathsheba's class today. I think they were suitably impressed. Maybe the history of the company's development and projected sales forecasts for the next 10 years were a little too detailed. Perhaps I shouldn't have dwelt so long on data protection legislation and company law. Still, the entire class of six- and seven-year-olds sat riveted throughout my PowerPoint presentation, complete with graphs and moving images. I resisted the urge to use my laser pointer to fry one little boy who sat picking his nose throughout the entire presentation. After talking for 40 minutes, I invited the class to ask me any questions. They all looked a little dazed.

'They're usually much livelier than this,' their teacher giggled apologetically. 'You really seem to have the knack of subduing them beautifully.'

'Can I ask a question?' Bathsheba raised her hand. I smiled and nodded encouragingly. 'How come you're so old and you're still not married? My Mummy thinks there must be something wrong with you.'

Saturday 23 January

Toyed with the idea of returning the moon-boots to the back of the wardrobe today, then the first flakes of snow began to fall. I was rather concerned about driving over to Ariadne's and Tom's for lunch, but decided to risk it. If I get snowed in there I can eat their food, benefit from the warmth of their central heating and watch their television – they've got cable.

Ariadne looked the picture of health. She's working as hard as ever, but seems to glow with energy. Tom, on the other hand, was a pale shadow of himself. While Ariadne went out to chop wood for their open fire, I sat next to Tom on the huge cream sofa.

'How are you, Tom? I can't help noticing you're looking a bit tired.'

'Oh, it's just this pregnancy, Theo. What with the back-ache, the swollen ankles, getting up in the night, the vomiting, the cramps. . .'

'But Ariadne looks remarkably well.'

'Oh, she's fine, blooming even. I don't know how she does it. It's me. I'm a wreck. And I know it's silly, but the least little thing seems to upset me. . .'

His voice cracked and he turned away, sniffing. I laid a comforting hand on his shoulder. If he's suffering like this during the pregnancy, I hate to think how he'll cope when she goes into labour.

Thursday 28 January

It's a relief to get the electricity back on after being stranded in snowdrifts with no amenities, and no chocolate, for four days.

It started snowing seriously on the way back from Ariadne's and Tom's on Saturday. I had to walk to the morning service on Sunday because the roads were covered with ice and snow. (And, Ariadne, if you ever get to read this, I was extremely glad of my moon-boots.)

St Norbert's, perched on the top of the hill, looked just like a scene on a Victorian Christmas card. The figures entering the building were no more than coloured smudges against a white canvas and the warmth inside the building radiated out through the stained glass. I slithered and skated my way up the frozen paving stones to join the coloured smudges.

It continued to snow during Sunday afternoon. It fell in large, stout flakes, country snow, which cloaked the buildings and landscape and muffled all sound. I was dreading the journey to work on Monday, with frozen points and bleak, polar platforms.

When I woke up on Monday, however, it was apparent that no one in the village would be going anywhere. During the night, the ponderous flakes had been whipped into huge drifts across the road at the point where the village dissolves into fields. The power lines and telephone lines were down, and the lanes linking us to the next village and the nearest town were also blocked. Thank goodness for candles, and for other people's mobile phones.

I ventured out mid-morning (wearing my trusty moon-boots) to see if anyone needed help. The normally busy roads were empty of vehicles as I crunched my way towards the post office. The village school was closed and children on sledges and trays caromed down the hill. Miss Chamberlain, wrapped in coats and scarves, was standing outside her house with a shovel, chipping away at the frosty mound. I took the shovel from her and dug a path from her front door to her gate. I have no idea where she planned to go or how she planned to get there, but it seemed very important to her that her path was clear.

After a cup of tea (she uses Calor gas) in her drawing room, I continued up to St Norbert's, where it was evident that most of the village had gathered. Candles had been lit in the church building and the church hall had been converted into a makeshift community centre. Mr Wilberforce and others from the congregation were manning a tea bar.

I recognized several people from the ecumenical service. One of the local farmers had used his tractor to drop off a generator, which supplied enough electricity for the tea urn and lighting and heat for the hall. St Norbert's regulars, young mums and elderly people sat and chatted with commuters and shopkeepers. Teachers, doctors and lawyers handed around cups of tea and pensioners played chess and dominoes with schoolchildren. It seemed that only the farmers were absent. Farm life seems to continue with no regard to the weather. I was surprised at how many people I didn't recognize, considering that I've lived in the village nearly all my life.

'Isn't this lovely,' beamed Mrs McCarthy. 'Just like the war!'

'In what way was the war lovely?' I asked. 'What about all the bombing and capture and death and destruction?'

'Oh yes, there was all that, but there was such a lovely community spirit. Everyone 'elped everyone else.'

'But wasn't that because everyone else's house had just been flattened by a doodlebug?'

'Some very good things come out of the war.'

'Like what? Rationing, concentration camps and the Berlin Wall?'

'There was always powdered egg. That was a very good thing. You never got none of that newfangled stuff in it. Not like you get nowadays in the eggs.'

'What stuff?'

'That semi-Nelly stuff.'

'No, you're right there,' I agreed. 'There's definitely no semi-Nelly in powdered egg.'

Digger Graves brought over a tray of tea in polystyrene cups and we each took one.

'Oh, I'm having a lovely time, Reverend,' said Mrs McCarthy. 'It's just like the war!'

His brow creased. I shook my head. 'Don't ask.'

I took my cup of tea and sat in a chair, looking round the hall at all the people who wouldn't normally come into the church. The staff from the baker's shop had set up a trestle table and were selling cakes and rolls. The milk, which had been delivered to the village by helicopter, was being sold from crates in another corner of the hall. Children played and old people chatted. Digger looked contented and relaxed as he talked and handed round the tea. His love of being with people shone from him like the Ready Brek glow.

The convivial atmosphere was shattered as the door of the hall swept open and the steaming figure of Jeremiah Wedgwood blew in. He was followed by a flurry of snow-flakes and an icy blast. He stomped over to the vicar, his eyes streaming as much with indignation as with the bitter cold.

'G'day, Mr Wedgwood. Sit down! You look as if you could do with a cup of hot brew.'

'I feel I must speak to you most urgently, Reverend.'

'Go ahead.'

Jeremiah's rheumy eyes scanned the motley collection of villagers. 'It's not right. It's just not right.' He drew a deep, hissing breath and pointed at Digger. 'And you, the worst of all, associating yourself with this . . . this devil's brood!'

'Oh, come on!' Digger gave a little laugh, trying to make light of it, but Jeremiah obviously saw nothing to laugh at.

'This place, Reverend, is supposed to be the house of God. You've turned it into a den of iniquity.'

Digger was no longer smiling.

'Now look, Jeremiah, there is a time and a place for airing your views and opinions, but this is neither. . .'

'Look!' Jeremiah pointed wildly at a young woman with a child on her knee. 'That harlot has brought shame on this place.'

'I think we'd better make this a private chat.' Digger attempted to take his arm and guide him towards the door. The conversation and laughter in the hall ground to a halt as all eyes turned towards the two men.

'Unhand me, you brute! You call yourself a man of God, yet you condone sin and attempt to silence those who speak out against it.'

'I don't care what you think about me, but I will not stand here and listen to you insulting these people who have turned to the Church for help.'

'They don't want help from the Church; they haven't turned to God.' Jeremiah's eyes blazed with a kind of fervour. 'They are here to milk us, to take all they can from weak and foolish men, then continue in their sin and depravity. Do you really think for one moment that these Sabbath-breakers, these idolaters, these fornicators, will want anything to do with this place once the snow has cleared?'

I held my breath, longing for this uncomfortable scene to end.

'I think you may be right,' answered Digger. 'I'm well aware that some people here may never set foot inside the building again.'

There was an embarrassingly long pause as he looked at the people in the hall.

'I'm also aware that many people here may have done things wrong. They may very well be all those things you say. And you are certainly right when you call me weak and foolish. I'm taking a risk. But I'm taking it because I'm try-ing to do what I think God wants me to do. I know it sounds corny, but I'm trying to do what Jesus would have done. He would not have turned people out into the snow, whatever they believed. He came to earth to show God's love and mercy to imperfect, sinful people and, God knows, I'm one of them.'

'You can say that again!' Jeremiah turned and stalked out of the door, flinging it wide and leaving it to slam closed behind him.

For a moment the room held its breath.

Then the silence shattered like ice on a pond as people coughed, looked away and resumed their conversations in guarded whispers.

'Oh, lovely, just like the war,' muttered Mrs McCarthy.

A child knocked over a cup of orange squash and I rushed to catch it, seizing the cup just before it hit the floor. After the cost of hiring the carpet shampooer to rectify the 'Bert Wilberforce Coffee Fiasco' last year, St Norbert's regulars have rivalled the England cricket fielders for their speed and dexterity in catching cups and the like to prevent spillage.

When I looked round, Digger had gone.

I went into the kitchen to find a cloth (in my 'Howzat!' celebration, I had accidentally slopped some juice). He was standing at the sink, staring out of the window.

'Well done! You certainly put old Jeremiah in his place. And you preached the gospel, too. Two birds with one stone,' I grinned.

'No, I didn't do well at all,' he replied soberly. 'I failed completely. I've lost Jeremiah's respect and friendship, and those people won't remember the gospel. All they'll remember is the day the vicar stood up and bawled out one of his congregation in front of the entire village.'

I didn't know what to say. I picked up a cloth from the draining board and slunk out to try to salvage the carpet.

Sunday 31 January

Just returned from a rather subdued morning service. Digger looked preoccupied and I couldn't help gazing at the empty pew where Jeremiah usually sat. No one mentioned the incident in the hall, but it felt as if everyone was thinking about it. I vehemently disagreed with almost everything that Jeremiah did or said, but I still felt his absence acutely and painfully. He was part of the family.

February

Monday 1 February

That woman, honestly! I'm sure she was sent to be the 'thorn in my flesh'. Charity Hubble, the human baby factory. She's expecting again! Eight kids and another on the way – surely that's plain greedy. She thinks that, just because she has single-handedly (well, not quite single-handedly; obviously Nigel had some input) doubled the population of the Home Counties, she has the right to criticize my lifestyle and relationships. I must learn to stand my ground.

She hunted me down in the post office, which doubles as a newsagent and general store, just as I was buying my copy of *Cosmopolitan* (I only get it for the recipes) and another tub of cottage cheese (this time with pineapple chunks to try to disguise the taste). Charity was lurking in her flowery frock on the other side of the magazine rack like a huge, prowling Laura Ashley sofa. I tried to dodge past before she spotted me and head round, via the crusty rolls, to the counter and out of the door. Unfortunately, it was 'Granny Day' at the post office counter and my escape route was blocked by a queue of OAPs collecting their pensions.

'Theodora, I'm glad I ran into you again,' she effused. 'How are you after all that dreadful snow?'

I shuffled my *Cosmo* behind the *Radio Times* and tub of cottage cheese in an effort to appear a more solid and respectable citizen. 'I'm fine thanks, Charity,' I said, glancing at her pansy-covered maternity dress. 'And you? Blooming again, so I see.'

'Yes,' she smiled coquettishly, patting her bulge. 'Children bring such joy and contentment to a woman's life. I can honestly say that I never felt complete until I had my family. When you get to our age, it's comforting to know that you'll never be alone with the warmth and love of a family surrounding you.'

She seemed to drift off into a *Little House on the Prairie* daydream and I seized the opportunity to wave a hurried little 'Must go, bye...' and scurried off to the checkout.

'When you get to our age' – honestly! I'm only 29.

Tuesday 2 February

CANDLEMAS
Everybody I know is having babies!

Wednesday 3 February

Well, obviously not *everybody* – not the men.

Thursday 4 February

Or the old women.

Friday 5 February

Or me.

Saturday 6 February

As I finished off my tub of cottage cheese with pineapple chunks, I thought about Ariadne and my conversation with the fecund Charity in the post office last week. It's not that I don't want children, in fact I definitely don't *not* want them. Just not when she thinks I ought to have them. The white lumpy cheese suddenly curdled in my mouth (actually cottage cheese is already curdled, isn't it?) as I thought of my biological clock ticking away. What if, when I feel ready to have children, I find I can't have them? What if years of sitting in draughty football grounds has had a detrimental effect on Kevin's reproductive capabilities? Even if I decide tomorrow that I want to have children, I still need to get Kevin to propose (say two years minimum), save up for a wedding (at least another five years), buy a house (10 years at least), earn enough money to be able to afford children (at this rate at least 20 years), allow a couple of years to conceive, plus nine months' gestation. Good grief. I'll be about 107 before I get to change the first Pampers!

Pineapple chunks do not disguise the taste. I wonder if you can buy chocolate-flavour cottage cheese?

Sunday 7 February

Family Service today. It was the sort of service which, in its desire to please the entire congregation, ended up pleasing nobody. The adults felt the children's sermon was patronizing; the children got bored during the prayers and started pinching each other and giggling. The elderly people complained about the number of choruses; the young people thought there were too many hymns. I think that God was probably the only one who enjoyed all of it.

Wednesday 10 February

Bought Kevin a Valentine's Day card with a picture of a cute teddy bear on it. It didn't seem very appropriate, but I couldn't find one with a picture of a slug.

Thursday 11 February

Booked a table at Amigos, a Tex-Mex restaurant, to celebrate Valentine's Day. Kevin wanted a curry, but I insisted he tried something different. Besides, they do some fantastic salads and they are rumoured to have cottage cheese fajitas on the menu. He spent the rest of the evening sulking.

'Oh, come on. It's got chilli in it. I'm sure you'll hardly notice the difference.'

'That's not the point. When I go out for an Indian, I expect Gandhi, not Sitting Bull...'

Friday 12 February

Now, I know that I think children are an abomination. I know that I'd rather juggle dead hedgehogs than hold a baby. I know that all children are smelly, impertinent, germ-laden organisms which rate only slightly above bacteria on the evolutionary scale. I know that I believe they should be sent away to boarding school, preferably between the ages of 2 and 20, but that doesn't mean I'd make a bad mother. Does it?

Saturday 13 February

It took nearly an hour to thaw Kevin out with a fan heater and a hairdryer this evening. He went to the match on the back of Jez's motorcycle. Apparently he couldn't bend his legs to sit down until half-time.

Sunday 14 February

ST VALENTINE'S DAY
Kevin at least had the grace to enjoy the meal at Amigos. I gave him the card with the teddy on it and he asked me if, by any chance, I'd happened to receive one. This morning a card came through my letterbox – a saucy picture of a French maid wearing black stockings, suspenders and a frilly apron. I knew it was from Kevin, even though he hadn't signed it. The greasy fingerprints and scorch marks from his blowtorch were a giveaway. The verse inside read:

> *I'd love you in yellow,*
> *I'd love you in red,*
> *But most of all, darling,*
> *I'd love you in . . .*

In what? Kevin refused to explain. What's the point of sending someone a message if they don't understand it?

'It rhymes with red, and it's somewhere I'd very much like to go with you one day,' was all the explanation he'd offer.

Monday 15 February

If, and I emphasize if, I ever have children, I will never be as inconsiderate with their names as my mother was with ours. Names become part of you and if you're unfortunate enough to be called Wincyette Pilchard or Algernon Grope, your personality, as you grow up, must be influenced by that name. As children, my sister, my brother and I suffered quite appallingly in this department. Ariadne, Theodora and Agamemnon! Honestly, what a burden to saddle your children with! No wonder we all grew up strange. I hope Ariadne and Tom decide on a *sensible* name for their baby.

Tuesday 16 February

SHROVE TUESDAY
Have decided to give up chocolate for Lent.

Arrived at work to find that Declan had neatly filed cold pancakes among the papers in my pending tray and filled my paperclip holder with maple syrup. If he devoted half the time he spends on thinking up his puerile practical jokes to his work, he would be Managing Director by now.

Wednesday 17 February

ASH WEDNESDAY
There was a special Ash Wednesday service this evening, including a distribution of ashes. Kevin was particularly scathing about our Antipodean vicar performing this ancient ritual.

'Hmm, it's about the only time we're likely to see the Aussies willingly handing over the ashes to the Brits!'

I advised him to stick to football.

The service itself was short and simple. I wondered if Jeremiah would come, but he didn't. At the end of the service, we went forward and Rev. Graves dipped his finger in the ash (last year's palm crosses burned and mixed with a little oil) and drew a cross on each person's forehead. I looked around at the familiar faces, each tainted with a little smudge of grey. I felt vulnerable, as if I'd just stood up in front of everybody and admitted to all the things I'd ever done wrong.

It wasn't just me, though. We all wore the mark that acknowledged our failures, our weaknesses, our sins. I looked at Charity Hubble's smudged forehead. She had, as far as I knew, never even returned a library book late. Slimy Roger Lamarck's leer was for once absent. Miss Chamberlain sat smiling, comfortable with her faults and content that she was forgiven. I longed to spit on my hankie and wipe the cross from her forehead. Surely she didn't deserve it? Even Digger looked grim. We were all joined in the kinship of imperfect humanity. I know that's always the case – it was just that today we owned up to it. Today we wore an outward sign of the side of us we usually try so hard to hide.

I cried.

Thursday 18 February

The message in the Valentine's Day card has clicked. I never thought that Kevin saw me in that way. Don't know whether to be flattered or affronted. Have decided on a bit of both.

Friday 19 February

Accidentally bought a cookie from the bakery with chocolate chips in it. Declan sat and watched, bemused, as I picked them out one by one and ate the remains of the cookie.

Sunday 21 February

Nigel Hubble preached the sermon today. I've never seen the congregation so riveted. Their eyes were practically popping out of their heads. He preached about three different Greek words for 'love' used in the New Testament, and illustrated each one with a slide on the overhead projector.

He had a picture of a church for *agape* – Christian love; a picture of a family for *phileo* – friendship; but for *eros* – sexual love – he put up a picture of a naked woman. It wasn't quite *Penthouse*, more *Cellulite Monthly*, but there was no denying that she was naked. Suddenly he had the full and undivided attention of everyone in the church. The women looked stunned, the men looked delighted, the teenagers giggled. Only Mrs McCarthy, who's a bit short-sighted, whispered rather loudly, 'She's pretty, but I can't quite make out what she's wearing.'

Still no sign of Jeremiah.

Monday 22 February

Nearly had chocolate powder on my cappuccino today. Managed to restrain myself just in time.

Wednesday 24 February

The training course started today: *Counselling in the Workplace*. Eight people from assorted departments in the building gathered in the small training room on the sixth floor. The trainer was an earnest-looking woman called Jules with freckles and rimless glasses. After the 'ice-breaker' (or 'creeping death') when we had to tell the person next to us what we had for breakfast, we learned all about counselling skills.

Jules started the session by talking about body language. She told me that sitting with my arms folded was a defensive gesture and meant that I wasn't at ease in my surroundings. She asked if I was suffering from 'anxiety neurosis' induced by stress in an unfamiliar interactive situation, and said I was not to worry, because the course would provide the ideal platform for addressing and dealing with it. I didn't like to tell her that the reason I had my arms folded was that my bra-strap had just broken and I was simply trying to hold everything in place.

I confessed to having an 'underwear insecurity syndrome', so Jules sympathetically offered to give me space within the medium of the course to explore and come to terms with my condition. I spent nearly all lunchtime with her in a corner of the training room. That left me only two minutes to dash to the loo and fix the strap with a safety pin. I was complimented in the afternoon on my more open, sharing posture. A victory for her counselling techniques and small, metal fastening devices.

By 4 p.m., I was getting extremely weary of Jules's high-pitched, pseudo-American voice. I was tempted to ask her how she would interpret my body language if I were to stand in front of her with my hands around her throat.

Someone passed a note round the group arranging to go out to the pub at the end of the day. Jules eyed us suspiciously as we passed the folded paper furtively from person to person when we thought she wasn't looking. We didn't invite boring Jules. As we filed out of the door, she shared an 'affirming' thought with each of us, saying how important it was to make a person feel embraced within the wider group. As we huddled in the lobby, organizing the kitty, Jules hung her head and trailed forlornly out of the building.

Thursday 25 February

There was a different staff trainer on the course today. Apparently Jules has taken some time off due to stress. She was replaced by Charles. Charles looked about 14 years old and proceeded to develop our counselling skills further. I was beginning to feel like a real expert – just like Clement Freud. The main technique we learned was called 'reflecting'. When the person you're counselling tells you something, you're supposed to 'reflect' it back to them, using slightly different words. Presumably the idea is to show that you're listening and sympathetic to their problems. I think it's to reassure them that you haven't nodded off yet.

I drifted off into a daydream where the distressed and depressed would come to me from miles around and, through my caring and patient counselling, would be liberated from all mental oppression. At last, I thought, I've discovered my ministry.

We were paired off and given imaginary scenes to role-play. We had to practise 'reflecting' by acting out the scene in front of the other people on the course. Unfortunately, one of the other course members had dropped out, so I was paired with Charles. He assumed the role of a colleague who was worried about his work and had come to me for help. This is how the conversation went:

> **Me**: Good morning, Charles. How are you today?
> **Charles**: Well, to be honest, I'm feeling a bit down.
> **Me**: So you're not on top form at the moment.
> **Charles**: That's right. I've been given some extra work to do and I'm not sure I'm coping with it very well.
> **Me**: I see, so you don't feel you're up to the increased responsibility.
> **Charles**: Yes, I'm worried that I'm not doing it right. Perhaps I could ask my supervisor for some more training.

Me: So you're feeling totally inadequate. You
don't think you're performing up to standard
in your job and you're contemplating admitting
this to your boss. You hope he will be
sympathetic and send you for more expensive
training to do something that *he* clearly feels is
well within your capabilities.

Charles: Well, that's not quite what I meant. It's
just that I've not been sleeping too well for
worrying about it, and I just thought having a
chat with someone might help.

Me: I understand what you're saying. You're
really depressed at the moment and you aren't
quite sure which way to turn. Your sense of
worthlessness is keeping you awake at night
and haunting your dreams. Your days are filled
with cold dread as you fumble your way blindly
through this extra work and the responsibility
sits like a lead weight on your shoulders. You
lie in the dark and cry out in your torment,
'How can I possibly go on?' Hopelessness is
stalking you like a ravenous wolf and you spend
many hours just sitting there, alone, thinking of
ways to end the torture.

At this point, Charles seized a bundle of tissues from a
nearby box and started sobbing uncontrollably. Well, to be
honest, it was all a bit embarrassing. Someone slipped out
to get him a drink of water, while someone else sat and
patted his hand sympathetically.

The course ended early and this time we all went straight
home.

Friday 26 February

On the way to work with Ariadne this morning, I described Charles's strange reaction to my attempts to counsel him.

'I'm sure I did exactly what they told me to do. I simply reflected what he said back to him.'

'You don't think you laid it on a bit?'

'No way!'

She shrugged. 'Well, all I can say is, it's the counselling world's loss.'

'Maybe I can find someone at church to practise my counselling skills on.'

'Are you sure that would be a good idea?'

'I dunno, maybe I should take a longer course first.'

'Maybe. Theo, promise me one thing.'

'What?'

'If you ever see a recruitment poster for the Samaritans asking for volunteer counsellors, give it a miss.'

The baby is obviously making her feel a bit negative about everything.

Sunday 28 February

Charity looked very worried at church this morning – not her bouncing, beaming usual self at all. Couldn't resist finding out what had caused this dampening of spirits and saving it up for use on future occasions.

'Hello, Charity, what's up? You look as if you've lost a talent and found a shekel.'

'Oh, hello Theodora,' she said, craning to peer behind me. 'I was really hoping to speak to Miss Chamberlain. Something dreadful has happened to Zilpah at school and I really wanted her advice.'

'Oh, poor thing, she's not getting bullied, I hope.' I thought of Zilpah's protruding teeth, thick glasses and curly red hair and her worst disadvantage of all – her parents. Surely, if there was a natural target for bullies, Zilpah would be it.

'Oh no, nothing like that. Zilpah won't stand for any nonsense. She knows how to put critics in their place. No, it's her reading book.' She wrung her hands. 'Oh, I can hardly bring myself to talk about it!'

Charity's cheeks became very pink and I was beginning to wonder if I should send for the smelling salts, when Miss Chamberlain appeared. Charity seized her by the arm and steered her towards a pew. As I now considered myself involved in the proceedings (and besides, my curiosity was mounting by the minute), I felt at liberty to follow them. I sat down on the other side of Charity.

'Miss Chamberlain, a dreadful thing has happened,' Charity began. 'Zilpah has been asked to peruse the most unsuitable reading material. I've been to see her teacher and the headmaster, and now I'm thinking of writing to the governing body. Oh,' she sobbed, 'and the worst thing is, *nobody* is taking me seriously! They think I'm just making a fuss, but I really feel we should stand against these dark forces. Don't you agree, Miss Chamberlain?'

I was intrigued. I really couldn't see the village school encouraging its pupils to dabble in the black arts. Miss Chamberlain, as usual, remained calm. In her antique china voice, she spoke gently and reassuringly.

'I can see you are very distressed, my dear. Do you feel able to tell me a few details? Then I'll see if I can suggest anything that might help.'

Charity sniffed and swallowed hard. 'One of the main characters in the book—' she peered round and lowered

her voice, '—is a witch. And there's all sorts of magic king-
doms and pagan creatures, and I believe it also promotes
the worship of animals!'

'I can see why that might upset you. Can I ask the name
of the book?'

'I've brought it with me. To tell the truth, I was concerned about even having it in the house. You never know
what powers these materials might have.'

Charity reached into her handbag and pulled out a copy
of *The Lion, the Witch and the Wardrobe* by C.S. Lewis. I
suppressed a snort of laughter. 'But that's a Christian book.
Even *I* know that!'

Miss Chamberlain glared at me. Charity burst into tears.
Then Miss Chamberlain turned and took Charity's hand.
'Theodora's right. It is a very famous children's book, written by a great man of God who used his gift of story-telling
to help explain the mysteries of our faith. This book is an
allegory, rather like Jesus' parables. I know there's a witch
in the story, but he uses her to explain how he sees the battle between good and evil.'

Charity nodded doubtfully. 'But the idea of a witch – it
seems so . . . evil. What might it do to a vulnerable child's
mind?'

I had difficulty envisaging Zilpah as a 'vulnerable child'.

'You need wicked characters in a book like this as well as
good ones. And believe me, just because there's magic in a
book, especially this book, it won't encourage little Zilpah
to dabble in the occult. Children are far too clever for that.
I think you're very wise to question what your child reads,
but believe me, if it was that easy to influence a child, just
by giving them a book, a teacher's job would be a great
deal simpler! No, children are very good at distinguishing
between reality and stories. Some people even advise that

it's a good thing for children to be a little bit frightened by what they read. If people in the story scare them, they can simply close the book. That can give them a sense of control over things that frighten them. Then, when something happens in real life which makes them afraid, they've had some practice in dealing with it. But I would say to you what I said to all my parents who were worried about what their children were reading or watching on television: read or watch *with* them. Then you can decide if you feel they're being influenced in the wrong way. Go back to Zilpah's teacher and just ask for a different book if that would make you more comfortable. That's what I would do. But make sure you read *The Lion, the Witch and the Wardrobe* yourself. I'm sure you'll love it when you understand it. Then, maybe when Zilpah is older. . .'

Charity nodded and thanked Miss Chamberlain for her advice. I had to admit it was very sensible. Rather a pity, though. I was looking forward to a ritual burning of the *Chronicles of Narnia* in the car park.

March

Monday 1 March

It's March. It's the first day of March. In 27 days' time I will be 30 years old. I know life is supposed to begin at 40, so technically I've got 10 years before it even starts. All the same, I can't help feeling that life is pulling out from Platform 1 while I'm standing on Platform 4, looking in the wrong direction down the track.

Wednesday 3 March

It's about time I started dropping hints to Kevin about what to buy me for my birthday. If I don't, I'll end up with another football video or football book or football T-shirt – and I can't risk the possibility of him buying me underwear. He doesn't wrap my presents, either. I don't think the man even owns a reel of sticky-tape. I do object to being given a birthday gift swathed in a Tesco carrier bag.

Thursday 4 March

A brilliant idea to solve the birthday present dilemma! I will buy the present, wrap it and give it to Kevin to give to me.

It won't be a surprise, but at least I'll stand some chance of getting something I actually want.

A few years ago, I tried giving him explicit instructions.

'Don't get me anything to do with football,' I said. 'I'm not remotely interested in football.'

'Not football.' He wrote carefully in a notebook.

'And I want it to be a surprise, something I'm not expecting.'

'Surprise,' he muttered as he scribbled furiously.

'And something useful. Not one of these gimmicky gadgets that are all the fashion for a few months then spend the rest of eternity in the back of a cupboard.'

'U-S-E-F-U-L-L. . .'

'One L,' I corrected.

I settled back, comfortable that I would not have to suffer another *Dirty Tackles – This Time It's War!* video.

That year he bought me an electric hedge trimmer. True, it fulfilled all my criteria, but I live in a flat. I don't have a garden.

Friday 5 March

Went out to buy a newspaper at lunchtime. Only just made it back past the confectioner's window. They have a display of Easter eggs, chocolate rabbits and boxes and boxes and boxes of the most delicious, luscious, delectable, mouth-watering. . .

Declan caught me looking in.

'Don't forget to wipe the drool off your chin before you get back to work,' he called cheerfully as he dodged my attempt to swipe him with the newspaper.

Looked up 'addiction' in the dictionary when I got home. It defined it as 'the condition in which a person is dependent on the continued taking of some drug, the deprivation of which causes adverse effects including an uncontrolled craving for it'.

That's it! I have a medical condition. I'm not just greedy. I'm addicted to chocolate and what I'm suffering from now is withdrawal. I need to attend a self-help group – Chocoholics Anonymous. I wonder if it exists? I can imagine the group meeting. A dozen chairs set in a circle in the village hall, the leaders with earnest, sympathetic faces, the clients looking pale and anxious, taking it in turns to rise and admit to their addiction.

'My name is Theodora, and I am a chocoholic. It's been 18 days since my last bar of chocolate. . .'

Sunday 7 March

It was Nigel Hubble's turn to preach again today and when he announced the topic of his sermon, 'Knowing God's Will for Your Life', I considered finding an excuse for a rapid departure. It isn't that I don't want to know what God's will is for my life, quite the reverse. I just had the uncomfortable feeling that Nigel's version of God's will and my version of God's will might not be exactly compatible. I whispered my concerns to Miss Chamberlain, who reassured me that she had known many occasions when God had spoken to people in spite of the sermon.

I sat back and listened as Nigel gave an example of how, when he was a teenager, he had 'sought and found the voice of the Lord among the many worldly distractions that can so easily ensnare the saints'. I tried to imagine Nigel being ensnared by worldly distractions. Had he cheated in a game of Monopoly, or bought a tabloid Sunday paper? No. Apparently his great deviation from the straight and narrow involved failing to switch off the television immediately after the nine o'clock news and spending time flipping through the channels. This, he said, had led him into a 'spree of covetousness, self-indulgence and carnality'. I made a mental note to check the *Radio Times* to try to work out what on earth he must have been watching. It turned out, rather disappointingly, that he had been watching the commercials. Poor Nigel. It became clearer and clearer that he just hadn't been able to cope with the modern world of advertising. So many voices advising him to buy so many things. My mind drifted and I imagined him as a character in a Jane Austen novel.

'Oh! Mr Hubble, I do declare that I am quite vexed concerning the variety of choices facing one regarding the magnitude of sweetmeats, fancies and luxuries paraded in front of one on the televisual viewing device nowadays!'

'Suddenly,' Nigel boomed, jerking me back from my daydream, 'I heard the voice of the Lord speaking to me through that television. I heard him as clearly as you can hear me now. "WE'RE WITH THE WOOLWICH," the voice from the television said, and I knew in my heart that it was God's voice.'

I glanced at Miss Chamberlain, who shrugged, and then looked behind me at Charity, who was sitting there captivated by Nigel's story of divine revelation.

'And I knew at once I must go to Woolwich. That very night I packed my case, said goodbye to my parents and caught a train to southeast London.'

This puzzled me. I wanted to know how he knew it was God speaking. I wanted to put up my hand and ask him, but you just don't do that in the middle of a sermon. What if the advert had been for the Halifax? Would he have boarded a train for Yorkshire? If it had urged him to 'Get the Abbey habit', would he have become a monk? I was beginning to have serious doubts about this calling.

'I arrived at about 11.30 at night and stood at Woolwich Dockyard station and prayed for guidance. I prayed that God would divinely reveal to me a dwelling of a Christian brother who would support and encourage me in my desire to follow God's calling for me. And after several hours of wandering the streets of Woolwich, I felt miraculously led to a house. I just had the assurance in my heart that it was a household where the Lord was glorified. I put my suitcase in the porch and rang the bell. After a few minutes the door opened and I saw a man whom I knew in my spirit was a brother in the Lord. He and his wife heard my story and let me stay the night in spite of not knowing me, and in the morning he talked to me and prayed for God to guide me away from that house in blessing and peace. They gave me breakfast, allowed me to ring my parents, and the gentleman even offered to drive me to the station. Isn't God's provision marvellous in the way that he upholds those who are willing to follow him?'

Nigel ended by saying that it was shortly after this experience (and no doubt after watching *The Vicar of Dibley*) that he felt called to put himself forward for ordination and the rest, as they say, is history.

I felt puzzled about what Nigel had said. I've always found Nigel's interpretation of guidance rather fanciful, but it was surely a miracle to find a house belonging to another Christian among all the houses in Woolwich. I mentioned this to Gregory Pasternak over coffee.

'Wasn't it amazing how God guided him to that house?'

'Yes,' said Gregory, 'but what he didn't tell us was the name on the front of the house.'

'You mean it was some kind of secret code, like the first-century believers used, that let him know the house belonged to a Christian?'

'Not exactly. The house was called "The Vicarage".'

Monday 8 March

Today's post consisted of a bank statement (so red I had to open it wearing oven gloves) and a postcard from a catalogue company informing me that I had definitely won a cash prize in their 'Fabulous Prize Draw'. Anything between £1 and £10,000 could be mine if I returned the card within 14 days, requested a catalogue, bought something from the catalogue, paid for the thing I had bought from the catalogue, recommended the catalogue to three friends, who also ordered and paid for items from the catalogue, and completed the sentence, 'I love to shop with Little Galaxy Stores because...' No fabulous prize for guessing which end of the financial spectrum *my* cash award would be.

The final item of post was an ivory-coloured envelope of heavy, embossed paper with my name and address written in beautiful copperplate script on the front. I opened it to find an invitation to my brother Agamemnon's wedding.

Ag is finally getting married and joining 'Club Conformity'. I couldn't believe it at first, but there before my eyes, in gold ink, embossed on a gilt-edged ivory card with a tastefully printed fleur-de-lis in one corner, was the undeniable proof:

Viennetta and Arthur Cabot-Whittle

Request the company of Miss Theodora Llewellyn
and partner

at the marriage of their daughter Cordelia
to Mr Agamemnon Llewellyn

At 2 p.m. on Saturday 22 May at
St Hector's Church, Marrow-on-the-Wold

That was the surprise he mentioned at Christmas. Ag has found a woman to take him on! I barely resisted the urge to phone him both to congratulate him for getting engaged and to berate him for not telling me he was even thinking of getting engaged.

I've always assumed Ag just wasn't the settling-down type. He holds down a job for a few months, serving in burger bars or doing courier work, teaching or even the occasional bit of freelance journalism, then he just takes off to a different country. We always joke that he should have been called Odysseus. The first indication that he's gone wandering again is usually a scrawled postcard from Kathmandu, Rotowaro or Mwanza.

Gave in to the temptation to ring Mum to get the full lowdown on Cordelia. He met her when they were both working in the Far East last summer. Apparently she lives in Wimbledon and she's in *television*. This is really exciting. I've never met anyone in television before. I wonder if she can get me Steve Chalke's autograph.

Wednesday 10 March

Looked again at the invitation. 'Miss Theodora Llewellyn *and partner*.' I don't know what to make of that. Sounds like someone I've gone into business with. I suppose 'partner' is the word people use to describe anything from 'common-law spouse' to 'any bloke you can drag along for the night with the promise of free food and booze'. I can't think of a word to describe adequately the relationship between Kevin and me. 'Boyfriend' sounds too adolescent. 'Sweetheart' just doesn't sum up someone who would present you with a gift-wrapped piece of David Beckham's used chewing gum. 'Lover' would be wildly optimistic and 'friend' sounds as if I actually *like* him. Flicked through the dictionary for a suitable term. 'Appendage' would probably be the best description – 'that which is attached as if by being hung on; a subsidiary but not an essential'.

Phoned Kevin anyway to tell him about the wedding.

'Oh, great, another one bites the dust,' he muttered and scurried off to check his fixtures list before deciding if he can come to the ceremony.

Why do I even bother going out with Kevin? Maybe Charity was right. Kevin and I have nothing in common, lead virtually separate lives and argue all the time we're in the same room. Come to think of it, we'd make an ideal married couple!

Friday 12 March

As I can't envisage our status as a courtship, I can only think of Kevin as a kind of ministry, a vocation. God has obviously given me Kevin for a purpose, a sort of test. Kevin is my project to prove to God that, although I may not be able to evangelize the world, I can be instrumental in frog-marching one person into the fold.

The first step in assisting Kevin in his transformation is to help him to conform, and to do that he must start to go to church regularly. He shouldn't spend so much of his time on Sunday mornings working. On Sunday mornings he does all the little plumbing jobs for the old people in the village that he says he can't fit in during the week, just to avoid going to church. To cap it all, he doesn't even charge them for the work.

I can't help feeling that Kevin is a rather major project, though – like an old car that needs to be stripped down and lovingly restored. I just hope that, like so many projects of this kind, I won't give up halfway through and leave him half-finished with bits going rusty in the corner.

Saturday 13 March

I'm going to start the modification with Kevin's image. I'll need to be subtle, so that he doesn't suspect anything. Obviously, in order to be a churchgoer, you need to look like one, which Kevin certainly doesn't. No one would pass the inspection of the old ladies at St Norbert's, let alone the scrutiny of the heavenly bouncer at the Pearly Gates, in a curry-stained football shirt and jeans with gaping holes in the backside. But what does a religious man look like? I'll check tomorrow at church. If I can get him looking smart for the wedding, that will be a good place to start and the rest is bound to follow.

Overdosed on jelly babies (well, they're not chocolate, and I didn't say I would give up all sweets) and ended up feeling sick. There's just no substitute for the real thing.

Sunday 14 March

Got to church early and sat in a strategic position, halfway down the aisle, in order to observe the men and their attire as they came in. First to arrive was Gregory Pasternak, the incredibly tall, thin, concave-chested organist, wearing a shirt so boldly striped in scarlet, peacock blue and sulphurous yellow that, if you laid him down and carefully arranged his long arms and legs, he could easily pass for a deckchair. Not, I decided, Kevin's new image at all.

Next in were Maurice and Doris Johnson, wearing matching his'n'hers greyish Arran sweaters, knitted, no doubt, by Doris herself from badger fur collected from the hedgerows. They looked like a 1960's folk duo. I expected them to burst into 'Wild Rover' at any minute. *Haute couture?* No chance!

Following a lengthy hiatus, the 'three wise monkeys' entered – Mrs McCarthy in a floral headscarf, Mrs Epstein in a creation which would have looked more at home at Ascot, and Miss Cranmer apparently wearing a knitted teacosy.

Roger Lamarck sauntered in and took his seat in the front pew. Roger has asked me out at least 10 times in the last two years. I eventually ran out of excuses and resorted to the old chestnut about washing my hair. By the time he stopped pestering me, I must have had the cleanest hair in the county.

The three old ladies, deep in conversation, sat in their customary positions at the back of the church in order to clock late arrivals and early departures, their headgear nodding apparently independently of the old ladies themselves. The pews began to fill up with other St Norbert's regulars. Roger leaned over the back of his pew.

'Well, well, the lovely Theodora,' he purred.

I smiled back weakly and tried to ignore the deep brown eyes that had Velcroed themselves onto the hemline of my skirt. This man is oilier than a Greek waiter's apron after a moussaka-juggling night at the taverna.

'Oh, morning Roger,' I acknowledged, giving a casual little wave with my right hand while tugging down my skirt with my left.

'And how are you on this fine, crisp, bracing morning?' he oozed.

'Just fine, thank you,' I returned sharply.

Then the thought hit me. In spite of his smug narcissism, and the fact that he has a face like a ferret, Roger actually dresses very well: classic navy trousers, a crisp, white linen shirt, understated tie and fine wool jacket. This was it – I'd found Kevin's new image.

'Roger, do you mind if I ask you something?' I cooed in my most beguiling voice.

'Not at all, my sweet. Any service I can render, just you ask away.' His eyes this time had fastened themselves just below my neckline.

The headgear in the back row became more and more animated, as three pairs of ears homed into our conversation.

'Where do you buy your clothes?'

Wednesday 17 March

ST PATRICK'S DAY

Declan says we have St Patrick to thank for the fact that there are no snakes in Ireland. Surely that's a bit like saying there are no dinosaurs in Hampshire because the New Forest ponies would form a vigilante patrol and frighten them off?

Saturday 20 March

Tried to take Kevin shopping today to get him something civilized to wear, Roger Lamarck-style, to the wedding. Needless to say, he wasn't exactly overjoyed with the idea. He believes shopping, especially clothes shopping, is some form of torture devised by women to try to control men through the twin processes of humiliation (i.e. being publicly measured by men wielding tape measures with stiff ends) and financial ruin.

I steered him towards the shop recommended by Oily Roger, a 'Gentlemen's Outfitters' with Georgian windows and a sign in Gothic script. He looked around nervously as I propelled him through the brass-furnished door. The shop interior reeked of furniture polish and leather. Racks of suits, sports coats and blazers stood to attention with military precision. A rather chinless young man was browsing through a selection of cravats, finally deciding on antique gold with maroon squares.

Kevin looked desperately uncomfortable. 'But Theo, I'd wear a *new* football shirt,' he whined, 'with a tie if you want.'

'Not good enough,' I snapped. 'I don't want you looking like a slob in front of my whole family.'

A grey-suited assistant slid up behind Kevin and cleared his throat resoundingly. Kevin jumped like a startled wallaby and spun round.

'May I be of assistance to Sir, or is Sir just looking?'

Kevin glanced over his shoulder looking for the 'Sir' the assistant was addressing.

'Can I help you, Sir, at all, in any way?' the assistant enquired obsequiously. He appeared to be wrestling with the urge to wring his hands and tug his forelock.

'Yes,' I replied, taking a firm grasp of the situation and an even firmer grasp of Kevin, who looked as if he was about to make a run for it. 'We'd like to buy a suit.'

The assistant turned his attention to me. 'Certainly, Madam. For a special occasion perhaps?'

'Yes, a wedding,' I smiled, clinging desperately to a now pop-eyed Kevin.

'And when is the happy occasion to take place?' he asked.

'It's on 22 May,' I replied, twisting Kevin's arm behind his back in a sort of armlock, smiling through gritted teeth and trying to make it look like a loving embrace.

'A registry office ceremony, naturally,' stated the assistant,

looking Kevin up and down as if he was something unpleasant he'd found stuck under a bus seat.

That riled me. That really riled me.

Who did that stuck-up assistant think he was, implying
that Kevin only befitted a civic ceremony?

'No, a full church wedding, actually. Organist, choirboys,
bells, overweight aunts in ridiculous hats, everything,' I
established. 'And there'll be a professional film crew in
attendance,' I added huffily.

'What, may I enquire, will Madam – or should I say Miss
– be wearing?'

'Well, I haven't decided yet.' I pondered, mentally cata-
loguing my wardrobe and envisaging my bank balance.
'Does it really matter?'

'Will it be a formal gown or a more casual, modern
trousseau? It is important to co-ordinate the bride's and
groom's outfits.'

Kevin suddenly threw back his head and roared with
laughter. 'No, not *us*! It's her *brother* what's getting married, not us. He thinks we're getting married, Theo. What
a laugh! Us, married? Ha! That'll be the day! Come on,
let's get out of here. I've had enough. I need a drink.
Married! That's made my day, it really has.' He shook his
head and wiped the tears of laughter from his eyes.

Aware of the condescending eyes of Mr Antique Gold
Cravat and the toadying shop assistant, I marched, red-
faced, several paces behind the still chuckling Kevin as he
wove his way past the clothes racks and out into the street.

Was getting married really such a ridiculous idea? I'd not
thought about it much before. I'd just assumed that one
day it would happen, a natural progression like summer
following spring or indigestion following a curry. Now the
bombshell had dropped. Kevin had no more intention of

marrying me than Peter Stringfellow had of getting a sensible haircut.

Am I so terrible that not even Kevin, who is, after all spiritually degenerate, will have me?

I sat in silence in the pub, staring into my lemonade as Kevin chatted about his team's new signings. I was devastated. Kevin seemed totally unaware that my whole life, my vision of the future, had just come tumbling down about my ears like an assemble-it-yourself wardrobe. He was so wrapped up in the new 'back four' that he was totally oblivious of the depths of misery into which he had just plunged me.

I said nothing on the way home either. I just sat there giving him loaded 'I'm extremely upset and you haven't even noticed' looks. He pulled up outside my flat and I slammed the van door, intending to stomp off dramatically. The effect was only slightly spoilt by the fact that I'd shut my coat in the door and had to bang on the window to stop him driving merrily away with me still attached.

11 p.m.
Have just spent the most miserable evening of my life without even a bar of chocolate for comfort. My hopes for the future, for marriage, a family, joint membership of the leisure centre, are all shattered. My life has come to an end and he doesn't even realize it. He's so insensitive.

1 a.m.
Just phoned Kevin's number and played 'I Will Survive' by Gloria Gaynor down the phone. That will teach him.

Sunday 21 March

Too depressed to go to church this morning. Sat in my pyjamas, ate cooking chocolate – yes, I failed there too – and watched *The Morning Service*. Why do they show church services on Sunday mornings when anybody who is interested in church would go to a service anyway?

I expect someone from St Norbert's will be round later to make sure I'm all right. They have a new system of pastoral care to fill the gap since Jeremiah's departure, ensuring that no one is left suffering or in need. Wonderful idea. It's at times like these that you really appreciate belonging to a caring Christian community.

8 p.m.
No 'caring pastoral visitors'. About half an hour ago someone dropped the following letter through the door on St Norbert's headed paper:

Dear... (Please insert name)

It has been brought to our attention that you (were absent from today's service/are ill/have recently had a baby/have converted to Catholicism*). Under our ongoing system of pastoral care, we would like to offer (to collect your shopping/to include you in our regular prayer diary/refer you to the appropriate professional services/arrange an audience with the Pope*). If you would like to take advantage of any of these services, please telephone the above number and leave a message on the answering machine. This message will be conveyed to the appropriate church sub-committee within three working days (four if falling within a week con-

taining a religious or public holiday). If the person
named on this letter, or their official representative, fails
to make contact within one calendar month of the date
of postmark, we will assume that our pastoral assistance
is no longer required and your name will be removed
from our list. In the event of the decease of the recipient
of this letter, the case will automatically be passed to
the vicar to initiate funeral arrangements.

Yours faithfully,
Xavier F. Huxley
(On behalf of the Parish Pastoral Committee)

*Please delete where appropriate

As I said, it's at times like these that you really appreciate
belonging to a caring Christian community.

Monday 22 March

Couldn't face work today. Rang up and said I was suffering
from 'the vapours'. I found it in an old medical dictionary.
Not quite sure what it is. That should keep them guessing
when it comes to filling in their staff sickness forms. I've
neither heard from nor seen Kevin since Saturday. That
proves my point. If he cared for me at all, he would at least
have rung. I'm better off without him. I WILL survive.

2 p.m.
Still no word from Kevin. Men are pigs.

8 p.m.
I want him back.

11 p.m.
No I don't. Not after the way he treated me.

1 a.m.
But I still love him.

Tuesday 23 March

8 a.m.
Couldn't sleep last night for worrying. I know I complain about him, but think I love Kevin and I miss him now he's not there. It's like having an itchy verruca: profoundly irritating at the time, but you miss having something to scratch when it's gone.

The truth is, I'm scared of being on my own, being left on the shelf. I'll become a spinster and have to start crocheting coat hangers and give up shaving my legs. I'll call everyone 'dear'. I'll grow roses, eat Rich Tea biscuits and wear lavender perfume and sensible shoes.

I phoned Ariadne because she was going into work early this morning. I know pregnant women shouldn't become distressed, but I felt this was an emergency. Tom, who seemed even more vague than usual, answered the phone.

'No thank you, I really don't require a horse.'

'Tom, what are you on about? Can I speak to Ariadne, please? It's Theo.'

'Oh, sorry Theo. I thought you were trying to give me a horse.'

Why on earth would he think that? There were rummaging noises and my sister's voice sounded rather irritated. Must be the hormones. 'What do you want, Theo? I'm late.'

'Sorry to ring you before work, but . . . the thing is . . . I've split up with Kevin.'

'Oh Theo, I am sorry. How are you?'

'Well, a bit upset really. Look, can I meet you for lunch?'

'Can't, I'm afraid, business lunch. Come round for supper.' She sounded more sympathetic. 'How's Kevin coping?'

'Kevin doesn't actually know.'

'How can he not know? You've been going out for nearly 10 years!'

'He doesn't seem to have noticed yet.'

'You didn't think to tell him?'

'It all happened so quickly on Saturday. I found out he didn't want to marry me. . .'

'You proposed and he turned you down?'

'Well, no.'

'But you discussed it.'

'Not exactly.'

'Let me get this clear. You haven't actually bothered to ask Kevin, but you've got it into your head that he doesn't want to marry you. Because of this, you've decided that you aren't going out any more, but you haven't thought to mention any of this to poor old Kevin.'

'It wasn't quite like that. . .'

'Theo, sort yourself out. See you tonight.'

The phone clattered back into its rest. I suppose it does sound a bit daft when you say it like that, but feelings are feelings and Kevin has trampled on mine like a muddy spaniel on a freshly hoovered Axminster.

Why should Tom think I was trying to give him a horse? I worry about that man. Is he fit to be a father?

11 p.m.

Didn't get much further in sorting out the Kevin thing at supper tonight. Pregnancy hasn't softened Ariadne. She seemed even more brusque than usual, telling me to pull myself together and talk to Kevin. She doesn't understand. Kevin is the last person I can talk to.

Forgot to ask Tom about the horse. Maybe this pregnancy has started affecting his mind.

Wednesday 24 March

I suppose I really ought to think about going back to work today.

No, I can't face it. I think I'll have a therapeutic day at the seaside. The sea air should blow away the cobwebs, if nothing else. What a silly expression. 'Blow away the cobwebs' makes me sound like a dusty attic. On second thoughts, that's exactly how I feel: neglected, full of old memories and only visited when someone wants something.

I rather optimistically packed suntan lotion, sunglasses and a book to read on the beach and set off, hoping my old car had the perseverance to make it all the way to the coast.

I'd just driven to the end of my road when I spotted Miss Chamberlain struggling with a parcel. I pulled up and wound down the window.

'Morning, Miss Chamberlain. Would you like a lift somewhere?'

'Thank you, my dear. I'm just on my way to the post office. That's very kind of you.'

I hopped out and placed the parcel in the boot, then took Miss Chamberlain's arm and helped her into the passenger seat.

'I'm just taking the parcel to the post office for my neighbour,' she explained. 'Poor old thing, she doesn't get out much. Arthritis, you know.'

Poor old thing! Miss Chamberlain couldn't be far off 90 herself.

'Not at work today, Theodora?' she said as I drove on.

'No. Actually, I was just setting off for a day at the seaside.' A compulsion seized me. 'Would you like to come?'

'I wouldn't want to hold you back. I know what you get up to, you young girls!' She winked knowingly.

What exactly did she think I was going to do in Dymchurch in March?

'Nonsense, I'd love to have some company.' That, at least, was true. Miss Chamberlain herself is like a breath of fresh air. The combination of the elderly lady and the sea breeze would be just what I needed.

After the claustrophobic grid of suburban avenues and drives with their ranks of uniform, double-glazed semis, it was a relief to hit the open road. Hedges flanked the grey tarmac and small villages passed in the blink of an eye. I decided to avoid the motorways and risk becoming stuck behind a tractor or flock of ambling sheep along the country lanes.

As it happened, we made good progress and, with Miss Chamberlain's companionship, the journey passed rapidly and very pleasantly. Even my recalcitrant car decided to co-operate on this occasion.

We arrived in Dymchurch at lunchtime. It appeared to be closed. The gaudy souvenir shops were shuttered against the brutal wind. Even the funfair seemed to be wrapped and muffled in winter tarpaulins.

'There's probably a pub somewhere along the coast,' I gasped as the wind snatched my breath. Miss Chamberlain's eyes were watering and it looked as if she would be blown off her feet. I took her arm and we walked along the top of the sea wall from the car park to a seafront pub next to the funfair.

The warmth and smell of freshly fried fish embraced us as we entered. I ordered two cod and chips, a bitter lemon for Miss Chamberlain and half a pint of shandy for me. We sat at a table in the corner to wait for our food.

'What's the matter, dear?' She placed a wrinkled hand on mine.

'Oh, nothing really, I just fancied a day out.'

'People don't just fancy a day out in arctic weather in the middle of March. Is it something to do with your young man?'

'You'll think this sounds silly,' I began. Then the whole story came pouring out. Miss Chamberlain nodded sympathetically and didn't laugh once.

'What should I do?' I implored.

'Well, you might wonder what a silly old spinster like me knows about young people. But, believe it or not, I was young once and I used to walk out with young men. One even asked me to marry him. I know it's hard to imagine, but he did.' Her cheeks began to glow as she remembered.

'What happened?'

'He proposed to me at the seaside. Not here – it was down at Brighton. I used to teach down there. He was a nice young man, lovely straight teeth and an honest smile. He'd bought me a diamond ring. He bought me dinner, then got down on one knee and asked me to marry him. But . . . but I turned him down.'

'Why?'

'I thought I could do better. I was a teacher and he was a fisherman. He asked, I turned him down, and no one ever asked me again.'

'Do you regret it?'

'I have sometimes wondered how things would have turned out. But regrets, no. Never hold onto regrets, they only make you bitter. I've led a full and blessed life. The Lord has been very good to me and I wouldn't change a thing.'

The landlord brought our meals over to the table.

'Just be aware that you need to make the most of opportunities when they arise. Make sure you make the best possible choices for the best possible reasons.'

We tucked into our fish and chips in silence. I narrowly avoided the double chocolate gateau. After lunch, the sun came out and Miss Chamberlain insisted she wanted to go down to the beach. 'I haven't come all this way to leave without having a paddle!'

I took her arm to steady her along the pebbles and shingle, until we reached the strip of sand. She took off her shoes and stockings and dipped her feet in the icy water. I wondered if it was really good for her, but if you can't do what you feel like when you're nearly 90, when *can* you do it?

I walked back to the edge of the shingle and sat facing the sea, with the wind wrenching my hair away from my face. My life is full. I don't need Kevin, or marriage, or babies. I just want someone to take me paddling in the sea in March when I'm nearly 90.

Thursday 25 March

Found out the origin of Tom's strange reference to not wanting a horse. Ariadne explained that, against her advice, Tom had answered an advertisement in his bird-spotting magazine and joined the 'Friends of Duntrotting Animal Sanctuary'.

'I told him not to. I knew there was something dodgy about that place,' she snapped. 'Now we get phone calls three or four times a week asking if we can take a retired dray horse or a lame mare.' She looked daggers at Tom, who visibly shrank under her glare. 'Now I suppose we'll have to change our phone number. Every day I arrive home from work expecting to find a Shetland pony grazing on the lawn.'

Friday 26 March

Kevin actually bothered to ring me today.

'Hi, Theo, how are you?'

'Where on earth have you been for the last week?'

'But I told you: Paul, Jez, Kev 2 and me arranged this European tour.'

European tour? Had they suddenly become the Rolling Stones?

'What tour?' Then it dawned on me. He *had* mentioned something about his team going to play in France, Holland and Germany.

So, that was it. He'd been living it up, sampling the finest of European culture, food and lager, while I'd been suffering the agony of emotional torment on my own at home. Any hopes I still entertained of continuing the relationship fizzled away like a second-hand firework.

'It's funny,' he continued, 'but everyone I've spoken to since I got back seems to think we're not going out any more. Come on, Theo, what's going on?'

'You and your precious football being more important than us. That's what's going on,' I retorted.

'I don't understand. I certainly haven't said anything to anyone.'

'I don't think you need *say* anything.'

'But they think it's all over.'

'It is now!'

I replaced the receiver with a satisfying clunk, rubbed my hands together – and burst into tears.

Saturday 27 March

No food. Nothing to spread on my toast this morning. Now I haven't even got any bread to toast. Ought to go shopping. Can't be bothered. Declan offered to take me out to the pub to celebrate my birthday. Probably feels sorry for me. Instead I sat at home and ate digestive biscuits with mashed potato. Digger has gone away for the weekend, to get 'renewed' or something, so I can't even talk to him.

Sunday 28 March

It's my thirtieth birthday. I have no man, no money and no marmalade. To cheer me up even further, I face the prospect of a sermon from Nigel Hubble followed by lunch with my parents. They aren't speaking again, due to my mother's insistence on doing the catering for my brother's wedding herself – Greek taverna-style, with a bouzouki player. My car is making funny noises and I've found my first grey hair.

I think I'll stay in bed.

Monday 29 March

Today I received a birthday present from Declan that didn't explode, turn parts of me black, or make raspberry noises when I sat on it. He must be slacking.

Why are people so cruel? I've been given no less than six boxes of chocolates for my birthday and I can't eat any of them for another 87 hours 48 minutes.

Now I truly understand the meaning of suffering.

Tuesday 30 March

No card from Kevin. If he'd had the audacity to send one I would have been obliged to burn it, of course. He's even denied me the satisfaction of doing that. The pig! The phone rang several times, but I ignored it in case it was him. I have nothing to say to him.

Wednesday 31 March

Eventually answered the phone today and wished I hadn't. Kevin said that he needed to talk to me and that it had all been a terrible mistake. I said I would rather talk to Attila the Hun as he was probably more considerate, and put the phone down on him.

Consoled myself by playing the CD that Declan gave me. It really didn't have any backward messages or rude songs on it. I checked by playing it several times. I'm worried about him. What if he likes me? He's quite good-looking and certainly has a sense of humour, but if I went out with him it would be like dating Jeremy Beadle.

Anyway, he's got a girlfriend.

And, as far as I know, he isn't a Christian.

And I'm not over Kevin.

I wish Digger was here.

April

Thursday 1 April

APRIL FOOL'S DAY
Checked the tops of doors carefully for buckets of water on the way from the entrance of the building to my office this morning. Examined my telephone for black ink on the earpiece. Scrutinized my answer-phone for messages to ring Mr C. Lyons at London Zoo.

Nothing.

No rubber snakes in my desk drawers, no rude screen-savers on my PC. Declan must, I decided, be saving it up for a really big one.

Twelve o'clock came and went. Still nothing. In fact, I hadn't seen him all morning. His jacket was hanging on the back of his chair, so I knew he must be lurking somewhere in the building. Somewhat disappointing, really, as I'd bought a rather spectacular nail-through-the-finger trick and was desperate to beat Declan at his own game.

At about 2.30, I overheard someone from accounts moaning that Declan had been in the records room all day and was he ever going to get off his lazy backside and do some work? This was my chance. I attached the nail so that it looked as if I'd hammered it straight through my finger, applied a generous quantity of fake blood and staggered

into the records room groaning in synthetic agony. Declan
sat on a low wheelie stool with his head in his hands.

'Aaaghh! I've just hammered this gruesome six-inch nail
right through my finger!' I wailed.

'Seen it before,' said Declan without looking up.

'But there's loads and loads of blood!' I waved the gris-
ly injury under his nose.

'Not in the mood.' His voice sounded thick and flat.

'Declan, what's wrong?' I knelt in front of him. His hair
hung over his face and I could see his eyes were rimmed
with red. 'What on earth has happened?'

'She's gone. She's finished with me.'

'Who? Katherine?'

'Gone back to Ireland.'

'But why?'

'Says she needs some time. Time to think about the two
of us. Got up this morning to find a note through the front
door. At first, I thought it was a joke. Well you would,
today being today and all that. But it wasn't a joke.'

'Declan, I'm so sorry. Do you want to talk about it? I'll
buy you a coffee in the canteen.'

'Nothing to say, really. Thanks, but . . . can you cope if I
go early today?'

'Of course. Look, if there's anything I can. . .'

'No, no. Thanks.' He heaved himself off the stool and
trailed towards the door.

'Will you be all right?'

Declan didn't turn round, but raised one hand in a half-
hearted wave. As much as his ceaseless practical jokes make
me want to stick sharp things in him, I hate to see him so
dejected. Especially with today being today and all that.

Friday 2 April

GOOD FRIDAY
Sat in church and thought about life. You only realize how much you need something, or somebody, when they aren't there any more.

That was profound.

I feel even more depressed.

Think I'll go out this afternoon and buy a self-assembly bookcase. That will stop me having any more profound thoughts.

Saturday 3 April

Kevin phoned again. Still can't bring myself to speak to him. This time I said he had the wrong number and pretended to be the Chinese restaurant. Perhaps this time he got the message.

Sunday 4 April

EASTER SUNDAY
CHOCOLATE!!!

Oh, and Jesus rose from the dead, of course.

Hallelujah!

Monday 5 April

EASTER MONDAY
Spent the whole of the holiday weekend assembling my bookcase. It looks really splendid now. The only snag is that you can't actually put any books on the shelves.

5 p.m.

Phoned Dad to ask his advice. He said I should have asked for one with gravity-proof shelves. I think that was his idea of a joke. Still, he came round with a screwdriver and a pot of glue and fixed it for me. Bless him.

Tuesday 6 April

Declan wasn't at work today. He'd phoned in sick with a migraine before I arrived. Toyed with the idea of phoning him at home. After all, I'm no stranger to a broken heart. Comforting the downcast could be my ministry.

Decided not to phone today. He probably needs the space.

Wednesday 7 April

Nearly phoned Declan, but chickened out at the last minute. What if he really has got a migraine? The last thing he'd want is someone from work pestering him. I don't want to turn into Jeremiah Wedgwood.

Thursday 8 April

Passed Kevin's van on the way back from the station this evening. It was parked outside Miss Cranmer's house. I resisted the urge to let his tyres down.

Friday 9 April

Declan came back to work today. I asked him how he was and he said he was OK.

When people say that, do they really mean it?

How can you tell?

I kept looking at him when he wasn't looking at me, but still didn't know if he was really all right. By lunchtime, I was worried in case he really wasn't, so I followed him to lunch and hid in the chemist's while he bought a ham sandwich and a coffee from the deli. I sauntered casually around the other side of the lake, carrying a newspaper in front of my face while he ate his sandwich and drank his coffee in the park. Then I followed him back to the office, but he kept turning round, so I had to keep ducking into shop doorways. I don't think he saw me.

After he had hung his jacket on the back of the chair, I walked nonchalantly to the filing cabinet next to him to observe more closely, examining him for signs of distress. He flapped the file he was holding down on top of the pile of papers on his desk. 'Theodora, I thought you'd like to know: I'm thinking of going to the toilet now, just in case you'd like to come with me.'

Saturday 10 April

Having finished all my Easter eggs several days ago, I discovered to my delight that the village post office is selling off its stock of Easter eggs at reduced prices. Bought more than I care to admit to on paper.

Sunday 11 April

There's a women's conference to be held at St Norbert's later this month. It's called 'Decide Now!' and promises to be 'a time of discovery, blessing, and ministry'. Can't decide whether to go or not. I always feel apprehensive about conferences. They invariably seem to be called something like, 'God's Warriors Charge into Battle with Swords Aflame'.

I never feel like one of God's Warriors. I feel more like the chap who goes around cleaning up after the horses.

Monday 12 April

Don't think I'll bother to go.

Tuesday 13 April

Today I bought pale blue nail varnish and matching lipstick from the make-up counter in a very fashionable department store. Does this mean I'm officially over Kevin?

Wednesday 14 April

Ariadne says my new lipstick and nail varnish make me look as if I'm suffering from heart disease.

Thursday 15 April

Ariadne wants to go to the conference and wants me to go with her.

Friday 16 April

I think I'll go. I think.

Saturday 17 April

Easter eggs all gone. I've worked it out. I think that, in the last two weeks, I must have consumed more than my body weight in chocolate.

Oh dear. Cottage cheese beckons.

Monday 19 April

Work hasn't been the same since Declan came back. He looks identical, with his floppy fringe of hair, and he's still as charming, but he's lost his sparkle. It's as if the pilot light has gone out. He hasn't played a single joke on anyone for weeks. A serious Declan. That's serious.

Tuesday 20 April

Ariadne and I are definitely going to the conference. Might get a zap from God and discover my ministry. What do people wear to conferences? I don't want to look like a novice.

Wednesday 21 April

Put a plastic spider in Declan's in-tray to try to cheer him up. Found it later in the bin.

Thursday 22 April

Replaced Declan's pens and pencils with rubber pencils and put a fake inkblot on an important document. No reaction.

Friday 23 April

Declan says he wants to talk to me. He's invited me out for a drink next Thursday. This means one of two things: he either wants to ask me out, or he wants to rebuke me about the practical jokes. Oh dear! I don't want to go.

Saturday 24 April

Ariadne looked nervous as we entered the normally subdued atmosphere of St Norbert's. She was wearing her maternity 'tent' for the first time and obviously felt underdressed without her tent pegs and guy ropes. The church was packed with women of every possible description and representing every continent. There were old ones, young ones, black ones, white ones, fat ones, thin ones, ones in flowery dresses and blue rinses and ones with shaven heads and purple dungarees.

Charity came bounding towards us through the crowd. She was wearing a dress so large and so flowery that I fully expected to see Alan Titchmarsh concealed within its folds. She patted her bulge and said to Ariadne, 'You must be Theodora's sister. I must admit, I was astonished when she told me you were joining us in the "Mothercare and coffee morning" set.'

I could see Ariadne's jaw tightening, but, to her credit, she managed to smile. 'And you must be Charity. Theo's told me so much about you. Blooming, I see.' She shot a glance at the cottage-garden-on-legs in front of her.

'I just wanted to invite you to join our Mothers Against Modern Alternative Lifestyles group – MAMAL for short. We seek to return to traditional roles for women, based mainly around keeping the home spick and span. For instance, in July we're having a lecture on how to get that nice red shine on your front doorstep and our consumer committee will bring the report of their road test on the latest models of dustpans and brushes. You'll need something to fill all that spare time when Baby is asleep.'

'Actually, I won't be staying at home after the baby's born. My husband Tom will.'

Charity's eyes widened. 'But do you feel that's in accordance with the spirit of Scripture? ". . .wives be in subjection to your own husbands. . ." There's great satisfaction to be gained from fulfilling your wifely duties.'

'Oh, I don't doubt that. I'm fully in subjection to my husband. I told him so only this morning while he was ironing my dress.'

I thought Charity would explode.

'Look, seriously,' Ariadne continued, obviously having decided that the sport of Charity-baiting was too easy to be real fun, 'Tom and I agreed this was the best way to run *our* household. I have a well paid job which I love, and Tom is wonderful with children and can't wait to quit his job. I know it won't be easy for either of us. It will mean big changes. But we believe and rejoice in the fact that God has made us all different and has given us different talents and strengths. For you, staying with your children and home-making is the way you fulfil God's plan for your life. Don't you see that it isn't right for everybody? Our child will be just as loved and cherished as your children obviously are. You're a very generous person, Charity, and I admire the way you devote yourself to your family and community. I wish I could be as selfless as you are, but I'm not there yet. Keep praying for me, will you?'

'Oh,' said Charity. 'Of course.'

I wish I'd said that to Charity. Why couldn't I have said that?

The meeting continued with a woman charity worker from an international aid organization talking about Third World debt and its devastating effect on the lives of some of the poorest women in the world. It made me want to seize a pen and paper and write to my MP. The next speaker talked about inner-city initiatives among the homeless in London. That made me want to quit my job instantly and go off to work with the homeless. After coffee, the third speaker encouraged women to devote more time to inter-cessory prayer and encouraged us to be 'a powerful force for change through supplication'. That made me want to get down on my knees.

After lunch, we split into groups to pray for each other. A very nice lady with orange hair and a pierced nose prayed that I would find my ministry. I prayed that she would find her family, whom she hadn't seen for five years. A group of five of us joined to pray for Ariadne and her baby. The group contained one very enthusiastic charismatic lady who stood and prayed with extravagant arm-waving gestures.

'Oh Lord, we beseech you, we implore you, bless our sister and this miraculous new life growing within her hidden places. Bring it forth with joy and thanksgiving. May this child be delivered singing your praises. May this womb open and bring forth this child with jubilant exultation!'

She went on praying, so graphically describing each stage of labour, that those women in the group who had not had children were turning green and those with children were crossing their legs and wincing at the memory. I glanced at Ariadne. She had one eye open and a look of sheer panic on her face. One particularly resonant exclamation of 'Bring forth!' nearly sent several of the group rushing for hot water and towels.

The meeting ended quietly with a hymn and a benediction. I had offered to stay behind and help clear up. St Norbert's had a slightly shocked appearance, like a bachelor uncle who has just been kissed and fussed over by a group of nieces. I collected coffee cups from windowsills and under pews and straightened the altar cloth. Ariadne sneaked up behind me.

'You know that woman with the vast knowledge of things gynaecological and obstetric who prayed for the baby?'

I nodded.

'When she finished praying, do you think we should have given her a "standing ovulation"?'

Sunday 25 April

Woke up at 4 a.m. and just couldn't get back to sleep. Things kept churning around in my mind like clothes in a washing machine. Every few minutes a different problem came to the front and I lay and contemplated it through the glass door. . .

Does God want to use me in His service, to give me a ministry, or is my spiritual application form at the bottom of the heap with hundreds of more qualified applicants piled on top? 'Thank you, Miss Llewellyn, we'll let you know when a suitable vacancy arises. Don't call us. . .'

Whirr, churn, slop. Another problem appears at the door. What if I've blown my chances with Kevin? What if, like Miss Chamberlain, I never meet a suitable man, never marry, never have children, never become tied down, have the freedom and money to go anywhere, do anything? On second thoughts. . .

Churn, slop, whirr. Declan. What about Declan? He looks all right, a bit like Hugh Grant, but with red hair, and shorter, and fatter, and more Irish ... OK, he looks nothing like Hugh Grant apart from the floppy hair. He doesn't like football – which is one major thing in his favour. I'm sure he's not attracted to me. If he were, I wouldn't always be the butt of his jokes. Anyway, I think he's a kind of lapsed Roman Catholic. And he's my boss. What if he's going to give me a rocket over the practical jokes? Maybe he can dish it out but not take it. Technically, he could give me a formal warning which would go on my employment record, permanently. He could even have me dismissed.

Feeling desperately in need of a final rinse and brisk spin, I decided to get up, get dressed and take my soggy thoughts for a walk.

Outside my front door I looked up at the drab sky. There wasn't a proper sunrise, no glorious dawning of a new day. The tone of grey just changed from dark dull grey to slightly lighter dull grey as the sun rose and a light mist of drizzle clung to my hair, face and coat.

I walked briskly up the hill to St Norbert's. I knew it wouldn't be open and that no one would be there. I just wanted to seek comfort in its solid bulk and familiar outline. I remember once hearing a child whisper to her mother as they passed the church, 'That's where God lives, isn't it?' Her mother didn't answer, but sometimes I think that child was right.

I found a bench in the churchyard, sat down and closed my eyes. The drizzle had stopped and the dripping sun started to overflow the banks of cloud, washing the morning in a few degrees of warmth. The scent of the flowers had begun to intensify in the tepid air. My thoughts finally stopped spin-drying and I felt peaceful for the first time in weeks. Yes, I thought, this is where God lives, and He's at home right now.

Thursday 29 April

It was neither a date nor a reprimand.

Declan was already sitting at a table with a pint of bitter when I arrived at the pub. His eyes darted from me to the floor and back. He bought me lemonade and there was an uncomfortable pause before he spoke.

'Theo, you must be wondering why on earth I invited you here tonight.'

I gave a noncommittal shrug.

'The thing is, I've been doing some thinking and I've come to some decisions. . .' He took a deep breath and wiped the palms of his hands on his trousers. 'I wanted to talk to you about them.'

'I'm all ears.'

'You and I have known each other for a long time and I feel I can say things to you that I couldn't say to anyone else. I know that you've been going through some difficult times recently and I've seen how you've got through them and how your faith has helped you.'

'It has?'

'Yes. And I know I can be a pain in the backside sometimes, with the jokes and all, but you've always taken it in good part.'

'I have?'

'Well, recently I've been thinking seriously about my life, about everything. I've started going to Confession again and I'd like to go to Mass. It's almost like God's been talking to me.' He looked at the floor and wrung his hands. 'Does that sound crazy?'

I shook my head.

'Thing is, I'm petrified and in need of a bit of moral support. The choice was eight pints, or ask you, and I couldn't afford the eight pints. I wondered if you wouldn't mind coming to Mass with me.'

'Er . . . OK.'

It certainly wasn't a date. I'd never been inside a Catholic church before and had certainly never thought of myself as an alternative to intoxication, but I was willing to give anything a try.

'There's something else.' He wiped his palms on his trousers again and looked up at me through a fringe of hair. 'I'm thinking of taking Holy Orders – you know, becoming a priest.'

'Oh.'

'Is that all you can say, "Oh"?' He looked disappointed.

My mind raced. This was certainly not what I'd expected. Here I was, wanting a ministry, and it felt as if God kept missing me and zapping everyone else around me. But this was no time to feel sorry for myself. It had obviously taken Declan a lot of courage to talk to me. I grinned broadly.

'Declan, that's wonderful!' I kissed him on the cheek. 'Are you allowed to kiss priests-to-be?'

'Of course.' He let out a big sigh. 'It's such a relief to tell someone, someone who understands. You will come then, to Mass on Sunday?'

'I'd be glad to. Honestly, I'm really pleased for you.'

We spent the rest of the evening chatting and laughing. I haven't seen Declan look so happy or relaxed for a long time. He even offered me a piece of 'snappy' chewing gum and laughed like a drain when it caught my finger, removing a sliver of my nail varnish and part of my nail.

Just after 10 p.m., he walked me to my car and gave me a peck on the cheek before he left to catch his train.

'You're an angel, Theo.'

I wish I were.

Friday 30 April

Miss Chamberlain's birthday. I baked a chocolate cake and took it round, along with a card and a packet of lace handkerchiefs. I've never seen her use them, but that's always what she says she wants when I ask. I wonder what old ladies do with all those handkerchiefs? I'm sure their noses can't run that much.

May

Saturday 1 May

Charity had her baby today. She gave birth at home and three hours later she was out pushing the child in a pram. I met her in the post office. She'd gone to post a letter for Nigel. She was still smiling and still wearing an enormous flowery frock. How does she make having a baby look so easy? Practice, I suppose. Apparently they've decided to call the baby Methuselah.

Sunday 2 May

Went to church with Declan who was, much to my relief, sober. St Semolina of the Divine Revelation was a large, modern building with tall windows and a stubby bell tower. Inside, it had the familiar furniture-polish-and-flowers smell common to every church I've ever been into. However denominations differ doctrinally, they seem to be united by this smell.

During the service, I got a bit confused about the genu-flecting and making the sign of the cross. I must have looked as if I was trying to signal in semaphore. Declan laughed at me.

'I'm sorry, I think I got that all wrong,' I whispered.

'I'm sure God will forgive you,' he whispered back.

'Yes, but I'm not sure *she* will.' I glanced at the woman next to me, whom I'd accidentally elbowed in the ribs.

I was struck by the similarity between the words of the Mass and St Norbert's liturgy for the Communion service. I even knew two of the hymns. Father Michael, a slender man in his sixties with a charming smile and blue eyes, preached the sermon. It was pretty much the sort of sermon Digger would have preached, but it was strange to hear it in a broad Midlands accent rather than Digger's Aussie twang. As Declan went up to receive the Host, I knelt in that strange, familiar place and prayed that God would guide him and help him decide what to do.

After the service, Father Michael stood at the door and shook hands as the congregation shuffled out. Declan introduced me.

'Ah, Theodora. You know that name means "Gift of God"?'

I hadn't known that. After hating my name for years, I now find out that it means something lovely. 'Gift of God.' Can't wait to tell Ariadne.

Monday 3 May

Went to see Ariadne this evening. For some reason, she was emulsion-painting the inside of the garden shed. Tom was indoors knitting. I took the paintbrush out of her hand and persuaded her to sit down.

'Did you know my name means "Gift of God"?'

Ariadne seemed unimpressed. 'Doesn't surprise me,' she sniffed. 'You always behave as if you think you're God's gift.'

If she hadn't been pregnant, I would have hit her.

Tuesday 4 May

I wonder what Ariadne and Tom will call their baby. It's due in just over a month and this is Ariadne's last week at work. It will seem strange commuting alone.

Wednesday 5 May

Supper at Mum's and Dad's. Ariadne and Tom came too. The subject of the baby's name came up over the stuffed vine leaves.

'Mum,' said Ariadne firmly, 'rest assured there's no way we're calling the baby Ajax or Aphrodite. And Dad, Morgan and Blodwyn are out of the question too.'

'Clytemnestra's nice,' said Mum.

'No!' Ariadne banged her knife and fork on the table with such force that the taramasalata nearly shot off into orbit. 'No, it isn't *nice*, Mother. It isn't nice at all. We're not having it, and that's final. No ridiculous Greek names; no silly Welsh ones. He or she will have a nice, normal name. One people can pronounce. One that doesn't have the rest of the class falling about laughing every time the teacher calls the register.'

'Hear, hear!' I piped. 'But Theodora's a nice name.'

Thursday 6 May

I haven't thought about Kevin for three days, four hours and 17 minutes now. I've broken my previous record by two hours and 23 minutes.

Friday 7 May

A new shopping centre has just opened a few miles from us and after work, Ariadne and I went to buy a present and outfits for Ag's wedding. The centre is called Tranquil Lagoon and from the road it looks as if an alien spaceship has landed in a field. I half expected a little green man to emerge and request that we 'take him to our leader'.

I light-heartedly suggested that our first call should be at the camping shop to find something for Ariadne to wear, but judging by the look she gave me, I sensed she was in no mood for that kind of comment. Our first stop was at a shop Ariadne insisted should be called Detached and Desperate. The music from its sound system could probably be heard in Reykjavik; you needed ear plugs to get through the door. It was full of 45-year-old women trying to squeeze into garments with far more netting and Lycra than was advisable. I reckoned Marks & Spencer was a better bet. After all, you can always return something there if you don't like it (unworn, of course).

Eventually, however, we found a little designer seconds shop. Ariadne held up a white two-piece suit.

'I can't wear white to someone else's wedding,' I protested. 'What if I turn up in the same outfit as the bride?'

'Firstly, from what I've heard, you'd need to get a tyre lever to get Cordelia inside this suit. Secondly, you're probably more entitled to wear white to her wedding than she is.' She looked at me as if she were peering over a pair of glasses. 'If you get my drift.'

Spurred on by Ariadne, I took the suit into the changing room and tried it on. To my consternation, it looked really good, quite elegant. The jacket fitted perfectly and the skirt *didn't* make my backside look the size of a small solar system.

'Great!' Ariadne enthused. 'All you need now are shoes and a bag – oh, and some sunglasses. You'll look just like a film star.'

Then I looked at the price tag.

'Oh, Ariadne, there's no way I could afford this! Not without a mortgage.'

She glanced at the price tag and sniffed. 'Might be less than London, but still overpriced. Watch this.'

We took the suit to the counter and stood in the queue. As we waited, I noticed that Ariadne was wincing and rubbing her back. Suddenly she became very pale.

'Ariadne!' I cried in alarm. 'Are you all right?'

I managed to support her as she slid gently to the floor. 'Can you help me? My sister's fainted.'

The assistant stopped mid-transaction and rushed round with a chair. We laid Ariadne out and raised her legs. Her eyelids flickered.

'Shall I call an ambulance?' asked the flustered assistant.

'I think she's only fainted.'

Another woman, the manager, appeared with a glass of water.

'I think we'd better leave this.' I handed her the suit. 'I ought to get her outside for some fresh air. I haven't got enough cash and I can't wait to pay for it by credit card.'

Ariadne, from somewhere in the region of my feet, began to groan.

'How much have you got in cash?' asked the manager. 'I'll reduce the price for the inconvenience you and your sister have been caused.'

'Oh, no, don't worry about it, we'll leave it,' I said.

'Take it!' Ariadne hissed through clenched teeth.

I fumbled in my bag and handed over the cash. The

assistant helped Ariadne to her feet and we staggered out of the shop to find a café.

In the café, I chided Ariadne. 'That was positively dishonest!' I ranted. 'Pretending to faint like that, just to get the suit reduced.'

'Well, it was obviously overpriced.'

'That's not the point; it's the principle of the matter. What you did just then not only deceived the shop assistant into selling the goods under false pretences—'

'You got your outfit, didn't you?'

'—but also confirmed stereotypes about pregnancy being an illness rather than a normal, healthy state of being, where women have no need for pampering and mollycoddling.' I folded my arms triumphantly.

'Theodora.'

'What?'

'I didn't pretend.'

Saturday 8 May

Emergency!

It's 11.30 p.m. and I'm suffering from an incredibly intense chocolate craving that won't leave me in spite of prayer, distraction activities and half a loaf of bread and butter. Got out of bed and searched the flat.

No luck.

Not even a Bourbon biscuit.

Not even a cream egg left from Easter.

All the shops are closed, so no chance of nipping out to replenish supplies.

There's nothing else for it. I'm reduced to the chocoholic's equivalent of meths – cooking chocolate.

Sunday 9 May

Today Nigel Hubble had organized a visiting speaker from Forthright Fundamentalists for Foremost Formation of the Firmament. The lady, who wore a dress the colour and texture of the English Channel, asserted that the account of the creation of the universe in the book of Genesis happened over six days in the year 4004 BC. She called Darwin, Huxley and other scientists 'liars and perverters of the truth'. Fossils were obviously God's way of decorating the earth and not evidence of extinct creatures. She said that carbon-dating was a 'conspiracy of falsehood' and, as dinosaurs were never mentioned in the Bible, they couldn't really have existed.

Obviously she was speaking total rubbish. Has she never seen *Jurassic Park*?

Monday 10 May

Declan left today. He's going to spend a year working on a project for homeless people, to test his vocation. At the end of the year he'll decide whether to train for the priesthood. There was no time to organize a proper leaving party, but someone bought a cake and someone else brought in a few bottles of wine. I wasn't in the mood for a party and sat in the corner of the office fiddling with a tray of paperclips.

When Declan was ready to go, he went round the office shaking hands with everyone. He came up to me and I flung my arms around his neck and howled.

'Theodora,' he chided gently, 'don't be after getting my collar all wet.'

'I'm sorry,' I sniffed, 'it's just that I'll really miss you.'

'Don't worry, I'll keep in touch. You won't be rid of me that easily.'

And he went.

Tuesday 11 May

Commuting without Ariadne has its advantages. I can eat a bar of chocolate at 7.30 in the morning without being made to feel guilty. Better not eat too many, though. I want to be able to fit into my suit for the wedding.

Declan's departure has left a gap in the office which, in spite of September's minute-taking fiasco, I have been asked to fill until a replacement can be found. It means extra money – not, of course, that money is my prime motivation for working. After all,

> ... the love of money is a root of all kinds of evil.
>
> (1 Timothy 6:10)

And,

> ... it is easier for a camel to go through the eye of a needle than for a rich man to enter the kingdom of God.   (Matthew 19:24)

Of course, on the other hand,

> ... the worker deserves his wages.   (Luke 10:7)

And,

> The Lord will grant you abundant prosperity ...
>
> (Deuteronomy 28:11)

Hmm. I'd better put down the concordance, or it will be 'God's arms' all over again.

Thursday 13 May

Miss Chamberlain is in hospital. She had a fall at home and has broken her ankle. She looked quite old and frail, her porcelain skin almost translucent as she lay sandwiched between the sheets of her hospital bed. I took her some chocolates and flowers and told her about my suit for the wedding. She smiled and nodded, seeming content to be there, not anxious to stay but not in a hurry to leave either.

'The nurses are lovely, Theodora dear. There's even one nice young male nurse. And I can choose what I want for breakfast, lunch and dinner. I feel as if I'm in a hotel.'

I smiled and took her hand.

'Reverend Graves has been to see me and even Jeremiah Wedgwood popped in. It was lovely to see him again, although I have no idea what I'm going to do with all the potatoes.'

'You're amazing,' I said. 'If I was stuck in bed for weeks, I'd soon sound like Victor Meldrew with toothache.'

'I have just one little complaint. I think the hospital have made a mistake. They've put me in a ward with all the old people. . .'

Friday 14 May

Ariadne and I have been invited to Cordelia's hen night tonight, even though we've not even met our future sister-in-law. I'm not sure whether to go. After all, she's supposed to be in telly and all her cronies are bound to be there. I'm not sure I'm going to be media-friendly. I wonder what she's like.

'It's just going to be an excuse for a drunken rampage.

There'll probably be a male stripper and everything,' I whined to Ariadne.

'Sounds great! Just what I need. Can't wait to go.'

I'm sure pregnancy is having a detrimental effect on my sister.

Saturday 15 May

Decided to give the hen night a miss and had an evening in with Mel Gibson instead. When I say Mel Gibson, I mean on video, obviously, not the real thing – unfortunately.

Got a postcard from Declan. He has a place as a volunteer helper on a project for the homeless in Manchester and is settling in well. A panoramic view of the Manchester Ship Canal now has pride of place on my fridge.

Sunday 16 May

I did the reading at today's service. I hadn't had time to read it through in advance. It was from I Chronicles and contained a list of the descendants of Adam. Nearly all of the names were practically unpronounceable. I felt like a five-year-old reading *Spot the Dog* in front of the entire school as I stumbled and stuttered my way through.

'Why did you give me that horrible reading?' I hissed at Digger on the way out. 'I would have had more chance of pronouncing the Albanian premier league football scores!'

Monday 17 May

Mum phoned to arrange transport to Marrow-on-the-Wold on Saturday. She and Dad are going up on the train the day before and Tom will drive Ariadne and myself up on Saturday morning. Apparently, no one trusts my car.

I tried on my white suit with some new shoes and a black top and was pleasantly surprised. I seem to have lost a little weight. I don't know how – I haven't so much as looked at a tub of cottage cheese for months.

I'm going to have my hair cut on Friday evening. I might even try a few highlights if I'm feeling adventurous.

Wednesday 19 May

Went to see Ariadne and Tom. My car started blowing out extravagant clouds of black smoke from the exhaust as I turned into their drive. Must remember to get it fixed. Perhaps I should start writing memos to myself:

MEMO

Phone garage.

Apparently the hen night was just as horrendous as I'd imagined and Ariadne insisted on describing it in graphic and explicit detail as she sat cross-legged on the settee with a large tub of ice cream resting on her bump. She looked rotund and vigorous and contented. Tom, by contrast, seemed pale and anxious. When he left the room to fetch Ariadne the ketchup, she explained that he'd been suffering from back pains and stomach cramps and had spent much of the night pacing the floor.

'I'm getting really worried about him. This phantom pregnancy business is going too far,' she confided.

'Do you think he should see a psychiatrist?'

'Hmm, perhaps an obstetrician would be more appropriate.'

The conversation was terminated by a cry of pain from the kitchen. I rushed out, with Ariadne waddling a few yards behind me. Tom was lying curled up on the kitchen floor like a giant prawn. His face was pale and twisted. Ariadne knelt on the floor rubbing his back until the spasm passed.

'It won't be long now,' he groaned, as Ariadne soothed and fussed.

Thursday 20 May

Poor Tom is in hospital with kidney stones. Ariadne is relieved that it's renal colic, not labour, but rather irritated because it means I shall have to drive her to the wedding as she doesn't fit behind the steering wheel any more. Still, we can use their car. Must remember to take mine to the garage.

Ariadne didn't seem to have much sympathy for Tom, chiding him as if he'd done it on purpose just to inconvenience her. Tom just lay there and groaned.

Saw both Tom and Miss Chamberlain tonight. Luckily they're in the same hospital. Feel rather like Florence Nightingale without the lamp.

Friday 21 May

8.30 p.m.
I knew it would be a mistake, I knew it. Why didn't I listen to myself? Why did I let that hairdresser persuade me? My 'highlights' would make Marilyn Monroe look like a mousy brunette. Mrs Barrie, downstairs, asked me if I'd just had a nasty shock or if premature greying ran in my family. I haven't got time to buy some hair dye or a hat for the wedding. Oh well, with any luck, no one will recognize me.

Saturday 22 May

9.40 a.m.

At 5.37 this morning, the shrill sound of the bedside phone dragged me from a dream that I'd gone completely bald. I put my hand to my head to check it really was a dream, then picked up the phone.

'What? Who is it?' I slurred into the receiver.

'It's me, you idiot,' came Ariadne's voice. 'I need a lift. I'm having the baby.'

'But it's too early.'

'Only three weeks. That's within the normal range.'

'No, it's 5.30. That's far too early.'

'Oh, go back to sleep. I'll call a taxi.'

I must have dozed off again, because the next thing I was aware of was the trilling alarm clock. I showered and put on my suit. My hair didn't look quite as bad as I'd remembered from the day before.

Then it hit me.

Ariadne was having the baby. Tom was in hospital. Mum and Dad had already gone. I quickly dismissed the idea of grovelling to Kevin. I had no alternative – I would have to drive my car to the wedding.

I rang the hospital to check that Ariadne was all right. I spoke to Tom, who told me, in graphic detail, how he had 'passed' his kidney stone the previous night and had recovered sufficiently to hold her hand and mop her brow. She was apparently at the 'pacing up and down the corridor, occasionally clinging to doorframes' stage of labour. It would be a while before the baby made an appearance. I offered to go to the hospital to be with Ariadne, but Tom bravely brushed me aside and ordered me to go and enjoy the wedding.

I did a little circuit round my car, caressing the paint-work, making encouraging sounds and whispering prayers.

I called in at Ariadne's and Tom's home to collect their wedding present, loaded up my own gift and, equipped with a map and a sense of foreboding, set off in my white suit and my blonde hair, clouds of smoke billowing from my exhaust pipe.

I must have driven a total of no more than four miles into the countryside when there was an enormous bang and the car stuttered to a halt. I got out and lifted the bonnet. I don't know the first thing about cars.

MEMO
Join the RAC.

I poked and wriggled some of the bits of wire and pluggy things, as if that would do any good. I turned the ignition key, but nothing happened. The engine was deader than a Tuesday night in Sidcup. I took the screwy lid thing off the bit at the front, and brown water surged out of the grey cor-rugated pipe, all over my suit. I threw the screwy lid thing on the ground in disgust. I peered at the car's grimy innards, then pulled out the bendy thing that tells you how much something-or-other there is in your engine, but couldn't find the hole to put it back. I flopped down on the grass verge in despair. I would have to look for a telephone box.

MEMO
Buy a mobile phone.

I walked about a mile to find a pub, with the time ticking away, my white suit grimy and the bendy thing still in my hand.

I found the only pub in England with no phone.

The landlord, however, was sympathetic to my predicament as I poured out my story. I tried to sound pathetic, which wasn't that difficult, in the hope that he would have pity on me and lend me his car or something.

' ... and then I took the bendy thing out and I can't even get that back,' I sniffed.

'Dipstick,' he muttered.

I know I must have been a sorry sight, but there was no need to be rude. He didn't offer to lend me his car, but drove me instead to the nearest phone box so that I could call the garage.

10.50 a.m.

It was clear that I needed to go home, change, and then try to get to the wedding by public transport. I suddenly felt overwhelmingly weary. I collected the presents and map, locked my car (why?) and began to trudge home along the lane.

On a particularly sharp bend, I suddenly came face to face with the front end of an ancient and rusty minibus with 'REPENT' painted across the front in huge red letters. Brakes screeched and Charity's bus slid to a halt, narrowly missing me. I was starting to wish it hadn't. Charity's beaming face peered out of the window.

'Theodora?'

'Don't say anything.'

'I didn't recognize you ... your hair ...'

'Yes, yes, I know. I look like Jezebel's promiscuous sister.'

'Actually, I think it looks very nice. Suits you.'

'Thanks.'

'Can I give you a lift anywhere, or do you prefer to walk?'

'Marrow-on-the-Wold, if you happen to be headed in that direction.'

'Well, I wasn't, but I could if you like.'

'Please, just take me home.'

I hauled myself into the passenger seat of the van and began to tell Charity the story. Baby Methuselah, who was sleeping peacefully in his car seat, gave a huge yawn. I glanced at my watch and sighed.

'My brother's wedding starts in just under three hours. Looks like I'll miss the service for sure. Oh well, perhaps I'll catch the reception.'

'There's no way you're going to miss that ceremony,' said Charity firmly, putting her foot on the accelerator, hauling on the steering wheel and pulling the bus into a creaking U-turn.

'What about Nigel?' I protested. 'And the children. They won't know where you are.'

'I'll telephone when I get there.' The bus was beginning to rock with speed as we bulleted along the country lanes towards the motorway.

'But my clothes! I can't go like this.'

'Look behind you. There's a bag of clothes. Some of them are quite new. Unfortunately, after Methuselah, I seem to have gained a few pounds, so I was going to take them to the Oxfam shop.'

'That's kind, Charity, but I really couldn't.'

'Nonsense.'

I reached behind me and grasped the carrier bag. I shut my eyes tightly, like a child taking a lucky dip.

I opened them again.

Flowers.

My worst fears were justified. The bag was stuffed with Charity's floral frocks.

I closed my eyes again, wishing the flowers gone.

I opened them.

Flowers.

'Charity, I don't think these dresses are really me.'

'I understand,' Charity sighed. 'They're rather old and tatty. I'm sorry, it's just that Nigel only earns a curate's salary and, what with the children to feed and clothe, there just doesn't seem to be much left for me.'

My heart melted.

'Charity, they're perfect. Thank you.'

MEMO

Take Charity to Tranquil Lagoon and treat her to a new outfit.

I rummaged in the bag for the least heavily bloom-laden garment and smiled at Charity.

'Thank you,' I said again.

And I meant it.

The bus rocked and pitched down the motorway like a yacht in a squall. I clung to the door, trying not to succumb to *mal de mer*. Methuselah swayed, lulled by the movement.

12.15 p.m.

We stopped at a motorway service station, where Charity fed Methuselah and I made a desperate attempt to salvage my beautiful suit with assistance from soap and the hand dryer. I failed. The dirty brown stains were just as evident and, in addition, the fabric had taken on a crumpled, abraded appearance where I'd tried to scrub at it.

I lowered Charity's ex-frock over my head. It was shapeless and flowery, and I would have fitted into it twice. I nearly cried.

'I wonder if we could just stop ever so briefly in the next town, just to have a tiny peek in Marks & Spencer?'

My suggestion was lost on Charity, who was beaming magnanimously.

'You look lovely, Theodora. Honeysuckle really suits you.'

I knew the battle was lost.

1.20 p.m.

When we arrived at Marrow-on-the-Wold, with 40 minutes to spare, the little church looked beautiful. It was a small, flint-covered, picture-postcard building, the sort of place where you could sit inside and wish away most of the last two centuries. I felt calm and relaxed in spite of the journey and the dress, and managed to slip away from Charity, who had taken Methuselah and gone to telephone Nigel.

I stepped through the wooden doorway expecting the cool tranquillity of the ancient building to enclose me. Instead, I was blinded by the most powerful light I had ever encountered. I was just about to drop to my knees, anticipating a booming voice demanding, 'Saul, Saul, why do you persecute me?' when the beam swung upwards in an arc, now illuminating the belfry. There was a squeaking protest and frantic flapping sounds, presumably from the bats, disturbed mid-slumber. I shaded my eyes from the light and could make out several figures, including one in a long, whitish dress wandering aimlessly around at the front of the church near the altar. I realized they must be the film crew. I hadn't expected so many people.

At my friend Tracey's wedding, there was just the registrar, the bride herself, a passing traffic warden who had been drafted in as a second witness, and me. It was touch-and-go whether the groom would turn up. I know the wedding had to be organized in a hurry, but a little more forward planning would not have gone amiss. At least the christening, six-and-a-half weeks later, was a more ceremonious affair.

That had to be Cordelia, cruising around in the low-cut ivory silk gown, like a heavily laden galleon in full sail, barking instructions to the film crew. She referred to them all as 'darling' or 'sweetie'. I suppose it's easier than remembering their real names.

She saw me, and I introduced myself. 'Theo, darling, come and meet the crew!' She grabbed me by the shoulders and hugged me into her cleavage, then kissed me on both cheeks and introduced me to the strange-looking bunch who were milling around. I'm sure there were more people than there were useful jobs to do. One lad's job seemed to be to go round with a large reel of silver sticky-tape, fixing down everything that might conceivably move. The woman who seemed to be wearing her underwear outside her clothes was in charge of 'wardrobe'. A young man practically shoulder-barged the ushers out of the way and chose the prettiest girls and best dressed young men to sit near the front of the church, where they were likely to be 'in shot', and sat the fat aunts and embarrassing old men who might dribble or speak too loudly during the service in the back rows. Unfortunately, Cordelia's rather elderly father was steered to the back near a pile of hymn books and had to be rescued by the indignant bride.

Agamemnon appeared from the back of the church looking taller, more tanned and far more handsome than when I'd last seen him. If he wasn't my brother, I could easily have fallen in love with him. I gave a little squeak and threw myself at him.

'Theo! You look so ... different.'

'It's a long story.'

He put his arm as far round Cordelia as it would reach and pulled her tightly to him. I held my breath in case the pressure forced her chest completely out of the front of her dress.

'Isn't it supposed to be bad luck to see the bride before the wedding?' she chided.

'I'll risk it,' he grinned.

The service itself was lovely and the stately ceremony was only slightly disrupted by the director's insistence on shouting 'Action!' before each of the vows, and 'It's a wrap!' when Ag was granted permission to kiss the bride. The poor vicar seemed a little distracted during the proceedings. I suspect it was partly due to the presence of the film crew, but I should think, as Cordelia knelt in front of him in her low-cut gown, it was mostly due to the sensation that he had unwittingly embarked on an aerial trip over the Grand Canyon.

I spent the service wedged between my mother and Charity, with Methuselah strapped to her chest in a kind of papoose. All three of them wept and snivelled continuously. Mum kept nudging me as if to say, 'When will it be your turn?' and Charity sang the hymns far too loudly with both hands raised in the air. Methuselah just wailed.

I thought about Ariadne and the baby, Declan, Kevin, Miss Chamberlain and Jeremiah. By the time we filed out for the photos, I felt thoroughly depressed. Ag and Cordelia looked so happy.

Standing among my family in Charity's dress, with my bleached hair and false smile, I'd never felt so lonely.

The reception at a nearby hotel passed, for me, in a fog of misery and self-pity. Charity ably filled the gap left by the absence of Ariadne and Tom, and enthusiastically consumed both their shares of the French onion soup, roast lamb with rosemary sauce and raspberry Pavlova, mints and coffee.

The evening buffet was yet another form of torture to be endured, another constant reminder that everyone in the world had a partner except me. Ag and Cordelia gazed at each other like a pair of lovesick spaniels. Even Mum and Dad seemed to have found something to talk about. But I had no car, no bloke, and was stuck instead with the human equivalent of the Chelsea Flower Show. I hated to admit it, but I really missed Kevin.

Everyone else seemed engrossed in conversation so I located the bar. In addition to the kegs of beer and bottles of wine, there were two large punch bowls, each filled with lurid red liquid. I picked up the ladle and scooped a large cupful from the bowl labeled "Non-alcoholic Fruit Punch" and found a table in a corner where I could cower until Charity took me home.

After my third or fourth glass of fruit punch, I could feel myself beginning to relax. I gazed contentedly around the hall. Everything seemed to have a warm glow. Everybody seemed a little bit nicer. I waved to Mum as she Zorba's-danced her way around the room shouting '*Yammas*!' with unrestrained bonhomie. Dad sat in a corner gazing thought-fully into his pint.

Two more glasses of punch. For a non-alcoholic bever-age, it was pleasantly soothing and relaxing. I guessed it must have had something herbal in it.

Ag and Cordelia clung to each other on the dance floor, gazing from time to time into each other's eyes and smooching to Status Quo's 'Rocking All Over the World' which was blaring through the sound system. They seemed absorbed in each other and unaware of the occasional jostling by the other guests, who, thumbs tucked behind imaginary braces, lurched around the floor like epileptic chickens.

I approached the bar for another refill. Maybe I could enjoy the party after all. Good punch, good music and, to add further to my feeling of wellbeing, I'd managed to disentangle myself from Charity's tendrils.

Returning to my seat, I noticed Charity, seated at a table near the door with Methuselah asleep in his carrycot. She was talking to a group of young men and women whom I assumed to be Cordelia's friends. Charity seemed completely at ease, smiling and gesturing, her audience smiling and nodding in response, totally engrossed in her discourse. I watched as Charity stood up, arms outstretched. Her audience hung on every word. The young people sat open mouthed and winced with imagined pain as Charity pointed to the palm of each hand.

She's doing it again, I thought. *She's telling people about Jesus in that easy, natural way of hers, and they're interested, they're actually interested.*

My initial amazement gave way to feelings of affront. How dare she elbow her way into my social scene and convert everyone? This was *my* family; *my* brother's wedding. If anyone was going to evangelize round here, it was going to be me. I slugged back the remains of my fruit punch and cast my eye around the room for a likely candidate. Most people were either involved in bellowed conversations or were on the dance floor, strutting their stuff to the ear-splittingly loud music.

On the far side of the room I spotted a youngish man with a pleasantish face. You couldn't call him handsome, but he had an open, friendly face that seemed familiar, although I was sure I didn't actually know him. Target located, I launched myself across the room towards him. To my surprise, my legs didn't seem to wish to go in the direction my brain told them to, and I ended up staggering crab-like towards the buffet table. In order to make my perambulation look more or less intentional, I seized a prawn vol-au-vent and stuffed it into my mouth. I took the opportunity of this pause to gain my bearings and started on my second attempt to navigate myself to the young man's table. I succeeded and sat down, listing to starboard only slightly, on the chair facing him.

'Good evening, my name's Theodora,' I said through a mouth full of vol-au-vent.

'Mike. Pleased to meet you,' he said, offering his hand, which I took and pumped vigorously up and down.

This was my opportunity.

'Are you washed in the blood of the lamb?' I blurted, still clutching his hand and staring earnestly into his eyes – of which there appeared to be three. He glanced down guiltily at his shirt, in search of gravy stains from the roast lamb dinner.

'Are your sins washed whiter than snow?' I was beginning to sound like a cross between *Hymns Ancient and Modern* and a washing powder commercial.

'I'm not quite sure. . .'

'Is there a crown and harp awaiting you in the land beyond the river?'

'Look,' he said, 'would you like another drink?'

'Yes please,' I slurred. 'I'm a Christian, you know.'

'Good. That's really . . . um . . . good.'

Mike disappeared while I racked my brain for an appropriate Bible verse to sum up my exposition of the gospel. The only verse in the whole Bible that came to mind was 'Love your neighbour as yourself.' Mike returned with a pint of beer and a glass of lemonade, which he placed in front of me.

'S'lemonade,' I slurred. 'I don't know if you realize, but I've been drinking fruit punch all evening. The non-alcloholoic one.' I winked lopsidedly.

'Really! I would never have guessed.'

'Do you have an anchor to hold you fast in life's storms?' Now I was sounding like *The Onedin Line.*

'Are you a friend of the bride or groom?' Mike asked in an overt attempt to steer the conversation towards some sort of recognizable territory.

'Acshully, I'm the groom's brother,' I assured him. 'No, tha's not right. I'm not sure exactly who I am, but I *am* int'mately acquainted with a variety of people in the imme-diate vishinity.' I moved my hand in a sweeping arc that encompassed most of the people in the room. The Bible verse from 1 Corinthians 13:13 about faith, hope and love and the greatest of these being love swam its way through my befuddled brain and reached the front of my mind. I paraphrased it.

'I really love you, d'you know that? I really, really love you. Faith, forget it! Hope, no chance. But love – s'some-thing c'mpletely different. Can I show you?'

He shuffled his chair backwards.

'Can I show you love? Would you like to come to church with me? S'good there. You can come tomorrow if you like.' I placed my hand reassuringly on his knee.

'That's inordinately kind of you, Theodora, but I'm afraid I really can't.' He removed my hand from his knee and placed it on my own knee.

'Oh, go on.' I punched him hard on the shoulder. 'Why not? What elsh would you be doing on a Sunday morning, eh? Lying in bed reading the papers? Washing the car? Going down the pub for a little drinkie?'

'Actually, I'll be rather busy at my own church tomorrow.'

He reached down, opened a sports bag by his feet and produced a clerical dog collar. He placed it around his neck. 'Look familiar?'

The realization hit me like a fly on a windscreen. That's where I recognized him from. He was the vicar who had just married my brother.

'So nice to meet you, Vicar. Mist go and mungle,' I stammered hastily, struggling to my feet. 'Look, I'm not wha' you think I am. I'm a nice person really. I'm one of you.' I lurched off across the room to find Charity.

I just wanted to go home. I was embarrassed, lonely, and becoming convinced there was something in that punchbowl that didn't agree with me.

Suddenly, I felt very sick. I ran to the Ladies, getting there just in time.

As I knelt on the hard floor and rested my cheek against the cold porcelain bowl, I heard a quiet knock on the cubicle door.

'Theo, Theodora, are you all right?' It was Charity.

My mind screamed, '*No, of course I'm not all right, you stupid woman! Go away and leave me to die here in peace.*'

'Yes, I'm fine,' I croaked.

'Is there anything I can do?'

I thought, '*Yes, you can go exploring down the nearest pothole with no rope, no torch and Dr Livingstone as a guide!*'

'No thanks,' I replied. 'I'll be OK in a minute.' I flushed the toilet and unlocked the door. Charity was still hovering like a multicoloured moth.

'Here, sit down, I'll clean you up.'

I didn't protest as she steered me to a small wooden chair and sat me down. She took a packet of baby-wipes out of her handbag and started swabbing my hands and face as if I was one of her own brood. I sat there, obedient as a child, and let her clean me.

Suddenly the day's events, my shame at getting plastered in front of everyone and my failure to live up to God's expectations overwhelmed me, and I burst into sobs.

'I got it all wrong, didn't I?'

'What do you mean?' she asked, brushing my hair from my eyes with her hand.

'I should have realised there was something funny about that punch. I should have stopped. I should have known what was happening to me.'

'It was a mistake,' Charity tried to reassure me. 'Perhaps someone switched the labels or perhaps some imbecile thought it a great prank to lace it with vile spirit.'

Nothing Charity said made me feel any better. I should have been more careful.

'I got it all wrong. I messed it up, let everyone down.' I stared up at the ceiling to try to stop the tears from falling.

'Who is "everyone"?' She pushed a tissue into my hands.

'The church, you, me, Jesus.' I sniffed and blinked. 'I feel so guilty.'

'The only thing you're guilty of is trying too hard.'

'It's not fair. It's so easy for you. I could see you tonight, talking about the crucifixion.'

Charity frowned, looking puzzled. 'What?'

'You had your arms outstretched like this and I saw you pointing to the nail marks on the palms. Those people you were talking to, they were hanging on every word. I just wanted to be like you.' The tears ran freely down my face and dripped into my lap.

'I don't remember saying anything about. . .' Suddenly the mists cleared. 'Fishing! I was talking about fishing, you silly thing! Nigel went river fishing for the first time last week and nearly caught an enormous eel. Apparently, it was this long.' She demonstrated by stretching her arms out wide. 'Then he got one of the fishing hooks stuck in his hand – here.' She pointed to her palm. 'When he tried to get it out, it stuck into his other palm. Eventually he had to go to the doctor to have it removed.'

I howled.

Not only had I made a hash of evangelism and in the process convinced the poor vicar that I was some drunken floozy trying to seduce him, but I'd confused a tale of 'the one that got away' with the crucifixion.

Charity patted me kindly on the shoulder. 'It's an easy mistake to make.'

I couldn't be consoled. I knew she was trying to be kind and that made it worse.

'But the vicar, Charity. I tried to convert the vicar!'

'By the look of him, he's had nearly as much to drink as you've had. He probably won't remember a thing about it in the morning.' She helped me to my feet and straightened my dress. 'Anyway,' she sniffed, 'just because he's a vicar, it doesn't necessarily mean he's saved.'

Monday 24 May

Birth Announcement

To Ariadne and Tom, a daughter
Phoebe Ann
3.42 a.m. Sunday 23 May.
Six pounds twelve ounces.
Mother, father and baby all doing well.

June

Tuesday 1 June

Too depressed after the wedding to write diary. Charity half dragged, half carried me to the van, drove me home and put me to bed. Even the news that several other people at the reception suffered at the hands of the "non-alcoholic" punch hasn't helped me feel any better. Work is boring, church seems deader than Lazarus second time around, and Ariadne keeps telling me to pull myself together.

Of course, I can't possibly speak to Charity after what happened.

Or Mum.

Or Cordelia.

Or anyone else in my family.

Or anyone at church.

Only God.

Wednesday 2 June

Ariadne brought Phoebe round today. She's very small and pink and has an amazing range of facial expressions. Ariadne is dotty about her and Tom is trotting around after the pair of them like a lackey. He hasn't stopped smiling since she was born and fortunately seems back to full health.

As I held Phoebe, she seemed to be coming to terms with some great internal dilemma, twisting her tiny limbs and grimacing. I wish I knew what she was thinking.

Thursday 3 June

Miss Chamberlain came out of hospital today. The ambulance brought her home and she is officially under the care of the community nurse. She has meals on wheels and a commode. She can hardly move and still seems incredibly frail.

'Could you not have stayed in the hospital a little longer?' I enquired.

'Oh, I think they needed the bed for someone else, dear. Probably some poor old thing who can't look after themselves.'

'But surely you could have stayed another week or two, just until you get back on your feet?'

'I must just be a cutback,' she said.

Friday 4 June

Went to get some shopping for Miss Chamberlain in my restored and now completely rejuvenated car. Tomorrow is Kevin's birthday and I felt obliged to buy him a card to show that I'm a mature adult and can handle the break-up of our relationship in an amicable way. It was harder than I thought to find a birthday card with a suitable message. Where can you buy cards for people you don't like? All the cards in the shop contained messages such as 'For a wonderful friend', or 'You are so special', or 'Wishing you all happiness on this joyous occasion'. Expressions such as 'Die in pain, you insensitive pig' did not feature greatly. I settled for a blank card with a picture of a fisherman on it and wrote:

> I hope you have a relatively tolerable birthday, reasonably free of calamity,
> but I'll still never forget how you treated me and I'll never forgive you.
>
> Yours, Theodora

That'll show him!

Sunday 6 June

Miss Chamberlain had set her heart on going to church today and wouldn't be dissuaded. I loaded her wheelchair and crutches, special cushion and footstool into my car and took her to the morning service. She sat in the front pew with her foot on the stool and radiated pleasure and contentment, even though she must have been in considerable pain. Everyone came to chat to her and say how much they'd missed her and how pleased they were to see her back.

By the time we reached the hall, the coffee had nearly run out. I parked her wheelchair near a wall display so she would have something to entertain her. The Sunday School had been studying the life of Moses and had made a poster showing the stone tablets with the Ten Commandments inscribed on them. When I returned with our coffee, I found that Miss Chamberlain had climbed out of her wheelchair and was foraging in her handbag.

'What are you doing?' I said in alarm.

'Adultery,' she said. 'It's wrong!'

'Well, of course it is.' I shrugged. 'But you know, the way the world is today . . .'

'No, on the poster. It should be adult*ery* and they've spelt it adult*ury*. I cannot *abide* poor spelling.'

She found a red pen, hobbled across to the wall display and proceeded to amend the seventh commandment.

Once a schoolteacher, always a schoolteacher.

Monday 7 June

A card arrived this morning from Kevin. On the front was a picture of flowers, which was a worry for a start. Kevin and flowers do not make natural bedfellows. Inside it read:

> Life without you is like a broken pencil
> ...pointless.

Why is he comparing me to a damaged item of stationery? It's either a very bad pun or he has totally taken leave of his senses. I thought I made it clear that I wanted nothing more to do with him. I wish I'd never sent that birthday card. Any feelings there were between us are now deader than Tutankhamen's granny.

Tuesday 8 June

Went to see Ariadne, who was breastfeeding little Phoebe. It's good to know that breasts have some purpose other than keeping the Wonderbra manufacturers in business and supporting sales of a certain group of newspapers.

I told her about the card from Kevin.

'Theo,' she said, '*ring* him.'

I'd hoped it wouldn't come to that. 'What do you think he means by it? Do you think he still cares about me?'

'Well, at a guess, he's either developed a stationery

fixation and is about to commit hara-kiri with a ballpoint pen, or he wants to see you again.'

I leaned forward anxiously in my chair. 'Which do you think?'

'Theo! For goodness' sake.'

She threw the phone at me. Fortunately, he wasn't in.

Wednesday 9 June

A very puzzling fax arrived on my desk this morning. It was headed 'Lambeth Palace' and was apparently from the Archbishop of Canterbury's private office. The gist of the information was that, in order to further their equal opportunities policies, the Archbishop's office were advertising for candidates for the position of Equal Opportunities Officer, reporting directly to the Archbishop. The job will involve reviewing the liturgy and hymns in order to remove anything that could be considered sexist, racist, ageist, heightist, sizeist or otherwise politically incorrect. Applications are invited from people with suitable administrative backgrounds and a good knowledge of the workings of the Church. Apparently my name came up on a list of possible candidates.

Well, of course I'm very flattered by the invitation, but I can't help thinking there's something strange about the whole thing. There's a number to ring if I'm interested. I think I'll leave it. It must be a hoax.

Saturday 12 June

Took Charity shopping to Tranquil Lagoon this afternoon to buy her a new outfit. Decided to avoid the boutique where I bought my white suit. After the incident with Ariadne, I can't risk inflicting Charity on them. It's funny: although the suit cleaned up admirably, courtesy of Sketchley's, I can't bring myself to wear it. I just want to blot that day from my memory.

We spent longer than I'd intended in Mothercare. Charity bought a brand-new outfit for Methuselah – his first previously unworn item of clothing. I suppose that, when something has worked its way through eight siblings, it must be a little depreciated. They had some gorgeous teddy bears and I couldn't resist buying one for Phoebe. I know she already has about 30, but I firmly believe you can never have too many cuddly animals.

We finally extracted ourselves from Mothercare and found a clothes shop. Charity browsed round the racks.

'They're all so plain and so *expensive,*' she protested. 'If we went to the market and bought some curtain fabric, I could run up six dresses for that price.'

That explained why Charity always looked like Laura Ashley's furnishing department.

'No, Charity,' I explained firmly. 'You're going to have something new *and* something you don't have to make yourself.'

A skirt and jacket caught my eye. 'What about this? It's smart and you could wear it anywhere. You could dress it up with scarves or jewellery to go out . . .'

'I don't have any jewellery, apart from my wedding ring, and we never seem to have the time to go out.' It wasn't a complaint, merely a statement.

'Well, it's about time you did. Choose a dress and, if you have a problem with babysitters, I'll do it.'

'Would you really?' she asked suspiciously. I wondered if she had needed to sandblast Ezekiel to remove the encrusted grot after the last time he was left in my care.

'Of course I would.'

We carried on browsing. 'What about this?' I held up a well-cut classic black dress.

'Oh, it's lovely. But I'm not sure Nigel would like it.'

'Nigel won't be wearing it. Do *you* like it?'

Charity nodded and went to try it on. I hate to admit it, but Charity looked stunning. Her eyes shone and she had untied her auburn hair from the restraint of its usual plait.

'That's the one,' I said.

Sunday 13 June

The theme of today's service was forgiveness. We all trotted through the prayer of confession as usual and were duly 'pardoned and delivered from all our sins'. Then Digger preached his sermon based on Psalm 103. He said it's sometimes easy to say sorry to people for things we've done wrong. (I'm not sure about that.) He said it's sometimes just as easy to forgive people who say they're sorry when they've done something to us. (Funny, I don't find it that easy.) We can get quite a 'warm glow' from forgiving others, he said. (I thought that was heartburn.) Often we have little problem believing that God can forgive us if we're truly sorry for what we've done to him. (To me this always feels as if I'm justifying my overdraft to the bank manager.) However, what we sometimes find nearly impossible, he said, is to forgive *ourselves*.

I felt as if I'd been struck by lightning. The rest of the world started rushing away from me at great speed and I felt as if I was the only person in the whole church and that Digger was speaking just to me.

He said it was much easier to go on punishing ourselves for all the times we got it wrong, for all the times we should have known better, and for all the times we knew the right thing and chose not to do it. I expected him to finish by saying, 'If God can forgive you, then it's all sorted,' but he didn't. He spoke instead about Jeremiah Wedgwood. He told of the number of times he had re-run the incident in the church hall in his mind, thinking of how he could have handled it differently. He told of the phone calls he had made and the letters he had written to try to sort it out. He told of the time he had seen Jeremiah in the street and had run after him to talk; of how he had begged Jeremiah's forgiveness.

A voice rang out in the silence. 'But it wasn't all your fault.' Heads swivelled and necks craned to try to see who had dared to speak out during the sermon.

'No,' replied Digger, 'I can see that. I know, in my head, that it was as much his fault as it was mine. But I feel in my guts that if I'd said something different, or if I'd done something sooner, it wouldn't have happened. Jeremiah feels he can't come to church any more and, although that may not be entirely my fault, I can't help thinking it's my *responsibility*. I feel as if I've somehow come between him and God and that's what I can't forgive myself for.'

I knew how he felt. Sometimes it's easier to be punished than forgiven. If no one else will get a big stick and beat us up with it – after all, that's what we deserve – we grab the stick with both hands and beat ourselves with it.

'I have an idea,' said the same voice. 'If somebody will push me, I think I know of something that might help.'

It was Miss Chamberlain. I leaped to my feet and seized the handles of her wheelchair. She directed us out of the church and we formed a snake down the hill. A serpent of people, with Miss Chamberlain at its head, slithered along the high street and out of the village. When we reached a stile, several people helped manoeuvre Miss Chamberlain over the gate to a piece of farmland surrounding a disused chalk pit. The pit was full of water and fenced off with the aim of keeping local children away. The fence, inevitably, was broken down and the pit quite easy to access. The snake coiled to a halt.

'How deep do you think it is?' Miss Chamberlain asked.

'Ooh, 100 feet at least,' replied Digger.

'What do you think are the chances of finding anything in there?'

'Pretty slim.'

'So you think, in time, that whatever went in there would be forgotten about?'

I had the horrible feeling she was about to do a 'Miss Marple' and reveal a long-forgotten murder in the chalk pit, but she didn't. Instead she reached down to the ground and picked up a stone.

'"As far as the east is from the west, so far has he removed our transgressions from us." This stone is all my sins and all the things I can't forgive myself for.'

She used all her strength to throw the stone, which landed with a satisfying plop a few feet into the pit.

'What do you think is the likelihood of me ever seeing that stone again?'

'About the same as an unopened tinny making it to the end of a barbie,' said Digger.

'So, it has effectively gone for ever. Like my sins. I have no reason to give either another thought.'

One by one, people began picking up stones and, like champion shot-putters, they threw them into the chalk pit. Oily Roger Lamarck selected a handful of small pebbles and threw them one by one. Mr Wilberforce found a stick and, for one horrible moment, I thought Rex was going to jump in to try to retrieve it. Digger moved away from the rest of the group and sat on the chalky ground for a long time with his eyes closed. Gregory Pasternak started to hum 'Amazing Grace' softly in his high, melodious voice and a few people joined in. Apart from the song and the sound of the stones splashing into the water, everything was still and quiet.

I chose the two biggest stones I could find and thought about Ag's wedding and, of course, Kevin. Then, with all the energy I could muster, I hurled them as far as I could into the dark, engulfing water.

We didn't go back to the church for coffee. Instead, each person drifted back to the village and to their own home. Digger was smiling. I pushed Miss Chamberlain to her cottage, settled her in and went home myself.

Then I put on my white suit and set off to see Kevin.

When I reached Kevin's house, I hesitated before knocking on the door. What if I'd got it all wrong? What if he didn't have any feelings for me and it was just a cruel joke? What if he refused to see me and I would have the shame of walking home, knowing that I'd been rejected for the second time? I thought of Miss Chamberlain and decided to take the chance. I tugged down my white jacket with determination and pressed my finger on the bell.

Kevin's Mum answered the door. She looked at me, completely bemused, invited me into the hall and scuttled off upstairs to get Kevin. Kevin jogged down the stairs beaming. He looked taller and slimmer. I didn't remember seeing that football shirt before. He had his hair cut differently, shorter and gelled, and he now sported a goatee.

'Theo,' he said. 'You look lovely in white – just like a dentist.'

I let it pass.

'It's good to see you again,' I grinned. 'I like the hair, and the beard. It suits you.'

'I've missed you.'

'Missed you too.'

'Can I take you out for a drink?'

'Yes please.'

'Just one thing. Can you pay? Only I've left my wallet round Jez's.'

'We could always call in for it on the way.'

'We could, but there's no money in it. I haven't been to the bank.'

'You're incorrigible.'

'Thanks.'

Tuesday 15 June

In my new, positive frame of mind, I decided to phone the number on the fax from the Archbishop's office. It was an answering machine. With the number of people they must employ, you'd think they could afford a real person to take calls. I left my name and phone number. The voice on the message didn't sound very Church of England. It had a soft Irish accent. Still, I suppose it's further evidence of their equal opportunities policy.

Wednesday 16 June

I suppose, if you had to reword the hymns and liturgy to avoid political incorrectness, you'd end up with things like, 'Praise to the Holiest in the vertically advanced and in the perpendicularly challenged be peace.' The Lord's Prayer would have to start, 'Our Person with Parental Responsibility who art in heaven...'

Saturday 19 June

Have had little time to write in the diary this week. I've been out with Kevin every night – Wednesday, cinema; Thursday, bowling; Friday, shopping. Kevin even bought some new clothes. I hope he isn't just doing it to please me.

I had a phone call from Ariadne this morning.

'Hi, stranger,' she said.

'Oh, hello. Sorry I haven't been round. I've been busy. Guess what? I'm going out with Kevin again.'

'Good! Um, is it good?'

'Yes, it's brilliant.'

'But I thought he was the sort of low-life, weasly scum you wouldn't be seen dead with if he was the only living organism in the entire universe. I thought he was a maggot who had just crawled out of the cesspit of life and as far as you were concerned could crawl back there and suffocate in his own putrefaction.'

'That was before.'

'And now?'

'I think I love him.'

'Theodora, you change your mind more often than most women change their knickers!'

Sunday 20 June

Kevin came to church with me today. He even sat next to me. Next time I may be able to persuade him to sing.

Monday 21 June

Declan phoned me today. *He'd* sent the fax from the Archbishop, and the reason the voice on the recording machine sounded so familiar was because it was his machine.

Of course, I'd suspected all along that it was one of Declan's jokes. Rewriting politically incorrect liturgy indeed!

'It's great to hear your voice again, Theo.'

'How's it going?'

'Fine, fine. As we speak, I'm filling in my application for training. I think I'm just about to pass the point of no return.'

'I only hope they're prepared for whoopee cushions in the confessional and stink bombs in the censers.'

'It won't be like that. I've changed. I just want to fulfil my vocation. I just want to make a difference to people.'

'I'm sure you will, Declan. I'm sure you will.'

'Theo . . .'

'What?'

'Never mind. It doesn't matter.'

Tuesday 22 June

Kevin has managed to get time off work and wants to take me to Italy for a long weekend. Says he's going to take me to a 'special place'. It'll be so romantic. I've insisted on separate hotel rooms, of course.

Wednesday 23 June

Miss Chamberlain is back in hospital. Suspected pneumonia. The church has set up a prayer vigil for her. Perhaps my ministry is prayer. I must admit, I haven't had much time to devote to thinking about my ministry recently – too busy trying to sort out other people's. I've signed up to pray for an hour a day. I even persuaded Kevin to put his name on the list.

I hope she'll be all right. I don't know what I would do without her.

Thursday 24 June

According to the hospital, Miss Chamberlain is a little better today. As I sat praying in a front pew in the silence of St Norbert's, I became aware of an eerie presence behind me. I swung round, and there was Jeremiah Wedgwood peering over the pew back.

'The Reverend rang me. He thought I should know – guilty conscience I shouldn't wonder – so I came here to pray for the poor dear lady in the midst of her suffering and anguish. You see what happens when pastoral care is allowed to slip in the name of "Community Relations".'

I leaped to Digger's defence. 'It's hardly his fault Miss Chamberlain is ill.' Then a thought dawned on me. 'I've missed you, you know. We all have.'

His watery eyes started to become even waterier. 'I could not let wickedness go unchallenged,' he said.

'Two of the people who sheltered from the snow that day have started coming on Sunday mornings,' I told him. 'One has even signed up for confirmation classes. I bet the Reverend didn't tell you that.'

'No, no, he didn't.'

'He cares very much about everyone at St Norbert's, you know. We're his family and, like any family, we don't always find it easy to get on with each other. But underneath there's something that holds us together. You really hurt him when you left.'

Jeremiah blew his nose.

'If you ever decide to come back, I'm sure you'll be very welcome.'

'We'll see. We'll see how the Lord guides.'

Friday 25 June

Miss Chamberlain is about the same.

I was in the middle of packing for Italy – chanting, 'I am only going for the weekend, I do not need to take the entire contents of my wardrobe,' like a mantra – when Declan phoned again.

'Theo, I wondered if you'd like to pop up to Manchester to see me sometime.'

'Yes, yes, that would be good,' I muttered absently, trying desperately to find a pair of tights without a ladder and deciding whether fluorescent pink leg-warmers were likely to be necessary.

'You've always been a special friend to me.'

'Have you been drinking?'

'Of course not!'

'Oh, I'm sorry, you were being serious. You're special to me too. You know that.' I stuck the phone under my chin and rummaged in a drawer for the sun cream and my straw hat.

'What about this weekend?'

'Sorry, I'm busy this weekend. Oh, I didn't tell you, did I. Brilliant news! I'm going out with Kevin again. As a matter of fact, we're off for a romantic trip to Italy this weekend. I was just packing.'

'That's ... marvellous, wonderful ... great. I wish you both all the best, really I do ...' His voice trailed away. 'Catch up with you sometime then.'

Funny, he suddenly sounded really offhand. It's not as if

I'd planned to visit him this weekend. I can always go and see him another time.

Saturday 26 June

11 a.m.
Hotel in Milan is beautiful. We flew in last night and had a romantic meal in a little restaurant – pasta and just the one glass of Chianti. Spent the morning sightseeing and shopping. It's wonderful to be with Kevin again. He may be spiritually degenerate, but I love him really.

12 noon.
FOOTBALL! The 'special place' he's taking me to this evening is the blasted football stadium, where England are playing Italy! Some stupid European match. I might have known. I really thought he'd changed. Men!

1 p.m.
Kevin finally resorted to calling to me under the locked door of my hotel room. 'Please come, Theo. You never know. You might like it.'

'I won't. I've already made up my mind not to. I can't *believe* you brought me here to watch football!'

'Please, just do this one thing for me. Come to the match.'

He sounded so pathetic that my heart melted. I unlocked the door. Besides, he had paid for the trip – I think.

'OK, but I'm not wearing the scarf and I'm not singing those songs.'

9 p.m.

The stadium looked enormous. We settled in our seats and waited for the match to start. We were in the away supporters' end and therefore surrounded, as I'd expected, by sweaty, yobbish Englishmen. To my surprise, there was also a large number of sweaty, yobbish Englishwomen. My summer dress and sunhat looked out of place in the sea of football shirts. Kevin saluted and grunted at some people he appeared to know. Then the whistle blew and the match commenced.

Whenever I had occasionally watched football matches on television at home, there had always been a commentator to provide information about what was happening on the pitch and make comments such as, 'Apart from the broken leg, he's perfectly fit.' Or, 'The number of goals each team scored made all the difference to the outcome of this game.' But here there was no commentary, helpful or otherwise. The events on the pitch happened with only the roaring, hissing or collective breath-holding of the crowd to give any indication of how the match was going.

'What's happening?' I called up to Kevin, who was on his feet.

'Well, our forwards are pushing up the wing and ... ooh!'

'Was that nearly a goal?'

'Yeah. Sshh.'

'What's happening now?'

'Now he's taking the corner, and ... YEEEEESSSS! Nice one, my son!'

I applauded politely, while the players on the pitch and the fans in the stands hugged and kissed each other.

'What's happening now?'

'They're starting again from the centre.'

The ball flew up and down the pitch. Players kicked other players, who in turn rolled around on the ground for a while. I began to wish I'd brought my knitting. Suddenly there was a cheer, which turned to a groan.

'What's happening now?'

'Offside! I can't believe it.' He sank into his seat with his head in his hands.

'What's offside?'

'I can't explain it now. Just watch.'

'That's not very helpful. I don't know why I bothered coming.' I folded my arms and stuck out my bottom lip in an exaggerated pout.

He took a deep breath. 'Well, offside is when a player is nearer to the goal line than the ball, unless he's either in his own half or there are two players from the opposing team who are nearer to the goal line than he is. But the referee will only penalize him for offside if he's deemed to be inter-fering either with play or with an opponent, or seeking to gain the advantage by being in that position. However, he can't be deemed offside directly following a goal kick, cor-ner kick or throw-in.'

'Oh, I see.'

'Do you?'

'No, not really.'

As he was explaining it for the second time, there was a roar from the home crowd. Italy had scored.

Then I felt it – the rush of disappointment; the feeling that, if I wished and willed a little bit harder, we would score.

Yes, *we*. Suddenly I was on the pitch with the England team in spirit, driving the ball forward, straining for the goal.

I was wearing the shirt with three lions.

I was saving the goal.

I was kicking the penalty.

I was there.

Play recommenced and I was out of my seat, shouting and cheering and jumping with the rest of the crowd. I chanted and yelled as the adrenaline pumped.

Then the whistle blew for half-time.

I sat down in the Italian sunshine while Kevin went to buy drinks. Today I understood what it was all about. Today I knew how Kevin had felt for all these years about his game. I realized why it was so important. For the 90 minutes of the match, nothing else mattered, the rest of the world stood still. On those few square yards of turf, the only thing of any significance unfolded minute by minute, kick by kick. It was victory or defeat. It was war.

Kevin returned with some iced lemon drinks.

'Have a look at the scoreboard, Theo.'

I shielded my eyes from the sun. A message flashed up on the illuminated scoreboard:

> **THEODORA**
> **I LOVE YOU. WILL YOU MARRY ME?**
> **KEVIN**

I gasped and looked around the crowd for all the other Theodoras and Kevins there must have been in the stadium. Then I looked down. Kevin was on his knees in front of me, wedged between the two rows of seats. My face burned scarlet as he opened a small box. All eyes were no longer on the pitch or gazing into empty fizzy drink cans. They were on us.

'Please say "yes", and say it quickly – this concrete is killing my knees.'

'Yes! Get up, you idiot.'

The people around us shrieked in delight and gave us a round of applause. The public address system played the theme from *Love Story*. Kevin clambered to his feet, grinning, and pushed a gold ring with a single stone onto the third finger of my left hand.

'It's lovely,' I said. 'Is it real?' I held up my hand so the stone caught the sunlight.

'Course it's real. Vague Dave down at the market swears it's genuine Hatton Garden.'

'If it's genuine Hatton Garden, what's it doing in the possession of Vague Dave down at the market?'

'Dunno. Dave was a bit vague about it. Still, if your finger goes green and drops off, I'll buy you another one.'

'Another finger?'

'You know what I mean.' He lowered his eyes and shuffled his feet. 'I'd do anything to make you happy, Theo.'

'Then shut up. The match is about to start again.'

'Don't I even get a kiss?'

I don't remember much about the rest of the match. Most of it was spent in Kevin's arms with his lips pressed against my lips. Which, at that moment, was just exactly where I wanted to be. The only slightly annoying thing was that Kevin kept swivelling his head towards the pitch to try to catch some of the action and ricking my neck in the process. I forgave him.

In the end we won 2-1. The winning goal was a blinder. The midfield players had just ... No, I won't go into that here. I'm in danger of becoming as bad as Kevin.

When we arrived back at the hotel, there was a message to ring Reverend Graves.

'I'm sorry to spoil your holiday with bad news,' Digger said when I called him. 'I just got back from the hospital. Miss Chamberlain ... well, it doesn't look too good, Theo love. I thought you'd like to know.'

'Thanks.'

'Jeremiah and I are taking turns to sit with her, you know.'

'Would you tell her something for me?'

'Course.'

'Would you tell her that Kevin and I just got engaged?'

'Congratulations! You certainly kept that one quiet.'

'It's only just happened. Would you tell her that I've taken hold of the opportunity and made the best choice for the right reasons?'

'I'll tell her as soon as I see her, I promise. God bless, and tell that Kevin to look after you.'

Sunday 27 June

Tom came to collect us from the airport this evening and was astounded to see the engagement ring. Frustratingly, he had no news of Miss Chamberlain. He drove us back to his house and Ariadne hugged me and squealed when we told her. She even hugged Kevin. I rang Mum and Dad and we all had a glass of champagne while I cuddled Phoebe.

Shortly after I got back to the flat, the entry buzzer sounded. It was Digger. I waited at the top of the stairs as he came up and ushered him into my flat. He perched on the sofa and indicated for me to sit in the chair opposite. His voice sounded strained. 'There's just no easy way to tell you. She died early this morning. I'm very sorry.'

I just nodded, unable to speak.

'She's with Jesus now.'

'That's no good, I want her here with me!' I shouted. 'There's so much I still wanted to tell her.' The tears burned down my cheeks.

'I know, Theo love. I gave her your message.'

'What did she say?'

'She was very weak. She sort of nodded and smiled. But I'm sure she was over the moon.'

The funeral is arranged for next Friday.

I walked past her cottage and everything looked exactly the same as always, except she wasn't there. Soon the place will be empty and she'll live on only in the memories and lives of those she touched.

Monday 28 June

As Miss Chamberlain had so many friends in the village, Digger has taken the unusual step of forming a committee to plan her memorial service. I think that by the end of today's meeting he was starting to regret this. The committee comprised Digger, Jeremiah Wedgwood (who sat at the opposite end of the table to the vicar and appeared to be there under sufferance), Miss Cranmer, Mrs Epstein (who brought her knitting), Mrs McCarthy, Alfreda Polanski (who owns the post office and whom Jeremiah insisted had pagan tendencies because she once allowed a maypole to be erected on the green outside her shop) and myself.

I felt honoured to be part of the group, as I'd only known Miss Chamberlain for a relatively short time (the whole of my life was probably less than half the time the rest of the group had known her). At the same time, it seemed very strange to be planning her memorial service. Just as Miss Chamberlain had never considered herself to be old, I could imagine her not quite admitting to being dead. She still seemed so present with us and, as the stories and anecdotes came tumbling out while we talked about her life, it seemed as if we were talking behind her back and that at any moment she would enter the room and bring us all abruptly to silence. But she didn't.

The meeting busied itself with deciding on the hymns
and readings, appointing someone to organize the flowers,
and designating stewards, people to make the tea, and the
like. We suspected that St Norbert's would be as packed as
a lift full of sumo wrestlers with Miss Chamberlain's friends,
acquaintances and former pupils, so the process began to
resemble a military operation in its attention to detail and
contingency planning.

I was stunned when, at the end of the meeting, Digger
took me to one side and asked me to say a few words at the
service about Miss Chamberlain.

'Why me? Other people have known her for longer.'

'I just think you'd be good at putting into words what
the rest of us are thinking. And anyway, although she had
loads of mates, I know she was especially fond of you.'

'That means a lot,' I said, fighting back the tears.

Tuesday 29 June

I have absolutely nothing to wear to this funeral. I was toy-
ing with the idea of the black suit I wore to Auntie Ivy's
funeral last year, but it makes me look too much like a
policewoman. Mum offered me her black hat, which could
easily have belonged to Morticia from the Addams family. I
declined. Anyway, black doesn't seem appropriate for Miss
Chamberlain. I've finally decided on a cream dress with
poppies on it. It reminds me of Miss Chamberlain's garden.
Help! I think I'm turning into Charity Hubble!

July

Thursday 1 July

Why did I agree to do it? The cliché queen, that's me. How is it possible to capture a life in a three-minute speech? Everything I try to write sounds so trite and obvious. Of course we all loved her. Of course we'll all miss her. Of course she's in a better place now. My speech is beginning to sound like a third-rate Victorian melodrama. I even researched some of Miss Chamberlain's early life and career, found out which committees and organizations she'd belonged to (just to list them would take a good two minutes), only to discover that Digger is already going to include all that sort of thing in *his* address.

Help me, God. Where are you when I need you?

Friday 2 July

I expected to wake up early this morning and spend time in quiet contemplation writing a proper speech before the service at 10 a.m. Instead, there was an overnight power cut and I woke to a blank alarm clock, a video recorder which had programmed itself to record an Open University programme about farming in the Scottish Lowlands, and a freezer full of defrosted chocolate ice cream. I had 20 minutes to get ready.

I disposed of the defrosted ice cream in a humane manner, showered and washed my hair, which had now thankfully lost its brassy taint and settled to a pleasant dark blonde. Then I pulled on my cream dress, dried my hair and opened the curtains. A rain shower had washed the village clean and the morning sun had dried and warmed it ready for the day. The scent of roses perfumed the air and the garden birds twittered and trilled the same songs they twittered and trilled every morning. Didn't they know that today was different?

The buzzer sounded. It was Kevin in a shirt and tie.

'You all right?'

'Yes,' I lied, and he gave my hand a squeeze.

I grabbed my Bible with one hand and Kevin's hand with the other, and we started up the hill to St Norbert's. Digger greeted us at the door, looking pale and tense, and inside everyone wore similarly pale, tense expressions, smiled briefly, then busied themselves giving out hymn books and adjusting floral arrangements. I found a seat near the front and Kevin went outside for a walk.

I still wasn't sure what I was going to say. I was afraid I was going to cry and look a fool in front of all those people. After all, Hollywood actresses aside, no one can look their best with smudged mascara round their eyes and a runny nose. I lowered myself onto a kneeler and prayed like I've never prayed before. I prayed that God was really there and that he could hear me. I prayed that what we hoped about heaven was true, and that Miss Chamberlain was really with him. I prayed that he would help me find the right words to say. I prayed for her friends, for Digger, and for Jeremiah, both of whom she loved and who both loved her deeply in their different ways. My hands were shaking.

I heard sniffing behind me and turned to see Jeremiah sobbing quietly into a large white handkerchief. The church was beginning to fill with people and I looked around to try to spot someone with a 'comforting ministry' who could sort Jeremiah out. I realized that I didn't know anyone there. Presumably these were her friends and relatives from other parts of the country. There was no one else; it would have to be me. I went and sat next to Jeremiah. I was going to put my arm around his shoulders, but thought better of it.

'We all miss her,' I said earnestly to the handkerchief, which was now entirely covering his face.

'You don't understand. She was different.'

'I know, she was a very special person.'

'Oh, shut up! What do you know?'

I sat up. I'd never heard Jeremiah speak like this before. 'Get thee hence, Satan,' perhaps, but never 'Shut up'.

'You and all the others make me want to vomit, with your Sunday Christianity and worldly attitudes,' he said sharply. 'None of you try to live by the Bible. I bet half of you never even read it!'

'I . . . I'm sorry if you feel this way, Jeremiah, but I'm sure. . .'

'You all hate me. You all laugh at me behind my back. Just because I try to stand up for the truth. She was the only one who really liked me, the only one who cared. Now she's gone.'

He took a deep breath, buried his face again in the handkerchief, and years and years of pain and bitterness poured out with his tears. I didn't know what to say to help him and decided, probably wisely, to leave him to sort it out with God.

'If there's anything I can do . . . well, you know where I am.'

I stood up to return to my seat near the front. The
church was full now and Kevin shuffled his way up the aisle
and squeezed in next to me. Then Gregory Pasternak
struck a chord on the organ and we shuffled to our feet as
Rev. Graves walked up the aisle in front of a small coffin,
carried on the shoulders of four men in dark suits and
almost hidden under flowers.

I sat in a daze, unsettled by Jeremiah's outburst and
uncertain of what I was going to say to all those people as
the prayers, hymns, readings and address flew by. Suddenly
it was my turn to get up and speak. Kevin nudged me and
Digger gave me an encouraging smile as I stood at the
lectern. I swallowed hard as I looked out at all the pale,
tense faces.

'I feel very honoured to be invited to stand here and say a
few words about a remarkable lady. I'm sure everyone has his
or her own special memories of her. I know she means so
much to everyone in this church and, I'm sure, to many
more people who cannot be here today. I know that a lot of
care and preparation has gone into today's service – the beautiful flowers, all the hymns and readings she loved so much.
When we were planning for today, I heard people saying
things like, "We must have pink flowers, she loved pink." Or,
"That was her favourite hymn." Truth is, much as she would
have appreciated the thought that has gone into the service,
she may have questioned what all the fuss was about. And I
know that she'll be far too busy in heaven to concern herself
with what's happening down here on earth.

'The things I remember most about Miss Chamberlain
were her insatiable search for knowledge – she wanted to
understand everything; her love of history – I'm sure she
has a few questions to ask God; and her genuine devotion
to people. Underlying all those things was her love for God,

whom she served willingly and faithfully for nearly 90 years. She didn't just love the lovable people; she loved the difficult people, the unkind people, the ungrateful people, and the people like me who spend so much time wrapped up in their own petty problems that they never have the time to care genuinely for others. That love didn't come from a sense of obligation or religious duty, but from deep inside a heart so wrapped up in Jesus that you felt you were a better person just for spending a few minutes in her company. I've never known her to knock on doors, give out leaflets, or even quote Scripture at anyone. She didn't need to. People came to her, they sought her out. She never told people – they always asked. She was, in that respect, like Jesus. She had wit, wisdom and genuine compassion. I only hope God knows how lucky he is to have her with him.'

I walked back to my place and whispered a prayer of thanks to God. I didn't have any sense of Miss Chamberlain smiling down on me – she'd be far too occupied for any of that.

At the end of the service, no one seemed to be in a hurry to leave. They sat in the pews and chatted, or admired the flowers and the stained-glass windows. I saw Digger and Jeremiah sitting together and expected to hear raised voices or to see Jeremiah sweeping to his feet and stomping out of the door. Under the pretence of collecting hymn books, I edged closer to where they sat. Jeremiah was weeping again and Digger had his hand on Jeremiah's shoulder. To my astonishment, I could hear that they were praying quietly together. It was hard to hear the words and, of course, not being a naturally nosy person, I didn't like to get too close, but they were actually praying together.

Perhaps at least one of Miss Chamberlain's prayers was answered today.

Saturday 3 July

Digger phoned early this morning to check I was OK. He said he'd been asked by Miss Chamberlain's great-niece to arrange for the cottage to be cleared as soon as possible before the niece put it up for sale.

'I've contacted one of those house clearance places, but I said I'd check round the cottage first. It's just that I don't feel it's appropriate, you know, a bloke going through her personal things. I'd be grateful if you'd give me a hand, Theo love, if you're up to it.'

I said I would, dressed and hurried down to Miss Chamberlain's cottage, where the roses and poppies in her garden were in full bloom. Digger met me at the door.

Inside, everything was meticulously tidy, just as she had left it. We checked inside cupboards and behind ornaments to check that she hadn't tucked any money away, like old ladies sometimes do. She hadn't. Miss Chamberlain wasn't like that. She never seemed the hoarding type. I suspect that, if she ever had any money left over from her pension, she would promptly and cheerfully have donated it to a worthy cause.

I went up the narrow staircase to her bedroom. The white embroidered counterpane was folded neatly away from the pillow, as if waiting for her to climb into bed. I opened the heavy oak wardrobe and started removing and folding her clothes to take to the charity shop, trying all the time to convince myself that this was what she would have wanted. The smell of lavender was almost overwhelming. One by one, I pulled open the drawers of her chest and packed up her underwear. I half expected to come across a drawer crammed with lace-edged handkerchiefs – Christmas and birthday presents, all still in their packages.

There were none. She had either used them or given them away.

Her silver brush, comb and mirror sparkled on her dressing table and by the triple mirror there was a small silver trinket box. I opened it to find a brooch, a string of pearls and a gold ring with a single small diamond. Miss Chamberlain's engagement ring. She'd kept it for all those years. I sat on her bed and cried.

Digger called up to me and I brought the silver box downstairs. He had just finished throwing away the last of the food from her kitchen cupboards. I showed him the box and sat down and told him the story of Miss Chamberlain's engagement that never was.

'I just thought . . . well, the ring might be valuable. Shouldn't we send it to her great-niece?' I asked.

'The niece wasn't interested. Just wanted the place cleared ASAP. Why don't you keep it? It's what she would have wanted.'

If I heard those words, 'It's what she would have wanted,' once more, I thought I would scream. How did he know what she would have wanted? If she'd wanted to give me those things, she could have done it at any time. I had no right to help myself to them now. I felt like a vulture.

It was as if Digger could read my mind.

'I know it feels funny, you just coming in here and taking her things, but isn't it better that they go to someone who knew and loved her rather than just ending up being sold in some shonky second-hand shop? Look, I'm keeping a few books, and her Bible.'

He pointed to a pile of books on the table. I picked up the Bible. It was old and very well thumbed, but I was surprised to see that there was not a mark in it. She had neither made notes in the margins, nor underlined favourite scriptures. When I thought about it, that was typical of the retired teacher. She would never, ever countenance writing in a book.

I opened the jewellery box again. Digger was right. I would keep the ring and think of her whenever I looked at it. Besides, considering the reputation of Vague Dave down at the market who sold Kevin my engagement ring, it might just come in handy.

Sunday 4 July

After church, Kevin came round for Sunday lunch and we set a date for the wedding: 30 April, Miss Chamberlain's birthday. We've booked St Norbert's for the ceremony and the church hall for the reception. I've started buying bridal magazines for ideas for the dress. I want something simple. I'm not keen on the 'galleon in full sail' look, like Cordelia. I've also politely declined Charity's kind offer to make me a wedding dress from net curtain remnants.

First things first, though. Strike while the iron's hot. I've decided that Kevin and I will go out on Saturday to buy him a suit for the wedding.

After all, I don't want people to think he's spiritually degenerate.

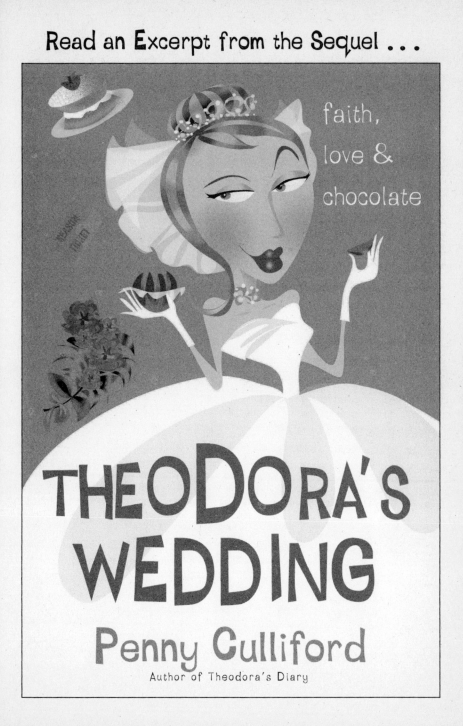

faith,
love &
chocolate

THEODORA'S WEDDING

Penny Culliford

Author of Theodora's Diary

JULY

Monday 5 July

Well, I've done it.

I've actually done it!

Nobody thought I'd persevere, least of all me. But I have done it. I've kept up my diary for over a year. Ariadne sneered when I started. She actually sneered. 'I'll give it a fortnight,' she said. My sister, my own flesh and blood, doubting my resolve. And now I've really shown her. I shall go and wave it under her nose and say, 'See, I'm not a flash in the pan, a five-minute wonder, a here today, gone tomorrow sort of person. I have written something lasting, something that will endure. Future generations will benefit from my incisive, yet entertaining, commentary on life.'

Actually, I think I won't. I can hear the derisive snort already and, having flicked back through last year's diary, I can see that a lot of it could come under the category 'neurotic ramblings'. Besides, poor Ariadne looks so exhausted, what with baby Phoebe and getting ready to go back to work, I don't think her eyes would stay open long enough to focus. I'm sorry to say she's also letting

herself go. She looks kind of tired and crumpled somehow. And she's rather plump. Perhaps she doesn't realize.
Perhaps I ought to tell her.

However, I think the diary has achieved its aim. I may
not have grown very much spiritually, nor am I any
nearer finding my ministry, nor have I been hailed as the
next British supermodel, but it has been an eventful year.
I have seen friends come and go, I have a new baby niece
and I have gained a fiancé, even if at times I think he is
spiritually degenerate. And to cap it all, I weigh half a
stone less than I did this time last year.

Tuesday 6 July

Cooking! Why on earth did Charity Hubble volunteer
me to do cooking? And baking cakes, at that. She knows
I hate cooking. She knows I would rather bungee-jump
naked from the bell tower or enter a Michael Jackson
look-alike competition than bake a cake. Just because
she's the curate's wife, is responsible for a one-woman
population explosion and dresses like Laura Ashley's furniture department, just because she was born knowing
how to make six different kinds of preserves from fresh
fruit, does not give Charity Hubble the right to conscript
me into baking for the produce stall at the flaming summer fete.

Wednesday 7 July

Confessed to Kevin about my cake problem. As my
future husband, I would expect a little support. Instead,

he laughed like a drain as usual (and being a plumber, I suppose he should know how a drain laughs).

'How do you get yourself into these situations in the first place?' he guffawed. 'If you didn't want to make a cake, why did you volunteer?'

'I didn't . . . it just sort of happened.'

'What's it for, anyway?'

'Oh, a good cause. The village fete. The church has got some stalls there, including a home-made produce stall. Just doing my bit,' I declared proudly.

'Village fete? Bit twee isn't it? I thought your church was into preaching the gospel, fighting for justice and setting the captives free. Where do village fetes come into it?'

I couldn't answer that one.

Thursday 8 July

I have been reading an excellent book. It's called *I'm Going to be Assertive Now, If That's OK with You.* It's written by Hiram B. Jefferson III who's got just loads and loads of degrees and diplomas from all sorts of universities, so he should jolly well know what he's talking about.

'Are you a human doormat?' Hiram demands.

'Yes, I am,' I answer.

'Do you say yes when you mean no?' he inquires.

'Yes I do – I mean no I don't, I mean yes but I want to say no!'

'Then take control. You have a right to your feelings and a right to express those feelings. Use positive statements such as "I am . . .", "I will . . .", to show those who would wipe their feet on you that here's one doormat who's gonna stand up and say "No more!"'

I decided, for once, to have it out with Charity. I'm not really a coward who shies away from confrontation; it's just that she is impossible to argue with. An encounter with Charity Hubble always seems to end with her making me say the opposite to what I really think. How does she do it? How will she stand up to Hiram B. Jefferson III?

Friday 9 July

Found a box of stink bombs, knife-through-the-head headbands and synthetic dog poop in the bottom drawer of Declan's old filing cabinet today. His practical jokes used to drive me up the wall when he worked here. I wondered how he had managed to become a section supervisor when he seemed to spend so little time working and so much time playing practical jokes. But since he left, work seems a lot duller. Safer, yes: there is no danger of finding the toilet covered with cling film or discovering your coat pockets are full of cold spaghetti or standing up to find that your shoelaces have been tied together – but for some perverse reason I actually miss all that. Even the extra pay and status (ha! It's all very well being made a section supervisor but I was the only person on the section so now I'm just supervising myself) doesn't make up for it. I wonder how Declan is getting on in Manchester. I wonder what kind of priest he will make.

Saturday 10 July

I finally tracked Charity down outside the post office, with baby Methuselah in a pram and three other hamster-faced offspring in tow as she stuffed Nigel's mail into the post box.

I pounced.

'Charity, why did you put my name down for baking a cake when you know I hate cooking?'

She paused for a moment to wipe a dribbly trail of slime away from baby Methuselah's mouth and to restrain Ahimelech, who was trying to climb the pillar box, then turned to me, beaming.

'I thought it would be a wonderful opportunity to practise. After all, you'll have to cook for Kevin after you're married, unless of course you're hiring help. One never knows with you "career women".'

Her eyes twinkled mischievously, and I suddenly saw a side to Charity I hadn't believed existed. If she hadn't been so unbearably holy I would have called it 'devilment'. She was really enjoying this.

'Of course not,' I retorted, much too quickly. Once again my mouth was moving faster than my brain and I realized that unless we planned to live on takeaways for our entire married life, cooking something at some point was inevitable. And Charity knew it. She just wanted to make me suffer. I panicked.

'Kevin can cook,' I blurted. This was a lie. Kevin can *eat*. In fact Kevin could eat for England. I have yet to find something Kevin won't eat; even Kippers in Garlic Mayonnaise somehow found their way down his gullet without complaint.

But Kevin can't cook. His mum has seen to that.

'Super! Then I can put him down for a cake too.'

'No! No, he'll be far too busy, what with work and everything. B . . . besides, have you thought about the places plumbers have to put their hands? Yuck, even I wouldn't eat a cake he had touched.'

'So you can make two, one for you and one on his behalf.'

'Charity! I know you're doing this on purpose. I don't *do* cooking. When I put my name on that list to help out, you know and I know that I didn't put it under anything to do with baking, boiling, fricasseeing or any other kind of food preparation.'

'Do you know where you *did* write it?'

My brain searched the archives. No record found.

Charity reached into her enormous handbag and pulled out a neatly folded piece of paper. She opened it and waved it under my nose. True, my name was not on the list of people volunteering to bake cakes. Nor was anyone else's. My name appeared at the bottom under 'anything', a section created for people who were either so versatile that they could turn their hand to any task or so ineffectual that they had no particular talents. I definitely fell into the latter category. My indecisiveness had once again become my downfall. Charity had spotted my weakness and gone in for the kill. I bet Hiram B. Jefferson III himself would be no match for Charity Hubble.

'Well, you *did* say you'd do anything,' she said, fluttering her eyelids coyly. At that point Ahimelech made a dash for the road and Charity had to scurry off to apprehend him. Otherwise I would have told her . . .

Sunday 11 July

There was a correction in today's *Church Organ*.

It was reported in last week's publication that the Street Evangelism Team would be offensive in spreading the gospel around the village in the next few weeks. This item should have read that the Street Evangelism Team would be <u>on the offensive</u>, spreading the gospel. The editor apologizes sincerely for this error.

I have the uneasy feeling that the editor was right in the first place.

Monday 12 July

Kevin's five-a-side team is taking part in an exchange with a French club this summer. First they're coming over here, staying with English supporters, then the English are going to stay in France for a fortnight. Kevin has *asked* me (a breakthrough in itself – in our relationship so far, I've been lucky if he's even *informed* me he's going) if he can go with them.

He has also decided to better himself and learn the language. He has an ambition to be able to order a beer in twenty different languages.

I hope he has more luck learning French than my mother has had learning Greek. Despite having a love for the country that borders on obsession, her attempts to speak Greek have been little short of disastrous. My mother is enough to make the Linguaphone lady resign. The other day she informed us that Archimedes jumped in the bath and shouted, 'Euthanasia!'

Theodora's Wedding
Faith, Love & Chocolate

Penny Culliford

I've actually done it! I've kept up my diary for over a year.

I may not have grown very much spiritually, nor have I been hailed as the next British supermodel, but I have gained a fiancè, even if he is football mad. And to cap it all, I weigh half a stone less than I did this time last year.

Welcome back to Theodora's world. Now a bit older but not much wiser, Theodora Llewellyn begins her second year as a diarist. And as usual, the results are endearing, hilarious and delightfully human.

In her search for life, love and a plentiful supply of chocolate, Theodora discovers that the course of true love never runs smoothly, especially when a voice from the past precipitates a crisis. But fear not – Theodora's humor and wit are up to the challenge. In the end, just one question remains unanswered: Exactly how much vitamin C is there in a chocolate orange?

Softcover ISBN 0-310-25039-0

Pick up a copy today at your favorite bookstore!

ZONDERVAN™

GRAND RAPIDS, MICHIGAN 49530 USA

WWW.ZONDERVAN.COM

We want to hear from you. Please send your comments about this book to us in care of zreview@zondervan.com. Thank you.

ZONDERVAN™

GRAND RAPIDS, MICHIGAN 49530 USA

WWW.ZONDERVAN.COM